Susan Breen lives in New York with her husband and children and teaches fiction at the Gotham Writers' Workshop in Manhattan.

the
Fiction
CLASS

by

Susan Breen

headline
review

Copyright © 2008 Susan Breen

The right of Susan Breen to be identified as the Author of
the Work has been asserted by her in accordance with the
Copyright, Designs and Patents Act 1988.

First published in Great Britain in 2008
by HEADLINE REVIEW
An imprint of HEADLINE PUBLISHING GROUP

First published in paperback in Great Britain in 2008
by HEADLINE REVIEW
An imprint of HEADLINE PUBLISHING GROUP
1

Cataloguing in Publication Data is available from the British Library

ISBN 978 0 7553 3721 7

Typeset in Garamond by Avon DataSet Ltd,
Bidford-on-Avon, Warwickshire

Printed and bound in Great Britain by
Mackays of Chatham plc, Chatham, Kent

Headline's policy is to use papers that are natural, renewable and recyclable
products and made from wood grown in sustainable forests. The logging and
manufacturing processes are expected to conform to the environmental regulations
of the country of origin.

HEADLINE PUBLISHING GROUP
An Hachette Livre UK Company
338 Euston Road
London NW1 3BH

www.headline.co.uk

For my parents,
Barbara and Bob Zelony

Acknowledgments

My deepest thanks go to the following:

Charlotte Mendelson and the team at Headline Review, who are mad about books in the best possible way. Thanks especially to Marion Donaldson, Leah Woodburn and Alice Shepherd.

Emily Haynes, my editor, who understood what I was trying to say and helped me say it.

My agent, Alex Glass, for his wonderful support and enthusiasm, and to all the lovely people at Trident Media Group, with special thanks to Lara Allen in foreign rights.

Michael Neff and his NYC Pitch and Shop Conference. Without him, none of this would have happened.

Alex Steele, for hiring me to teach my first fiction class, even though I gave a lousy lecture, and the whole Gotham Writers'

Workshop team, among them Andre Becker, Dana Miller, Linda Novak, and Stacey Panousopoulos.

My students, for trusting me with their stories. Special thanks to the cheering section in Wednesday afternoon Advanced Fiction.

My many friends, who listened to me dream year after year, among them Maureen Brady, Sarah Cox, Melinda Feinstein, Terry Gillen, Joanna Grosodonia, Leslie Mack, Kay Spinella, and Trish Waters. Special thanks to Rev. David Harkness and the Irvington Presbyterian Church, whose prayers have literally kept me going.

My brother, Robert Zelony, who has always been so good to me, and the rest of his dear family, Beth, Meghan, and Taylor.

Also, thanks and love to all the Breens, Bucks, Murcotts, and Turchettes, who are such an important part of my life, and to my aunt, Dr Lee Burnett, who introduced me to Mexico City and fortune-tellers and ghosts and many other wonderful things worth writing about.

Lots of love to my husband, Brad, who has been the hero of my own particular romance story these last twenty-five years, and to my children, Tom, Kathy and Chris. You are my treasures.

Finally, to my dear son Will, all my gratitude for teaching me that life should be an adventure, and that I should not be afraid to live it.

First Class: Getting Started

'YOU'VE KNOWN THERE was something special about you for a long time, haven't you?'

Arabella lets the question hover over the classroom for just a moment. Eleven pairs of eyes stare back at her warily.

This is the first day of class, and they're not sure if she is mocking them. But she's not; she's absolutely serious.

'Ever since the third grade,' she goes on, because for some reason it always is the third grade, 'ever since the teacher chose your story to read aloud on Parents' Day. She was so excited by your facility with words. Facility! She even used that word in the letter she sent home to your parents inviting them to be guests of honor at the reading, although in my own particular case, my father couldn't come because he was in the hospital, and my mother didn't make it because she fainted in the school

1

hallway and banged her head on the water fountain and had to be taken by ambulance to the Nassau County Medical Center. If my mother let me down, there was always an ambulance involved; no lame scheduling conflicts for her.

'But anyway.'

Arabella pauses for a moment and surveys the class: eleven people staring down at their notebooks, terrified that if they make eye contact, she might call on them. She recognizes Conrad from last semester, and she is touched that he re-enrolled even though, especially though, she never felt as if they connected. Everything he wrote was about transsexuals – transsexual nursery school teachers, transsexual police officers, and so on. The obvious explanation was that Conrad himself was a transsexual. Not that Arabella would ever suggest such a thing; the etiquette of a writing class requires that everyone act as though what the author is writing is an absolute fiction.

'Teacher,' one woman cries out. Her face is flushed, and her white hair stands up like a Q-Tip. 'I have to share this. I won a contest in the third grade, and I've wanted to be a writer ever since. I can still remember the story; it was about plums and—'

'Actually, I won one, too,' another woman breaks in, this one young and thin and glamorous. 'Actually, it was in high school. First place. Five hundred dollars. End of story.' Her name tag says she is Mimi, and she shimmers with pride, and rightfully so, Arabella thinks. She's beautiful, with that type of toasted tan skin that never ages. She is obviously bright, and she is probably a great writer. Probably better than Arabella – there's always one in every class. Her descriptions will be incandescent, perfect little nuggets of phraseology, and there will probably be lots of sex in her writing – the clinical type of sex with labias and clitorises and tongues going everywhere.

'Good for you,' the woman with the white hair says to Mimi, and Arabella is touched. She is always touched when people are generous.

A red-faced woman in the front row raises her hand.

'Yes, Pam?' Arabella says, squinting as she reads the name on the tag.

'I never won anything,' Pam says, 'not even a scavenger hunt.'

'That's all right. Neither did I,' Arabella responds, although that may have been the wrong thing to say. She can see Mimi looking at her, obviously wondering why she is paying money to take a writing class from someone who has never won anything, an unpublished teacher who is standing in the middle of a nursery school classroom in Manhattan surrounded by cutouts of snowflakes on the wall and occasionally interrupted by the thumping of an angry-looking bunny in a cage.

Arabella sighs and moves on.

'The point is that for many of us the desire to be a writer starts young, but then something happens, doesn't it?' Arabella asks. 'Maybe you found you couldn't get a job with your English degree, or you got married or had a baby or went into law, because that's what English majors are supposed to do for money, and somehow that dream you had of being a writer went away. Or, even worse than disappearing, it came to seem like something foolish, something childish and self-indulgent – like wanting to be a fairy princess or a movie star.'

There is a lot of nodding now, which is encouraging. If Arabella can get the students to like and trust her and each other, the class will be a success. But she knows she must move slowly, carefully. A new class is a fragile thing. This is New York, after all; people are prickly, competitive, strange – which is why Arabella almost snarls in irritation when she notices two people in the front row whispering to each other. Nothing disrupts the mood of a class more quickly than people whispering.

'But here's the strange thing,' Arabella says, looking at the two whisperers as she speaks, hoping to shame them into silence. 'No matter how hard you've tried, you can't quite get that dream of being a writer out of your head. You still feel something special every time you pick up a book. You still connect to characters in ways you've never connected to people you actually know, and you still think there's something special about you even if no one else in this whole wretched world can see it. You know you're more than what you appear to be. You have to give it one more shot; you have to see if you can be a writer.

'Welcome to the Fiction Class.'

Unbelievable. The two of them are still whispering. She

glares at the two whisperers: an elegant gentleman and a woman drenched in a black shawl. Her name is Alice Dutton. Dark Alice, Arabella thinks.

'My name is Arabella Hicks,' she shouts, 'and I will be your teacher. Yes, I can see you smiling. I know it's a ridiculous name, but my mother loves Georgette Heyer romance novels and I'm named after one of her heroines. The real Arabella, the true Arabella, is married to the aristocratic rake Robert Beaumaris. You can only imagine how delighted my mother is that I'm thirty-eight and single.'

The class laughs at that, thank God. Is there anything more wonderful than having a class laugh at your jokes? Even the whisperers laugh.

'I'm fifty-five and married,' a woman in a red leather jacket calls out. Bonita Carbone. 'It's not all it's cracked up to be.'

'My girlfriend wants to get married, but I'm resistant.' This from Justin Szymanski, who has been sitting quietly, one of those boys on the verge of manhood. He could be anywhere from twenty to forty, and he's holding a copy of *Bleak House*. Arabella is tempted to tell him that's her favorite book, but now she notices that the elegant whisperer is smiling at her.

He alone is not wearing a name tag, and he is dressed more formally than anyone in the room. He is wearing a white shirt, white sweater, a soft navy blue jacket, and weathered jeans that hang perfectly against his legs. Arabella suspects his clothes were purchased just for this class, that he told a salesman at Brooks Brothers he wanted to look like a writer. She can tell he is not a serious man; she imagines he is taking this class because it is too cold outside to garden. Either that or he is planning to write some thinly disguised memoir about the women he has known and loved.

Arabella looks down at her class roster; his name is Chuck Jones. She can almost hear what her mother would have to say about this man. 'A civilian,' she would call him, meaning he was not engaged in the battle of life. And a rich civilian at that, judging by the cut of his clothes and the air of self-satisfaction about him. Arabella has never liked people like him. It seems to her that if fate hands you money and health and looks, you are obligated to do something with them as a way of giving thanks. Not sit here like some self-satisfied letch, interrupting the class with whispering and making faces at the teacher.

'Excuse me.' A young woman is waving her hand. Her name is Ginger Clark, and she has added three exclamation marks to the name tag. She has a brand-new laptop in front of her.

'You have a question, Ginger?'

'Can we move that bunny? I've heard they carry avian flu.'

They all turn and look at the rabbit. His name is Thumper, although he is usually too exhausted to do much thumping. Generally he just lies there, sprawled out on his stomach, gazing out on the class with a jaded expression. He has the air of someone who has heard one confession too many, like a bartender at a cheap bar. Arabella is fond of him.

'The bunny stays,' Arabella says, 'but you can change seats

if you like. Now, should we get started with the first lesson?' But before she can begin the lecture, another student raises his hand, this one wearing a security jacket with a name stenciled on the pocket, a name that looks like Demon.

'Demon?' she says.

'D'mon,' he says, 'like the devil but without the e.'

'I see.'

'Will we be talking about how to get an agent?' he continues, and Arabella surprises herself by snapping back: 'No. This isn't a class about publishing,' she says. 'This isn't about making money. This is about learning to write.'

'Okay,' D'mon says, shrugging genially.

'I don't mean to be belligerent,' Arabella says. 'It's just that writing is something holy to me. Quite honestly, it's something I've been doing for a very long time and without any financial reward. I spend half my life copyediting annual reports so I have enough money to live. You can't think about success.'

'So we're not going to be published?' D'mon asks.

'Well, no, I don't want to quash your hopes. I just wouldn't plan on it.'

Again, Arabella is conscious of Mimi's eyes on her, appraising, analyzing. She wonders what this young woman is doing in her class; she seems more the type of person who would be in an expensive graduate program. Maybe she is looking for material for a book; maybe she's going to write an exposé about writing programs. The bunny begins to suck on his water bottle, and an insistent gurgling sound fills the room.

'Let's get started,' Arabella says. 'Literally, let's talk about how you get started writing.

'The writer Katherine Anne Porter told a wonderful anecdote about how she came to write the classic story 'Flowering Judas,' and it's worth thinking about as you begin to write.

'Porter was living in Mexico, and one night she went out for a walk. As she did so, she happened to pass the window to her apartment. There she caught sight of her roommate in an unguarded moment. The expression on her roommate's face was one of desperation. Until that moment Porter had never realized how unhappy this woman was and how desperately she loved the man with whom she was having an affair. The sight of the roommate in the window set up what Porter described as a 'commotion in her mind.'

'So, my question for you is, what sets up a commotion in your mind? What do you agonize about at night before you go to bed?'

Arabella catches Conrad's eye and blushes. She wonders if he would do better with a transsexual fiction teacher. His writing is good, yet superficial; he needs to go deeper, but there is only so far she can press him without sounding like a voyeur. *Can you try to explain why your character is so eager to wear his mother's panties?*

'So,' she continues, 'you need to try to figure out what topics obsess you. It might be something big, like war and peace, or it might be something small, such as the fact that people keep cutting you on line. Or perhaps you think about Mr Right. I can see you nodding over there, Ginger. Or maybe you think about your mother; you wonder what sort of crisis is going to be going on when you visit her today. Is she going to accuse the nurse of stealing her engagement ring again? Is she going to be having an allergic reaction to some new medicine? Is she going to be convinced that the little old lady who sits in the corner and cries all the time is trying to cheat her at bingo?'

The elegant gentleman laughs at that and nods at her approvingly, but Arabella is not appeased. She is still annoyed that he was whispering, and she refuses to be seduced by his charms. She thinks, as she always does when she meets someone like this, of her father, a true gentleman who was confined to a wheelchair for his entire adult life and suffered for so many years without complaining at all. She has no patience for people who expect everything to come easily – which is why she became a writer.

'My point is that if you write about things that are important to you, you will find it much easier to get started. Write about the thing that sets up a commotion in your mind, and you will find that words come flowing.

'So here is the first exercise for the class. I'd like you to make a list of the five things that obsess you.'

The room is suddenly quiet. D'mon raises his hand.

'Do you have to have five obsessions?' he asks. 'Could it be four?'

'No,' Arabella says, just to be disagreeable. 'It has to be five. Hemingway would have had five, and so should you.'

D'mon nods and pulls out a pad of paper. Conrad doesn't move, and Ginger, who has already moved once to get away from the bunny, now asks if she can move again to be nearer the socket. 'I have to charge my laptop.'

Arabella shrugs, sits down at her desk, and figures she will let them have ten minutes to write. Then there will be half an hour more of class, and then it will be time to drive up to see her mother. She visits her every Wednesday. It's too bad that this semester the class she teaches is on the same day as her visits to her mother, but there is no point in changing it. Her mother is not flexible about these things. If you say you are going to visit on Wednesdays, then you show up on Wednesdays. You do not begin shifting things around. Once you begin shifting things around, you might shift yourself right out of a weekly visit; you might shift yourself right out to California and never visit her again. This is her mother's reasoning.

'All done?' Arabella asks when the time is up.

'So soon?' the woman with the Q-Tip hair cries out. She is a large woman and seems out of place in this nursery school classroom.

'The nature of obsessions is that you shouldn't have to think about them for too long,' Arabella says. 'They ought to jump right into your mind. Who'd like to read first?'

The class stares at her. There is a sullen intransigence about them that puts Arabella in mind of a child at a dentist's office: no one seems willing to open his mouth. 'I know it's hard,' she says, 'but reading aloud is an important way we build up trust in the class. You'll be amazed at how easy it gets.'

She smiles at Mimi, confident Mimi, who shakes her head slightly. She nods at a sleek young man who is dressed all in black. His name is Byron Stark, and he hisses, 'no.' She glares at the elegant whisperer, thinking to shame him into reading aloud, but he smiles gently and looks away. Of course. Arabella is reluctant to press anyone too hard. This is the first exercise, after all, and she wants to respect people's fears.

'Would someone please read his or her obsessions?' she says. Ginger is looking at her laptop screen so intently, one might suppose she was about to enter the code to start a nuclear attack. Conrad looks like her best bet, yet she does not want to hear his list about transsexuals because she is worried that will scare everyone off. She automatically starts to fold her arms across her chest and then stops. Never show fear. The first rule of teaching.

The bunny begins to thump against his cage, and a little pinecone, stuck on top of the cage by some mischievous nursery school student, goes cracking to the floor, the noise making everyone jump. She will just have to call on someone.

'How about you?' Arabella says, nodding at the red-faced woman with low self-esteem. Maybe if she reads, she will be proud of herself. Maybe it will set a good tone for the class, a tone of overcoming obstacles. She does so want this to be a successful class, with people reaching into themselves and coming up with something wonderful. And, anyway, she can see that Pam has drawn up a list of her obsessions. Arabella can see the list, can almost make out the words.

'Pam Mahoney?' she tries. 'Will you read for us?'

But Pam looks absolutely appalled. She clenches her hands into fists and presses them across her chest. She has quite literally locked herself into opposition. 'I can't,' she hisses through clenched teeth.

'Just one obsession,' Arabella whispers. 'Nothing big. Your favorite TV show?'

'No,' Pam murmurs.

There is a moment of silence, and then Q-Tip calls out, 'Why don't you tell us about your obsessions, Arabella?'

The class rumbles in agreement, and Arabella forces herself to smile genially at this rabble-rouser, this rebel, this cold sore on the healthy body of her class. She has the discouraging feeling that this woman is going to be getting her into trouble for the next ten weeks. She can almost picture the evaluation forms that the students will fill out at the end of the semester. *Was the instructor receptive to new ideas?*

'Of course,' Arabella says.

Now the class leans forward, probably hoping to hear something tantalizing. Arabella can feel them observing her, guessing her weight, thinking she should lose ten pounds and get a manicure, and wondering why she wears her hair that way. She wishes she had thought to brush it; she wishes she had gotten it cut last week instead of staying home, at her desk, working on her novel.

'My first obsession is my mother,' she says, smiling slightly so as not to look too pitiful. 'That would probably be my second obsession, too. My third obsession is writing and writers, and most particularly Dostoyevsky who is, as far as I'm concerned, the best there is. Fourth would be Manhattan; I love the city and have never wanted to live anywhere else. And fifth . . .' Here Arabella pauses. Her last obsession would be illness. Her father had Multiple Sclerosis and her mother has Parkinson's, and she has often written about people who are ill and how they deal with the healthy world. Yet she can't bring herself to say that to the class. It seems too much like a bid for pity, as though she is begging people not to drop her class, and it also seems fairly sad. She is only thirty-eight; she should be obsessed with something fun – sex or shopping. She can't bring herself to say sex, not in front of a bunch of writers. They will all imagine her in bed.

'And my fifth obsession is shopping,' she throws out, shrugging slightly. The bunny seems to shrug back at her, but then he's a bunny in a nursery school so exclusive that the children have to be interviewed before they can attend. He has heard his share of lies.

Now she can breathe deeply. Almost done. 'So,' she says, 'I've gone. Now wouldn't someone else like to read what he or she wrote?'

The class twitches. They're tempted; she can see it. And

then she notices that the elegant gentleman is whispering again to Dark Alice.

'Excuse me, Chuck Jones,' she snaps, 'but is there something you'd like to share with the class?'

He grins at that, a boy's grin, and although he looks to be about fifty, she can imagine him playing soccer, scoring a goal. She pictures a long-legged boy with curly blond hair, the handsome father, the genteel mother, the easy life.

'Does it relate to your obsessions?' Arabella presses.

He laughs at that. 'I'm sorry. I was just telling Alice here that you're the cutest teacher I've ever had.'

Writing Assignment

ARABELLA HICKS – THE FICTION CLASS

Make a list of your five obsessions.

1.

2.

3.

4.

5.

Now write a few paragraphs about one of them.

Chapter One

AFTER THE CLASS is over, Arabella gets into her car, which she has succeeded in parking on West Ninety-third Street, no easy feat, and heads north, in the direction of Westchester, in the direction of her mother who is in a nursing home in Port Chester. She stops off at a Wendy's along the way and buys two hamburgers, two medium French fries, and two Diet Cokes. This is the one and only thing she does that brings her mother pleasure. When you live in a nursing home and are forced to eat nutritious food all the time, the taste of a fast-food hamburger is like nectar – or so her mother says.

The parking lot at the nursing home is never crowded, but Arabella always parks in the same spot, next to the same Dodge Caravan with the bumper sticker that reads: 'Proud Parent of an Honor Student at Port Chester H.S.' She has noticed that almost every car in the nursing home parking lot has a bumper sticker; every car seems to need to screech out its owner's identity. I am not a bad person, each car seems to yell. I may have put my parent in a nursing home, but I support our troops, give money to breast cancer, brake for small animals, and am a member of the Irvington curling club. Her own car is a beat-up 1994 Cadillac which proclaims that in 1998 she had a pass to Jones Beach.

For just a minute Arabella sits in the car collecting her thoughts. The smell of the hamburger is nauseating. She checks her face in the mirror, pulls out a tube of lipstick, and smears it on, although the color doesn't look right to her. Her skin is so pale, the lipstick is so pink, and her eyes look so tired. She does not look cute. She has never looked cute, not even when she was a girl, with her brown hair in pigtails and her skinny legs covered in bright pink tights. She was the sort of child who everyone called 'Little Woman'. Adults invariably came up to her and said, 'What's wrong, dear? Not getting enough sleep?'

One of her boyfriends was convinced she would be gorgeous if she just took a little care of herself, but Arabella never saw the point of it. So many of the people she loved had major issues with their appearance, truly frightening and alarming issues, and to spend a lot of time worrying about the shape of her eyebrows or the cut of her hair just seemed ridiculous. She finds herself wondering what this Chuck would make of her best friend from childhood, a girl with a case of polio so extreme that it was as though God himself had reached down and twisted her body. She finds herself wanting to shock Chuck, to erase that smug expression. She wipes the lipstick off her face.

The nursing home is a two-story brick building that looks like an elementary school from the 1950s. There is a barren trellis at the side and two gigantic urns by the front door. Several sprigs of old Christmas holly jut out of the urns, bits of color for a cold day, although the effect is negated by the fact that the January winds have blown the sprigs sideways. The berries look stunned and harassed.

A woman is standing by the front door, which is odd, given that it is freezing out and she does not have the look of someone outdoorsy. She is wearing a fur coat and tiny black boots, and she has a scarf wrapped around her head. She is the sort of person Arabella associates with brick houses, marble floors, and formal mahogany dining room furniture. A haughty woman, and yet, even from the parking lot, Arabella can see there is something lost about her, too.

If she were one of Arabella's students, she would probably be writing a sensitive coming-of-age story about a young woman growing up during World War II. There would be a boy who had not gone to war because he had a weak heart. The girl's name would be Betty, and she would have a fiancé fighting in the Philippines. She would feel a love for this boy that transcended anything she had ever known. Perhaps there would be a child. His name would be Edward.

Arabella is so swept up by the woman's story she's imagining that she is surprised to find the woman walking toward her. She is even taller up close; the fur is more voluptuous, and the scent of her is spicy and rich.

'Excuse me,' Arabella says because the woman is now blocking her way into the nursing home.

'You're the daughter,' she says, 'aren't you?'

'What's she done?' Arabella immediately gets the burning sensation in her stomach that she associates with conversations having to do with her mother.

'She's gone after my husband, that's what she's done.' There's a trace of Long Island in this woman's voice. She has huge brown eyes and brassy blond hair, and Arabella remembers her mother saying that a doctor recently entered the home. 'A neurologist,' she had said, her eyes goggling with pleasure. Her mother comes from the generation when to be a doctor was to be a form of god, and to be a doctor's wife was the greatest honor of all – better even than catching one of Georgette Heyer's rakes.

'You're Bernard's wife, Camille?'

'So she told you!'

'She told me she'd made a new friend.'

Arabella can't help glancing at this woman's engagement ring, a huge pear-shaped diamond surrounded by smaller diamonds. She is a walking jewelry store.

'What sort of woman goes after another woman's husband?'

'I really don't think there's anything for you to worry about,'

Arabella says. 'I think it's just a harmless sort of thing. I suspect my mother is just looking for friendship.'

It's freezing out, and Arabella wants to go inside, but she can hardly walk past this woman.

'He told me she wants to get married.'

'No,' Arabella says, shaking her head. 'That's ridiculous. She was very devoted to my father, and I know she doesn't want to remarry. She would never say—'

'He asked me for a divorce. He said I was not worthy of him.'

The words make Arabella cringe because they sound exactly like something her mother would say, and yet it still seems unbelievable.

'Does she think I don't love him anymore?' Camille is saying. She's beginning to cry, but she isn't wiping away the tears. They slide down her cheeks, onto her coat.

'I'm sorry,' Arabella says.

'He is the love of my life.'

'I'm sorry,' Arabella says again, and she is. She is sorry for this woman and for her mother and especially for herself, a woman who has done absolutely nothing wrong, who only wants to bring her mother a hamburger and then go home to her little apartment in Yonkers, read through Alumco's optimistic annual report, looking for errors, write her novel and sip some scotch. Is that so much?

'We were married for forty years. He was my life. He was my soul. I would have done anything for him; I would have died for him. But he got this terrible, terrible illness. He became someone entirely different from who he was, and I still loved him. I never stopped loving him,' Camille whispers. 'But I couldn't keep him safe. I would come home, and he would not be there. He would be standing in the middle of Searington Road directing traffic – in his underwear. I hired an aide. She couldn't keep track of him. I hired two aides. He eluded them. This man is a genius. Even with this illness, he is a genius.'

Camille throws back her head, and now there is something biblical in her dignity. She is a queen addressing a peon. 'What could I do?' she demands. 'What could I do? Was there any punishment greater that God could have given me than that I should have had to make the decision to put my husband in this place?'

She is quiet for a moment and closes her eyes. The wind has died down, and the sun is on Arabella's face, although it brings her no warmth.

'We had no children,' Camille says. 'He is all I have. He is all I've ever had.'

Now Arabella feels her own tears welling up. She feels this woman's pain, and she thinks how terrible it must have been for her to put her husband in this home. She says the only thing she can say, the only thing she ever can say: 'I'll talk to her.'

Talk to her mother; she will scream at her. Arabella is so angry as she walks into the nursing home that her body is actually vibrating. How can her mother do such a thing? How can she trifle with this man's affections?

Where she was freezing just a moment ago, now she is hot, sweltering. She wrenches off her coat as she strides in the direction of her mother's room, past a cluster of residents sitting harmlessly in the hallway. Her mother's room is in the West Wing; a little paper tag marks it as her own: Mrs Vera Hicks. Arabella pushes open the door, walks in, and almost yells in frustration when she sees her mother is not there. She actually goes to slap her hand against the wall, stopping herself only when she realizes that her mother's roommate is sleeping. Actually, Lily is in a coma, but still it doesn't seem right to make a loud noise.

Her mother knows she is coming. Her mother knows the exact time she is coming because she has called twice to remind Arabella not to be late. How can she not be here?

There is a scattering of tissues on the floor near where her mother had been sitting. There are a few plastic cups filled with water and some wrappings from the Werther's candies she eats all the time. Two little shoes sit pointing out from under the bed, and for a moment Arabella thinks of the wicked witch's shoes in the *Wizard of Oz*. She looks at the nightstand, at the stack of Georgette Heyers, the collection of little angels, and some photos. One picture of her father catches her attention. He stares kindly at Arabella, and that makes her all the angrier. What if someone had tried to steal him away? What if someone had been as cruel to him as her mother is being with Bernard?

Arabella sets the bag of food from Wendy's on the nightstand, the bag now as sodden and flat as roadkill. Then she slams out of the room and heads in the direction of the dining room. It is the only other place her mother could be. The head nurse walks by, pauses for a moment as though intending to talk to her, undoubtedly to tell her about some other infraction her mother has committed, but then seems to think better of it and lets Arabella go. Two little dogs scamper by, solemn little Yorkies who live at the home and are there just to bring pleasure to the residents. At the sight of them, Arabella forces back a sob and then continues on.

She can hear the sound of the TV as she gets near the dining room and the urgent voices of the soap opera that is always on. When she hears the jangling of the bingo wheel, Arabella knows what her mother is doing. She knows what she is going to see, and, sure enough, as she walks into the dining room, she finds her mother sitting at the head of the table, looking for all the world like a queen on her throne.

She is dressed up, but then her mother always dresses nicely. Today she is wearing a blue skirt and a white top trimmed with lace. Her hair has been recently coiffed, and tiny little curls rest on her forehead. She has a fine aristocratic nose and high cheekbones, but the elegant effect is somewhat diminished by the eyebrow pencil she has overused, which gives her the appearance of being surprised.

There is a man sitting in a wheelchair alongside her, a man

with an arrogant face and mystified eyes. He is wearing a button-down shirt and a sailor hat, and he is staring at her mother adoringly, although her attention is completely focused on the bingo wheel.

'O sixty-four,' the nurse calls out, and her mother cackles with glee as she sets the red marker on her card.

'I almost have it,' she croons. The woman sitting across from her is trying to put the bingo chip in her mouth, all the while shouting, 'I'm winning. I'm winning.'

'You are not winning,' Arabella's mother snaps. 'I'm winning.'

'I'm going to get the prize,' the poor old lady cries out. Bingo chips are trickling out of her mouth. The nurse comes running over and pounds her back.

'You are not winning,' Arabella's mother snaps. 'I just need a B four.' At that moment she looks up and catches Arabella's eye and smiles. 'Just one more chip, and then I'll get the trophy.'

'It's time to go,' Arabella says. She thought she was speaking softly, but the words came out like a scratch. 'Game's over.'

'What!'

'B four,' the nurse calls out. No one except Arabella's mother is actually paying attention; no one except her mother can pay attention. 'Stop whispering,' one of the other women shouts, an aggrieved old lady with a stuffed animal on her lap.

'That's the one I need,' her mother says, but Arabella is beyond caring. She steps behind her mother's wheelchair and wrenches it backward, although, of course, the brake is on, so she can't move it anywhere. One of the nurses moves forward to offer help. She has a kind look on her face and is a kind woman; everyone here is kind except her mother.

'I've got it,' Arabella says, flipping the brake off and pulling her mother back. The residents are ignoring all the activity; their attention is on the game that is still going on in front of them. You could die here – people do die here – and the game goes on.

'What are you doing?' Her mother is shouting, putting her feet down on the floor, trying to stop the wheelchair from moving. 'I've won. I'm going to get the trophy.'

'You are being ridiculous,' Arabella hisses. She pushes her mother down the hall, past the little dogs who look up at her so hopefully, smelling the hamburger on her hands. They arrive back in her bedroom. It is only 4:30 in the afternoon, but it is dark outside; the window pane is a black slab.

'What is going on?' her mother asks, her pale blue eyes hard with anger. 'Have you lost your mind?'

'How could you go after a married man?'

Her mother presses her lips together. 'I'm parched. If you're going to kidnap me, could you get me something to drink?'

'I've just had a conversation with Bernard's wife. She's distraught. She asked me how you could go after her husband, and I have absolutely no idea. You of all people, after all those years of telling me how important it is to honor the marriage vows and after all those years of devotion to Dad. How could you do such a thing?'

Arabella can't help but look at the picture of her father that sits on her mother's nightstand. There is a cluster of pictures there, a habit her mother picked up from the days when her father was in the hospital all the time: Keep a lot of pictures alongside you so that people will know you are loved, and the staff will treat you better. Now Arabella looks at her father, sitting quietly in a wheelchair, as he sat for so many years of his life, hands folded neatly on his lap, the most gentle and loving expression on his face.

'Her name is Camille,' her mother says. 'What type of name is Camille? That's a courtesan's name. Didn't you tell me that? That's the name of someone from an opera.'

'You named me Arabella. Who are you to talk of names?'

Her mother puffs up her chest at that, making her look like the angry winner of a cockfight. 'Arabella is the name of a romantic heroine. Arabella does not die of consumption at the end of the story. She marries a wealthy man. She marries.'

'I'm not getting into this argument, Mother. This is not about my not being married. This is about you.'

Her mother looks at her quizzically, and Arabella can feel how ugly she must look now. Her face always turns bright red when she's angry; her hair is ragged because she hasn't had time for a haircut; her nails are torn; and for just a moment she thinks of Chuck smiling at her, telling her that she's cute. He has no idea, she thinks; a man like that could never understand who she is.

Arabella speaks slowly. 'It is upsetting to come to visit you and find a woman standing by the front door who is in tears because you have stolen her husband.'

'Did you see the ring on her hand?'

'Yes, I did. She has a big wedding ring, so what?'

Her mother tucks her head down and presses her tongue against her dentures, causing them to click up and down. 'A woman with a ring like that can afford to hire round-the-clock help. She can afford to have a nurse live with her. She doesn't have to put Bernard in here.'

'She had two aides. They couldn't watch him.'

Her mother puffs out a bit of air. 'Then you get a third aide.'

'So what are you, the avenging angel for husbands who are not well taken care of?'

Now her mother is angry. 'You take a vow for better or worse,' she says, 'not for better or better. So he's difficult now. So he wanders around, and he doesn't always know where he is. That's when he needs his wife; that's when he needs her to look after him. But what does she want to do? She wants to travel. She didn't tell you that, did she? Did she tell you she was in Egypt on a tour? That's why he kept escaping.'

She is breathing rapidly now, panting as though she had just gone running. 'Was it easy for me to look after your father? Would I not rather have gone on a tour of Egypt? It's so easy to let people go.' She's shaking her head now, looking at the picture of her husband. She fingers the necklace that he gave her for their twenty-fifth anniversary, a beautiful necklace that he designed himself – a spray of diamonds in the shape of a V. It is the only possession her mother cares about.

'You don't seriously want to marry this man?' Arabella says.

Her mother makes a clucking sound, 'I will never love any man but your father,' she says. 'I don't break my promises.'

Arabella feels the familiar buzz of confusion that she always feels with her mother, the strange pull of love and admiration that runs under all their conflict. She stands up to set out the cold hamburgers, to take care of her mother. The sound of classical music comes from the hallway, something soothing and sentimental.

'So now,' her mother says, settling back into her wheelchair, 'tell me about this new class of yours. Any husband material?'

Second Class: Character

'YOU LOVE BOOKS,' Arabella begins. 'You love the characters in books. In fact, I suspect for most of us who want to be writers, those characters were our first true friends. Have you ever felt as though the people in books understand you better than the people you actually know? Would Elizabeth Bennet criticize you for wanting to read a book on a Saturday night? Can you imagine Jane Eyre telling you to buy a push-up bra and go out there and make some noise? And Atticus Finch. Don't get me started. I became engaged to two separate men because they reminded me of Atticus Finch, although in the end all they really had in common with him was that they were lawyers and spoke slowly. In some respects there was more of Boo Radley in them than Atticus; it turns out that using literary characters as a guide to dating is not such a good idea.

'But my point is that when a writer creates a character, that character becomes alive. Readers will identify with her, and, hopefully, they will love her and want to be with her. This is not some idle intellectual exercise we writers are engaged in. We are like God; we are powerful – we are creating our own world and the people in it. So you don't want to blow it; you don't want your characters to be boring or stereotypes. You want them to be deep.

'Yes, D'mon?'

He is wearing the same outfit as last week, a blue shirt with his name embroidered on it. His skin is dark brown, and his hair is braided into a cluster of ropes.

'Has someone dropped out?' he asks. 'The class seems smaller this week.'

Arabella scans the room and counts ten people. 'Mimi's out sick,' she says, 'but I think everyone else is here.'

'No, I'm sure someone else is missing,' D'mon says. The rest of the class begin to turn their heads, counting the empty seats. Arabella thinks how odd it is that the students are always so conscious of attendance. She suspects they are all trying hard to be brave and not quit, that the thought of someone else succumbing to fear is quite terrifying. Either that or everyone just enjoys a disaster.

'There was another woman,' Ginger says. 'A redhead.' Ginger is the one who changed seats twice in the first class, and now she is sitting in yet another seat, which has thrown everyone off. Most people sit in the same seat over the course of the class; they stake out their turf and stick to it. But Arabella admires Ginger for bucking the trend. It is not easy to do something that's different. It hints at hidden depths. Either that or the woman is a complete lunatic.

'I really don't think so,' Arabella says. 'We started off with eleven, and now we're at ten. Could we get back to character?'

'I could take notes and send them to the absentees,' Dorothy says. This is the woman with the shock of white hair.

Absentees? 'There's just one missing,' Arabella says, picturing Mimi, a college-age woman, who was undoubtedly out drinking last night and is sleeping it off today.

'Do you have their addresses?' Dorothy asks.

Arabella wants desperately to get the class back on track, but before she can proceed, Chuck raises his hand. He is wearing a soft silver sweater today, a dark pair of jeans, and shoes that must be Italian. In fact, they look hand-sewn, and Arabella imagines him flirting with the young salesgirl at Barneys. *I've always loved all things Italian, he'd croon. Perhaps I could take you out for a biscotti and a caffè?*

'Yes?' she says, nodding at Chuck, wondering why a man who spends half his time whispering feels compelled to raise his hand to say something out loud.

'I just want to say that it's their loss. They're missing a good time.'

Dark Alice nods in agreement. 'Amen.'

Arabella is starting to feel that hysterical sensation she gets at times of stress. She has a feeling that she's going to start laughing. She remembers laughing at her father's funeral, and her mother laughing, too – the two of them cackling over the open casket on that horrible day. It was actually one of the few times she felt truly close to her mother. Their shared inappropriate laughter created a bond between them that gave them strength – for that day anyway.

'The question is,' Arabella says, gulping down her nervous laughter, 'how do you create characters who will resonate? How do you bring your characters to life? One way is to build up a dossier for them. We call this the iceberg theory; you have to know much more about your characters than will ever appear on the page. You may have to use only ten percent of what you know about the character in your writing, but it's important for you, the writer, to know everything. So let's create a dossier now.'

The angry woman with the hair like a Q-Tip raises her hand. It seems so odd to Arabella that this woman's name is Dorothy. That's a name she associates with Kansas and pigtails and a dog named Toto, and this woman is the antithesis of all that. She's Dorothy after a bad marriage.

'In my last class,' Dorothy says, 'the teacher said that character begins with a visual cue.'

'What do you mean?'

Dorothy takes a huge breath; she is getting ready to spew. She's a big woman with an active body, hair that shoots up, lips that look voracious, and hands that constantly smooth the smock of her plus-sized shirt. Arabella wonders what her story is. She doesn't wear a wedding ring. Is she someone who has been left in the lurch? Someone wounded but unable to find help – a science fiction writer, perhaps; someone who needs a new world to live in?

'In my last class,' Dorothy is saying, 'the teacher said that most writers find their characters when they see something that triggers an idea.'

'I think that's true,' Arabella says. 'You see a woman dressed all in white at the airport, and she has a white briefcase and white shoes, and you wonder who she is. Joan Didion started a novel with just that image. Or you're at the supermarket, and you see a couple. She's young and he's old, and you wonder if he's her father or her boyfriend or her parole officer.'

Chuck laughs at that and whispers something to Dark Alice. Meanwhile, Dorothy is busy writing notes on what Arabella said. She has written more words than Arabella has actually spoken. She'll write one of those long evaluations at the end of class, one of those screeds in which she analyzes everything Arabella has done wrong, and then she'll wind up with, 'But I thought as a person she was very nice.'

'But once you have the idea for the character, then what do you do?' Arabella asks. 'That's what I want to talk about now, and we'll do it together.'

'What?' Dorothy asks, looking alarmed, but Arabella turns to the blackboard and picks up a piece of chalk. She can hear people laughing in the next classroom; that's the screen-writing class. They are always so cheerful in screenwriting; the memoir class is always in tears, and the fiction class seems to be confused.

'Let's fill out a dossier together,' she calls out, hoping she sounds cheerful and enthusiastic. They are in a nursery school classroom, after all, surrounded by primary colors and easels and finger paints. It seems right to be cheerful.

'Dorothy, we'll start with you. What sex shall our character be?'

Dorothy doesn't answer. She is busy writing in her notebook. She is writing so fast, she looks as if she's taking dictation, and then she stops and underlines something so hard that Arabella can hear the paper tearing – a squeaking noise that seems to surprise the bunny, who thumps his legs against his cage.

'Dorothy,' Arabella whispers. 'Sex?'

Dorothy looks up at her with a look of utmost concentration. Whatever else one might say about Dorothy, you cannot say that she does not take this class seriously. She closes her eyes, then runs her hands through her hair, causing the white shock to stand up even straighter. 'Male,' she cries out.

'Male it is.' Arabella turns to the blackboard and writes *Male* in big letters, but as soon as she is done, Dorothy calls out: 'No, no, no. I mean female.'

'Okay.' Arabella picks up the eraser, and some white chalk falls on her blouse. 'Female it is.'

'No, no, no,' Dorothy calls out again, but Arabella holds up her hand. 'We can't do this all afternoon. Let's move on to Byron, is it?' She looks at the catlike man with the pencil in his mouth. Like Arabella he is dressed in black, but his clothes are soft, made of velour. His skin is a rich tan color, and he is wearing a bright gold necklace and watch.

'What is the name of our character?' Arabella asks, and then, giving him a moment to think, she looks at the rest of the class. 'You want to give a lot of thought to naming your character. The best example I can give you is that Margaret Mitchell based the main character in *Gone with the Wind* on her grandmother, but her grandmother's name was Annie. She changed the name to Scarlett, of course, but just think how different that book would be if the main character was called Annie.

'So, with that in mind,' she looks again at Byron, 'what shall we name our character?'

'Pussy,' he says.

The class titters at that. Arabella can feel herself blushing. She is not sure what to do. If she tells him to pick a different name, she will look like a prude, and people will be making suggestive remarks for the rest of the semester. If she's quiet, she will spend the day with a character named Pussy.

'Pussy it is.'

Dorothy writes something in her notebook and underlines it fiercely three times. Arabella moves on to the next student, the next question, and asks where Pussy lives. As she goes around the class, it turns out that Pussy lives in Las Vegas, her favorite color is red, she drives a Corvette, she shops at Victoria's Secret, and she is not married.

With a whole universe of characters to come up with, the class has put its collective minds together to create a stereotype that should be on a detective show on television. Arabella feels herself getting more and more impatient with each question she asks. This is not a character who interests her. This is not at all the sort of person she writes about. She doesn't have anything to say about such a person who has no inner life and no anxieties. And then, having gone all around the classroom, Arabella gets to the last person, who is Chuck Jones; as always, he is beaming genially at her. It is just one big party for Chuck.

'All right, how old is Pussy?' she asks him.

He grins at her. 'Sixty-three.'

The class moans, but Arabella is intrigued in spite of herself. It seems to her that a sixty-three-year-old Pussy is very different from a twenty-one-year-old one. The older Pussy will have many more dramatic possibilities, will have a past, will have regrets, will have something for her to write about.

'And, if I may be so bold,' Chuck Jones says, 'why don't we give Pussy a twenty-one-year-old daughter named Sheila?'

'Very nice,' Arabella says. Suddenly this woman is taking shape in front of her eyes. She is like a ghost flickering into view. She can actually see Pussy standing at her job, maybe at the front desk of the MGM Grand Hotel. She sees a tall woman with long gray hair; it is in an inappropriate style, and yet it looks oddly attractive.

'She would have been pretty old when she had Sheila, forty-two or so.' This comment from Ginger Clark of the traveling chairs who has dressed carefully for this class in gray slacks and sweater and a scarf tied neatly about her neck. She looks as if she is going to church after class. She's from Connecticut.

'It's not impossible,' Arabella says. 'In fact, that's how old my mother was when she had me. The question is, what does this tell us about Pussy?'

Ginger frowns and rubs her forehead. 'Oh, I don't know. Maybe she was a spinster, a virgin. And a traveling salesman came to town from Las Vegas, and she offered herself up to him, and this beautiful child was the result.'

So Ginger wants to be a romance writer, Arabella thinks.

'Now the daughter wants to be a stripper,' Byron calls out. 'She wants Pussy to be one, too. The first mother-daughter stripping act in Las Vegas.'

'I think we're getting a little far afield,' Arabella says. She has allowed this man to name her character Pussy, but she is not going to allow a mother-daughter stripping act. 'We are writing literary fiction, not pornography.'

'Why?' Byron says. 'Pornography is much more fun to read. In fact, I'm writing a book about the sex industry, and I've already had some nibbles. It's called *Spread Legs*,' he says to the class, stroking his chest. For one very bad moment Arabella thinks he is going to rub his crotch, but he doesn't.

'That's the title?' Conrad asks, rousing himself from his usual silence.

'The title and the name of the main character. No point in beating around the bush, right? I want everyone to know what they're going to get,' Byron says. 'No one is going to pick up this book and be surprised. If you don't want to read it, you don't have to, but' – here he leans forward dramatically and looks at Ginger – 'lots of people are going to want to read it.'

He winks.

'I do not see this woman at all,' Dorothy calls out, irritated. 'I think this is a farce. I don't believe in Pussy.'

'What if this lady has a gambling problem?' This is from the young man who has been sitting very quietly next to Conrad. He has a hat pulled down over his head and is clutching a copy of Hemingway's short stories. Last week it was *Bleak House*. Arabella hopes he can write; he's holding himself to very high standards.

'So Pussy is trying to protect her daughter,' Arabella says, thinking out loud, 'but she's having trouble taking care of herself because she has a gambling problem.'

'Oh, come on. Make her a lap dancer at least. This is Vegas.' Byron's mouth is twisted with exasperation. 'Let's have some fun. Come on, people.'

But Dorothy is shaking her head. 'She wouldn't be a lap dancer,' she's saying. 'I don't believe in that.' Dorothy is looking toward Arabella, waiting for her to resolve the problem. Is Pussy going to be a wild woman having a great time or a tortured soul with a gambling problem? Arabella is tempted to make her a lap dancer just for the fun of it. Why

39

shouldn't literature be fun? But she thinks that Dorothy is right, that this character is turning into a cliché. Even more important, she feels that whatever she chooses will mean more to Dorothy than to Byron. Dorothy is obviously a woman who is used to having her choices dismissed.

'We'll give her a gambling problem,' Arabella says, but when Byron groans, she smiles at him. 'You can do whatever you like with your own writing. I give you permission to put a mother-daughter stripping team into *Spread Legs*. So now let's move onto one last question for Pussy, and this is the most important one. What does Pussy want?'

There is the briefest of pauses, and then Byron shouts out, 'To get laid.'

'That's enough,' she says to him. 'Get your mind out of the gutter.' For just a moment she sounds so much like her mother that she almost covers her mouth. She is losing control of the class. She is losing control of herself.

'You!' she says to a middle-aged woman who has been sitting quietly through the last ninety-minute discussion, the same woman who would not recite her obsessions last week. Hopefully, she has recovered by now; hopefully, she is ready to say something. 'Yes, you, Pam Mahoney. What do you think Pussy wants?'

Pam breathes deeply. She looks down at her notepad, at the black ink that she has scrawled all over it. At least she hasn't crossed her arms on her chest. That's progress.

'Any thoughts?'

Pam stares up at her, wild-eyed. How hard is this? Arabella thinks. All you have to do is come up with anything. You can even agree with Byron and say that she wants to get laid. You can say anything.

The class is quiet, waiting. Pam is staring at Arabella, who shrugs at her encouragingly, and then Pam stands up, picks up her notebook, and walks out of the room. It all happens so seamlessly that it takes Arabella a few seconds to realize that one of her students has just run out on her.

Arabella starts after her but then stops at the door. What is she going to do? Chase her down the west side of Manhattan, wrestle her to the ground, and force her to be a writer? Type, damn you, type!

The best thing would be for someone else to chase after her, but no one else seems to care. She looks back at the class, ablaze with irritation. How can no one care? We're writers. We're supposed to care. She can almost hear the sound of her mother cackling. *We live in an age of cowardice. No one has the courage to stay anymore. The first hint of trouble, and people go running out.* And now the boy with the Hemingway book raises his hand. Maybe he will offer to go, Arabella thinks. Hemingway would have run after her, wouldn't he?

'Yes, Justin?'

'What she wants is love,' he says.

For a moment Arabella is flummoxed. Why would Pam want love, and why would that make her go running out of the classroom? But then she realizes that he is still on Pussy. The class is still thinking about Pussy. They don't care about a desperate and invisible middle-aged woman who went running out of the room. They just care about themselves. And isn't that the way of the world, she thinks.

'She does want love,' Arabella says.

The rest of the class goes by smoothly. No one else goes running out, anyway. The class ends on time, and Arabella hands out the take-home assignment, which is to think about a famous character from history and write a scene in which he or she is eating lunch. 'Just make up the details,' Arabella cautions. 'Don't go Googling for Abraham Lincoln's favorite pastry. Think about what you know about these people and try to make it up.'

She feels spent as the class files out and suspects that she will remember the image of Pam running out for a long time. Chuck stops by her desk, and he is smiling. She looks at him warily. How can anyone be so damned happy all the time? Has the man no self-doubt, no angst, no depth?

'Do you think that woman is all right?' he asks. 'I wonder what came over her.'

'I imagine she got scared,' Arabella says.

He shakes his head and smiles ruefully. She can smell the leather of his shoes; she finds herself thinking of her father's shoes, his beat-up loafers stretched out of shape by her mother, who struggled to cram his unbending feet into them.

'What could she be scared of?' he asks. 'This is adult ed, and you're not exactly a Tartar.'

'I don't think it's me she's afraid of,' Arabella snaps, irritated that he finds the whole thing so amusing. 'I think it's herself. She's probably terrified that she's not good enough, and if she's not good enough, what is she going to do with the rest of her life? What is she going to dream about?' She can feel her voice catch, and the emotion surprises her. What is it about this man that agitates her? She has the oddest desire to fling herself at him and smack him, but before she can do anything, Justin interrupts. 'Sorry. Excuse me.'

'Not at all,' Arabella says, perversely glad to have an excuse to turn her back on Chuck. 'How can I help you?'

Justin is a pale young man with an intense expression, Raskolnikov from Scarsdale. There are always boys like this in her class, and she always worries about them; they seem doomed to disappointment. She is never sure what happens to them after the class is over, but she has the feeling they wind up doing some horribly venal thing and feeling contempt for themselves the rest of their lives.

'Can I get your opinion about something?' he asks.

'Sure.'

'I have this job as a messenger, and the owner is really messing me up. I'm thinking I might quit. You've read my stuff. Do you think I could make it if I quit?'

'No,' Arabella says, with visions of bounced checks in her head. The poor boy winces as though she has slapped him. 'It's nothing to do with you, Justin. No insult intended. It's just that it's really, really hard to make enough money to live on as a writer. And then you have to worry about health insurance. Do you have any idea how many annual reports I have to proofreead to set aside enough money? Even worse is that when you quit your job, you put yourself under all sorts of pressure. It causes writer's block.'

She can see by the expression on his face that he doesn't care about health insurance.

'Really, believe me. Try to find a way to write and work at the same time.'

He shakes his head and bites his lip, obviously annoyed. He must have thought she would applaud his decision and praise him for his daring. She catches the bunny's jaded gaze. Without shifting his eyes, he tips his head up slightly and licks his water bottle. *We are all creatures driven and derided by vanity*, she imagines the bunny saying, assuming the bunny quotes James Joyce.

'Well, good luck,' she says to Justin. 'I hope it works out for you.'

Writing Assignment

Arabella Hicks – The Fiction Class

Think of a person from history who intrigues you. Napoleon? Cleopatra? Martin Luther King?

Write a two-to-three-page description of that person eating a meal. What would s/he eat? How would s/he eat? What would s/he be thinking about as s/he ate? Would someone be sharing the meal with him or her? What would they talk about?

Remember: Bring Your Character to Life!

Chapter Two

THE WIND IS so harsh when Arabella gets out of her car that she is flung forward in the direction of the nursing home. It is the third Wednesday in January, about as wretched a time of year as there is. The cold seems to be attacking her body, biting her cheeks, stabbing at the fillings in her teeth, slicing into the very marrow of her bones. The only source of warmth comes from the bag from Wendy's that Arabella is pressing against her chest. She feels like someone in a Jack London story; she imagines herself slumping into a snowdrift, clutching the Wendy's bag for warmth, her own life force seeping out as the hamburger gradually cools.

She is feeling a little depressed.

She keeps seeing Pam running out the door, and there is something horrifying about that image that she can't get out of her head. But if Arabella is honest with herself, which she tries to be, the terrible thing is that there is also something ridiculous about Pam. She thinks of Chuck's words: *This is adult ed, and you're not exactly a Tartar.* He's right, of course. Who goes running out of a writing class? Her emotions twist inside her: mockery, anger, and sadness. She agrees with Chuck, and yet he angers her, too, because he is a man who will never go running out of a writing class. It just doesn't matter enough to him. He doesn't even do his homework.

The wind nips at her while she struggles forward. Head down, hamburger pressed against her chest, she catches a whisper of some music that must have escaped from the nursing home when someone opened the front door. It sounds like a waltz. The music jars her; suddenly it carries her back to a night when she was young and happened to be standing outside the door of her parents' bedroom. She heard her father singing. He had a lovely, deep voice, and it stayed strong throughout the course of his illness. As she listened from behind the closed door to her father singing, she could imagine that her parents were like everyone else. He started off singing drinking songs from the army, moved onto Gilbert and Sullivan, and wound up with Arabella's favorite, the song that had been on the radio when he proposed to her mother. 'Waltzing Matilda, waltzing Matilda, you'll come a-waltzing Matilda with me.'

She hums the music to herself; it comforts her as she presses forward.

*

'Would you like a cookie?'

Arabella, caught up in her reveries, snaps to and finds she has walked into the lobby of the nursing home, and the receptionist, Dotty, is standing in front of her, holding out a butter cookie.

'Take one,' she's saying. 'I have a whole plateful.'

Arabella, looking over at the front desk, sees that this is true. There is a large silver platter filled with bakery cookies and two silver urns and a tray of china coffee cups.

'I can't. Thanks. If I put on any more weight, I'll explode.'

'You!' Dotty exclaims. 'But you're so tiny.'

She pops one into her own mouth by way of encouragement, and Arabella can't help but follow suit. They're the buttery type of cookies with hardened cherries in the middle. The blast of sugar warms her.

'That is good.'

'See, you looked as if you needed a cookie. Have another one.'

Dotty is a small woman who wears huge pieces of jewelry, giant wings of silver that creep around her neck and doughnut-sized earrings that shimmer. From their previous conversations Arabella knows that Dotty used to be a saleswoman at Tiffany's. Then she got married and had a daughter, her husband left her, and she got cancer. Now she's okay except that she gets tired a lot. Arabella's mother says she's a whiner.

'Do I smell hamburger?' Dotty asks, twitching her nose like a rabbit.

'You do.' Arabella opens up her coat and withdraws the bag, which is now pressed into the shape of a flat disk. 'Oh, damn, I have it all over me.'

Her blouse is black, so the stain is not visible, but the hamburger grease feels damp, like an open wound. It is warm and sticky against her skin; it is disgusting.

'Wendy's,' Dotty chirps, nodding her head. She walks over to her desk and pulls open a drawer. 'That's such a treat for your mother, isn't it?' she mutters as she rummages through her supplies. She lifts up a bottle and then another, and meanwhile the little dogs have flopped down at Arabella's feet and are staring up at her mournfully. 'What a good daughter you are. So thoughtful. They do love their fast food, don't they? Such a treat.'

All the time Dotty is muttering and rummaging and searching, lifting up Chap Sticks, threads and needles, a thimble, a CD, lipstick, and curlers. Then she cries out: 'Here we go. Found it.'

She teeters over on her high heels, grabs hold of Arabella's shirt, and begins to rub at it with a white pen. All the while she is humming some formless tune; it is probably a habit of hers while she's working. Arabella finds herself wondering what sort of fiction Dotty would write if she were in her class. People do surprise you. The most innocuous-looking people write the most alarming fiction, and women are the worst. Many women seem to seethe with a deep, violent anger. Many times Arabella has read some little gray-haired lady's story and found it a screed of rage and anger. Yet she cannot believe that Dotty is something other than what she appears to be. She feels certain that Dotty would lean toward a gentle romance, something along the lines of Georgette Heyer, something in which the women are pert and beautiful, and the men strong and reliable. And somehow Arabella's shirt is clean.

'Good as new,' Dotty calls out.

'That's amazing.'

'Just a little Clorox in a pen. You never know when you'll need it.' Dotty twitches her nose again, goes back to the desk, and puts the Clorox away. Arabella feels oddly calm now, taken care of.

'That was very kind of you,' Arabella says. She can feel her voice cracking. Anytime anyone does something kind for her, she feels as if she's going to cry. She takes another cookie, and Dotty takes one, too. Then Arabella asks her how she's doing, and she tells her a horrible story. She has a lump. It is probably nothing, but the doctor wants to do surgery. Her insurance company has changed, and she is not sure she will be able to have the operation. She also has a ringing in her ear that makes her think the cancer has spread to her brain.

'You're late,' her mother says when Arabella walks into her room. She is sitting at a small table next to the window. Her reflection shimmers ghostlike against the night-black pane.

'Well, hello to you, too,' Arabella says, walking over to the little table and setting down the Wendy's bag.

'It's almost seven o'clock. I thought you were in an accident.'

'I was talking to Dotty at the front desk.' Arabella clears away some of the stuff that has accumulated on the table: the stacks of Georgette Heyer romances, the newsletter from the home, the reminders from the social worker to come to the book club, an old birthday card from the church her mother used to go to, and the red family Bible. 'Dotty's having a terrible time.'

'I hope this means you're going to stay later. I hope this isn't one of your mini visits.'

'No visit with you is a mini visit,' Arabella says, smiling, although in the reflection in the window it looks as though she's grimacing. 'Every single one of them is a full-length novel.'

Arabella pulls out two paper plates and sets the hamburgers and French fries on the table. She has eaten so many cookies that the sight of the food is not appealing, but there is no point in telling her mother that.

'I see you once a week, and you spend the time talking to someone you wish was your mother. You're going to stay for five minutes.'

'I'm going to be here more than five minutes, and I don't need another mother. One is fine.' The roommate's respirator is making a steady, soothing sound. Arabella wheels her mother over to the table, sets a napkin on her lap, and holds up the hamburger to her lips. Sometimes her mother can hold her food herself, but not if she is upset, and Arabella knows this is not going to be a great visit. She will probably start to gag on the hamburger. The Parkinson's is always worse when she is worked up, and then the gagging reflex starts.

'I see Lily has flowers. Is it her birthday?'

'You have to stay until eight o'clock. It's the least you can do. You have to watch *Wheel of Fortune*.'

She takes a bite of the hamburger and chews it greedily. Her hair is a little floppy today, which is not like her, Arabella thinks. Her mother has always been adamant about taking care of herself and her husband. He might be in a wheelchair, but that was no reason that he couldn't be well dressed. Never give people a reason to pity you, she used to say. She would have liked the shoes that Chuck was wearing today, Arabella realizes. She would have found them 'spiffy'.

Outside, the wind is blowing so hard that the birch tree seems to be bending over. It is going to be a rough ride home, and driving a 1994 Cadillac in the snow is not the same experience as driving a four-wheel-drive SUV. Suddenly a passage from a story Arabella read flashes into her head. It was a gruesome story about someone who haunts car graveyards looking for used parts. He comes across a car that has been in an accident and sees teeth marks, apparently the driver's, impressed into the steering wheel. Arabella can't help herself; she rubs her teeth.

'So what's new with Dotty? Why is she having a tough time now?'

'The doctor thinks the cancer might have spread to her brain.'

'Might have. Remember when they told Debbie Ranes that she might have ovarian cancer, and it turned out she was just pregnant?'

'Yup.'

Arabella opens the little container of ketchup and squeezes some onto the fries. She thinks of Pam, and suddenly all the sympathy she had been feeling for her drains away. What a coward to run out of a writing class. How could the anxiety of being in a room with a bunch of writers possibly compare to being in a room with her mother?

'People shouldn't pay so much attention to doctors,' her mother is saying. 'You have to make up your own mind. You have to learn to think for yourself.' She clicks her tongue against her teeth, a sharp, irritating noise.

'Mom, that's ridiculous. If a doctor tells you that cancer may have spread to your brain, how are you supposed to ignore that?'

'I'm just saying that Dotty does seem to have a flair for the dramatic. What was it last year, a cerebral hemorrhage?'

'But she did have a cerebral hemorrhage.'

Her mother turns toward Arabella, her expression exasperated. A small bit of ketchup is on the side of her lip. 'Well, it couldn't have been that bad, or she wouldn't be back at work, would she?'

Arabella looks over at the little dimpled angel that sits on her mother's nightstand. Her mother used to be obsessed with angels; she would buy them whenever they went shopping – solemn plaster ones and shimmering sparkling ones, and this little cute one who looks more grandmother than angel.

'I'm just saying she might not be the pillar of society you think she is,' her mother adds.

Arabella looks back at her mother. 'I can't keep arguing with you, Mom. I think it's killing me. I feel as if I'm drying up inside, you know? I feel as if this constant level of anger is killing me. I mean really killing me. In fact, I'm convinced there's some tumor forming inside me even now. Isn't there some way we can stop this?'

Her mother swallows, sniffs, and licks the ketchup off her lip. She folds her hands on her lap in a gesture that reminds Arabella of her father, always sitting so patiently, waiting, waiting. 'Of course,' she says.

'I'm not saying it's your fault,' Arabella adds. 'It's mine, too. I'm just saying I'd like to get past it.'

The wind is forcing the birch trees against the window; their branches claw for support. Her mother seems to deflate, and her skin pales. The blouse hangs loose on her, but her gray slacks are pleated; her shoes stylish. Her mother is adamant about not wearing nursing home sneakers; she will not surrender. She has fought so hard and has had so much to fight. She has had a tough life. Guilt seethes through Arabella, but there is no way to make amends – not at this point.

'I'm sorry, Mom. I didn't mean to upset you.'

Off in the distance one of the residents is calling for her mother, a sad, forlorn sound. On the wall there is a computer-generated calendar for the month of January, and someone has colored in a picture of a snowman.

'There's nothing to apologize for. Certainly I don't want to be responsible for giving you cancer. God knows I have enough guilt to deal with. Why don't you just tell me about your day? What did you do with your class?'

Arabella hears the quaver in her mother's voice, a tortured sound. 'I'm sorry. I shouldn't have said anything. I don't know what I was thinking.'

Her mother is silent. This is not Pam; her mother is much tougher than Pam. Her mother will not run from the room. It will be Arabella who goes dashing from the room; it will be Arabella who is going to pay for her indiscretion, so she might just as well do what her mother wants and tell her about the class.

'I talked about character,' she says, 'and we worked together to create a composite character, which wound up being this strange woman who lives in Las Vegas. Then one of my students went running out of the room.' She throws that part in intentionally because she knows her mother will love it. And she does spring to attention.

'Why?'

Arabella shakes her head. She sees Pam in her mind again, those wide-open eyes, the terror. 'It must have been hard for her to come to the class in the first place. In fact, I have a feeling her husband gave it to her as a gift, maybe for their twenty-fifth wedding anniversary. She probably always dreamed of being a writer. He thought he was doing something nice for her and had no idea of the anxiety it might cause.'

The music from the hallway has changed to something melancholy, perhaps something by Schumann. Arabella can hear the rolling wheels of the medicine cart; the nurses are making their rounds, handing out sleeping pills and Benadryl. It is bedtime at the nursing home; soon the lights will start clicking off, and the quiet will be filled with the moans of patients calling for their mothers. It's a scary time.

'Do you think she'll come back?'

'No,' Arabella says and shakes her head, thinking of the look on Pam's face as she ran out of the room and the rancid smell of her panic. 'I doubt it. I wouldn't. I mean, it would be kind of embarrassing after all that.'

Her mother sniffs at that, and Arabella laughs. The one thing she and her mother have in common is a shared belief that you do not quit, that come hell or high water, you see things through. She suspects that is the one solid tie that binds her and her mother together. She also suspects that is why she has never married. Every time she dates a man, she wonders if he would stay with her if she got sick. It sort of puts a crimp on going to dinner and a movie.

'Was she a good writer?' her mother asks. The querulous

look is off her face. Now she's intrigued. Her hands are shaking less, and she is able to pick up the French fries. She is munching them thoughtfully. Arabella can't help but smile at her mother. She does love a story.

'I don't know. It was too early in the class to tell, but I doubt it.' The few things Pam wrote were generic, and that may be part of why she ran. She may have sensed that. It is always a shock for people to meet other writers, to realize there are other people trying just as hard or even harder.

'I don't see how you can teach someone to write,' her mother says, but she is speaking thoughtfully. She is not looking for an argument.

'It's not so much about teaching them the craft of writing,' Arabella says, 'because they could probably figure that out from reading a book.' She is speaking urgently; this is something she thinks about a lot. 'It's about creating an environment in which they think they can write. That's the secret of a writing class. A good teacher makes her students feel secure enough to write their stories.'

'And that's what you do?' her mother asks.

'That's what I want to do. In practice, it's hard, and I can't always figure out how to bring everyone together. This is New York, after all. People are prickly.'

The lights in the hallway are dimmed. The nursing home is shutting down, getting ready for bedtime.

'Maybe I should write my story,' her mother says. Her eyes are challenging. It is the same expression she wore when she

Susan Breen

fought the doctors: *What do you mean there's nothing you can do for my husband?*

'Maybe you should.'

'You don't think I'd be any good.'

'I never said that.' The medicine cart is coming nearer. Soon the night nurse will be here with the blue pills mashed into the little cup of applesauce.

'I used to get As in English. You get your talent somewhere, you know.'

That surprises Arabella. She never knew her mother thought she had any talent. She is not one to hand out compliments.

'I'll tell you what,' Arabella says, the compliment making her feel expansive, 'I gave the class an exercise. You might like to hear it.'

Her mother nods.

'I asked them to think about a character from history who intrigues them and then try to bring that character to life.'

Her mother puts her finger to her nose, a sign that she is thinking. She does something similar when they watch *Wheel of Fortune*. She continues thinking, and Arabella is not sure whether or not she should say something. Her mother does not like to be interrupted.

'Marie Curie.'

'The scientist?' Arabella says with more vehemence than she had intended.

'Why not?' Her mother purses her lips. 'I used to think that

58

if I could have had a college education, I would have liked to be a scientist. She worked alongside her husband, but after he died and she was left a widow, she continued her research. She had a full life.'

'That's interesting,' Arabella says, suddenly remembering that her mother used to talk about Marie Curie a lot. That was probably why Arabella had started off wanting to be a doctor.

'So,' her mother says, haughty, eyes heavy-lidded, 'did I pass?'

Minutes later the aide pushes the medicine cart into the room and then the night aide comes to get her mother ready for bed. This is always Arabella's signal to leave. Her mother likes privacy when she is being changed and gotten ready for bed, and Arabella does not like to witness the intimacy. There is something about seeing a stranger take your mother to the bathroom that is very unappealing, so she packs up the leftover scraps of Wendy's and kisses her mother's cheek.

'Love you,' she whispers.

'Love you, too,' her mother whispers back.

This visit has actually not been that bad, but the relief Arabella feels as she leaves her mother's room is transcendent. She is free for a week. There may be errands to run; she usually has to pick up Polident or Werther's candies. There may even be phone calls, but that's never as bad as the visits because she can always hang up. The simple clean lines of her week stretch in front of Arabella. She can work on her novel; she can try to figure out an end for it. She is meeting with an editor who has a museum brochure for her to proofread. She is going with an old friend to a lecture at the Mercantile Library on Friday night; the friend is in even worse shape with her book than Arabella because she is stuck on the opening chapter. Saturday she is taking a knitting class, and Sunday is church. And one of the members is going to be giving a lecture on how parables are portrayed in art. She is looking forward to it.

Arabella is in such a good mood that she stops at the nurses' desk to check in with Marvel, the head nurse for the West Wing. She tries to keep up with her mother's doctor visits and cholesterol levels and so on, not that there is ever any change. She checks so that the staff knows that she cares, so that they will take better care of her, and so they will not feel contempt for Arabella. That's important to her. She feels contempt for herself for having her mother in a nursing home, but she can't bear that anyone else would feel it.

'Ah, Miss Bella,' Marvel croons. 'I've been wanting to talk to you about your mother.'

Arabella immediately feels like smacking herself in the head. What was she thinking, stopping off at the nurses' desk? Isn't that one of the first rules she learned as a child? Don't go looking for trouble. 'I know all about Bernard,' Arabella says. 'I talked to his wife last week, and then I talked to my mother. I think the whole thing is straightened out.'

'No, no,' Marvel says. She is a huge black woman with a Jamaican accent and a face that seems carved. There is something as solid as a statue about her, something godlike, actually. God without the attitude. Arabella likes her, but she is scared of her, too.

'Let's go in my office and talk.'

What has she done now? Arabella thinks. Could Camille be suing her? Could it be something really bad, like the time two years ago when she persuaded one of the male nurses to bring her some sleeping pills? They almost threw her out of the home for that. What if they are going to throw her out of the home? She doesn't have any more money; she can't go anywhere else. What if she has to live with Arabella again?

Arabella's knees feel weak. She is actually shuffling as Marvel puts out her hand and guides her in the direction of the office, which is no more than a very large closet. On the wall is a calendar from a pharmaceutical company as well as a framed photo of several children on a beach and a postcard from Las Vegas, which makes Arabella think of Pussy. Poor Pussy who just wants to find love. Why on earth did she stop by to talk to the nurse?

'Have a seat,' Marvel says, gesturing toward a gray metal chair that moves back slightly when Arabella sits down on it. She jams her feet on the ground, seeking support. Suddenly she is starving; suddenly she wishes she had eaten the hamburger and fries.

'How are you, Bella?'

'I'll be doing much better when you tell me what my mother's done.'

Marvel clasps her hands together as if in prayer. 'I'm sorry to tell you that the doctor heard some abnormal heart sounds during the checkup today.'

Those words are so far from the ones that Arabella is expecting that she can't quite take them in. 'I thought the medicine was taking care of that.'

'She's had Parkinson's for more than thirty years. It's taking a toll on her heart.' Marvel wears her hair ironed into a neat flip, which makes her look like something out of the 1950s.

'Well, I remember the doctor talked about surgery to repair a valve. I guess we could think about that,' Arabella says, trying to remember what it was the doctor did say so many years ago. She took notes. They're somewhere.

'Oh Miss Bella,' Marvel says. She puffs out her cheeks and blows a gust of air. 'Your mother is in no condition to have surgery.'

Arabella starts, unintentionally causing the chair to jolt. One of the photographs falls to the floor, and she stares at it — two dark children smiling up at her from a sunny beach. She is tired. It has been a long and upsetting day, and she has to drive home in the dark and the snow.

'What are you saying then, Marvel?'

'I'm saying that perhaps now would be a good time for you to try to settle up with your mother.'

Something swirls inside of Arabella, something that feels like a tornado ripping right through her. Suddenly Arabella has had enough. Suddenly it seems to her that this long, terrible day must come to an end. Perhaps because she trusts this woman, she is more honest than she otherwise would be.

'What do you think I'm going to do with my mother? Take her to Disney World? Everything there is to say to my mother I've already said, and believe me when I say that she hasn't left much unsaid, either.'

She can't let it go at that. Her heart is ramming inside her, sending hot streams of blood racing around inside her veins. It is as though her body is in rebellion, as though her very insides are screaming in protest.

'I love my mother. I've loved her my whole life. I'll do the best I can for her. I'll take her to extra doctors if you think I should, and I will deplete my meager savings. But don't say I should do something if you mean I am going to wave some wand and make everything all right between us because I just don't have it in me.'

Arabella sags against the chair, dropping her weight against it in surrender. 'I just can't,' she says to Marvel. 'I just can't do it.'

Chapter Three

ON THURSDAY MORNING Arabella wakes up and goes directly to her computer. This is her regular routine: Sit down at the computer, stare at her bookshelves, look at the computer screen, play three rounds of Spider Solitaire, stare out the window at the Hudson River, open up the document she is working on, read the last chapter she wrote, and change some of the punctuation. Pick one of the books on her bookshelf, look at the ending of it, and try to figure out why that ending works. Look at the framed picture of her mother that she keeps on her desk, an eight-by-ten glossy from an old church directory. Play Spider Solitaire. Delete the changes she just made to the punctuation. Stare bleakly at the last chapter of her novel.

She is so close to finishing it. Twenty good pages would

probably do it. The problem is she has been working on it for so long that she can't tell what's good and what isn't. It is like being caught in a boring marriage; it is not bad enough to jettison, but she can't figure out how to fix it. She can't think of an ending, or she can think of an ending but nothing good. There is a main character who wants to get married, and she does. Somehow it seems as though something more should happen, but she can't think what. Arabella has a terrible feeling that the problem is not with the ending but with the beginning.

She jumps to the first page and sees the novel's title: *Courting Disaster*. She still likes the title, but she has to change it because she just saw an ad for a book in the *New York Times* with the same title. But that is the least of it. She reads the first paragraph for the three thousandth time:

> *Jack Hastings would have been the fourteenth man to propose to me, the sixteenth if you count the Dorsey twins, which I don't. They were so desperate, they would have proposed to anyone, and when they saw that I was not afraid to look at them or touch them, it was only natural that they fell in love with me – if* natural *is a word you can use in that context.*

Arabella wonders once again if she should switch to the third person. She wonders if the tone is right. She wonders why on earth she ever decided to write a novel about such a snide person and if it wouldn't be better to delete the whole thing and start over. But how do you delete seven years of your life? Surely there is some way to salvage this.

She plays another round of Spider Solitaire. She wonders what the people who program Spider Solitaire do when they are loafing. Do they read books on the sly or, most likely, go to porn sites? She thinks of Byron and wonders why he is taking her class. She looks up at the picture of her mother. It was a Christmas present from a few years ago.

'What a large photo,' Arabella had said.

'I know,' her mother had replied. 'It's a ridiculous picture, but you'll be glad to have it after I'm dead.'

For a while Arabella kept it in the back of her closet, but every time she went to get her winter clothes, she'd stumble across it and be startled. She finally figured it would be better to have it out in the open. It is always better to face your demons – or *D'mons*, as the case may be.

She wonders if Marvel is right. She wonders if her mother really could be dying. The thought of it makes her feel cold, as though it were she who was dying. There is a void opening in front of her.

Enough of that. Arabella turns her attention back to the computer and clicks to the last paragraph. She stares at it until her eyes tear.

Third Class: Plot

'YOU'RE SCARED OF plotting out your story, aren't you? You're not so worried about character because you've been interested in people all your life. And description doesn't concern you because you like words. That's why you want to be a writer. But what are you going to do about this plotting, this maneuvering your characters around in ways that seem arbitrary to you? The outlines and the index cards and the computer programs and the narrative arc? It all seems cold and artificial.'

Arabella smacks her hand against the desk. 'You're an artist, for God's sake, not a conductor. Who are these philistines who are expecting a plot? Why can't they just appreciate good writing when they see it?' The class stares at her, bemused, all nine of them. Pam is not there, of course, and Mimi e-mailed this morning to say that she was sick again, although Arabella suspects she is just hung over. She is twenty-two years old and applying to graduate programs. She explained in her e-mail to Arabella that she's taking this class just for fun. She wants to meet normal people, she wrote, without the least consciousness that one might consider that an insult. She is hung over for sure.

'The problem is that when there is no plot, there is no story, and when there is no story, things get just a little bit boring.'

'A craft question,' D'mon calls out.

'I haven't said anything yet. How can you have a question?'

Arabella can hear the edge in her voice, and she knows the class hears it, too. She has not been getting enough sleep. She has been dreading today's visit with her mother. But there's no point in taking that out on the class. 'All right, what's your question?'

'Does the plot start with page one?'

'You can start it on page 267, but that would defeat the purpose, wouldn't it?'

He smiles genially at her and writes down the answer. He is a very good-natured man, and she can't figure out why he asks so many ridiculous questions. Is it because he's a security guard; because his job is to enforce the rules, so it is important to him to understand them?

'You do want to get the story going quickly,' Arabella says, trying to force her voice to sound warm and friendly and trying to get the image of Marvel out of her head – Marvel looking at her with those liquid eyes, expecting her to do something. It has been a week, and nothing has been resolved. Everyone is always expecting her to do something, but no one ever tells her what to do.

'We live in the age of MTV,' Arabella says, accidentally looking right at Chuck as she speaks. She blushes and hopes he doesn't think she's implying that he doesn't live in the age of MTV, that he's older, which he is. She shakes her head and goes on: 'People do not want to wait too long to find out what happened. Victor Hugo goes more than eighty pages before introducing the main characters in *Les Misérables*, but I don't think that would work today.'

She nods at D'mon. He nods back. Crisis averted, hopefully.

'The good news is that most stories follow a very similar pattern, and we call that the narrative arc.' She writes the words on the blackboard and then draws a long diagonal line and puts a big, fat X at the bottom of the line. 'First,' she calls out, 'we start with the inciting incident.'

'Slow down,' Dorothy mutters. 'Slow down.'

D'mon's hand is up again.

'Yes?'

'Does the inciting incident take place on page one?'

She wonders if his mother didn't pay enough attention to him. Maybe she had a full-time job and couldn't afford a good babysitter, so he spent too much time by himself in front of the TV. He decided to enroll in this class to make up for all the attention he did not receive as a child. She wonders if he knows she wants to smack him.

The problem is that Arabella knows Marvel is right. She has been given the gift of time. She does have a chance to make things right with her mother, no matter how impossible that seems. She has to try. It would be terrible to lose another parent the way she did her father, who slipped away before she had a chance to tell him she loved him. One minute she was at his birthday dinner; the next minute she was kissing him good-bye, telling him she had to get back to college, she had an exam to prepare for, though in fact she just wanted to get back to her boyfriend. Her last words to him were a lie, and then he died that night. What she would give to have one more conversation with him and tell him how much she loved him.

Suddenly the whole room seems to spin in front of her. The colors dim, and the whole place seems unreal – the strange-looking rabbit with its marble eyes and floppy little tail, the swirl of crazy colors against the wall, children's rantings as though they can see some other world that is closed to adults. Why can't she teach at a normal school? How is it possible that her mother is about to die? It is too large for Arabella to take in. It upends the nature of the universe, and, to cap it all off, there are nine people staring at her now, looking at her warily.

Then D'mon raises his hand.

He is leaning forward, grunting, the way children do when they need to go to the bathroom. She turns away from him, catching sight, as she does so, of a poster on the wall that tells what to do in case of fire: 'Stop, Drop, and Roll.' She may have no choice but to deal with her mother, but she is damned if she is going to call on D'mon Williams again.

'An inciting incident is something that happens that gets the story going.' She is resolutely looking away from D'mon, turning her attention to Dorothy, who is scribbling and scribbling notes. She can hear shouting from the screen-writing room and assumes they are working out one of the scenes.

'It might be that you find out a meteor is headed for Earth,' Arabella says loudly, over the shouting. 'It might be you meet a man on the corner and fall in love. Or you get a letter from someone unexpectedly. Or you inherit money or lose money on a bet. It might be that someone you love is dying.' Thirty-eight years of arguing, and she is supposed to fix it all.

D'mon's hand is up again. For such a soft-spoken man he is very stubborn, and she feels a twinge of guilt. He happens to be the one African-American man in the class, and it doesn't seem right that he's the one person she is not calling on. She wonders if maybe race is behind all these questions. Maybe discrimination has taught him the importance of knowing all the rules. Maybe he is just trying to figure out how to navigate his life safely. She wants to reach out to him, but if he asks another foolish question, she's afraid she's going to scream.

Not today. She promises herself that she will call on him as much as he wants next week.

'Let's go back to our character from last week,' Arabella says, catching Chuck Jones's eye yet again. When you teach a small class, you are always making eye contact with someone, and if she's looking away from D'mon, she is forced to look at Chuck. These are the sorts of dilemmas in teaching they don't tell you about in college. Do you look at the student who is driving you crazy, or do you look at the elegant man who keeps smiling at you, which will undoubtedly make him think you're coming on to him? He is wearing another one of his gorgeous outfits today, a creamy yellow sweater that makes Arabella think of Italy even though she has never been to Italy. She can't help herself. She peers down at his shoes and sees butterscotch leather loafers with a crisscrossing pattern. They look like an incredibly expensive version of saddle shoes, and she blushes yet again when she sees that he has noticed her admiring his shoes. Oh, God. This man is driving her crazy.

'Remember Pussy?' she says. Chuck nods as though she is speaking to him, which she is in a way. 'Let's say, for the sake of argument, that what Pussy really wants is to go back to Buffalo, which is where she's from. But we know she has a gambling problem, and so the inciting incident could be that she loses a lot of money in a game and has to sell her plane tickets.

'Does that sound good, or does anyone else have an idea for an inciting incident?' Arabella asks.

Ginger's hand goes up. Her blond hair is tugged back with a scrunchy, and she has on a cute bolero jacket and soft black pants. Her mother would love that outfit, Arabella thinks; in fact, her mother would love Ginger Clark.

'She meets a man?' Ginger asks.

Byron snorts at that, but Ginger does not pay attention to him. Her eyes are focused entirely on Arabella. 'She meets a man where she works?' Ginger asks. 'He's one of the dealers? At the MGM Grand Hotel?'

'Pussy is not going to meet a man,' Byron says, lips curled down in contempt. The top buttons of his shirt are open to expose his chest and a huge gold chain. 'What is she, in her sixties?'

He looks around the classroom, trying to win support for his position. His contempt for Ginger is something solid, something angry. She is not at all the sort of woman this man would like, although it is hard to imagine what type of woman he would have patience for. Probably his mother; he probably has one of those adoring mothers who drove him to doctors' visits until he was twenty-five.

But, surprisingly, Ginger, who speaks in question marks, is not deterred. 'Sixty is the new fifty,' she says. 'She could so meet a man. He could be a widower? Someone whose wife died a long time ago? Maybe he's been lonely for a long time, and he thinks she's beautiful?'

Byron snorts at that, but Chuck Jones is nodding. 'I like it,' he says. Ginger beams at him. In her excitement, her ponytail has come loose, and she looks ten years younger. There is something romantic and hopeful about her. She is not just a woman her mother could love, Arabella realizes; she is the woman her mother once was. Before all the sickness and

73

disappointment, this was her mother: happy and innocent and dreaming of romance. This is the unlined face that stares out at her from the wedding photo. This is the woman who married her father because he was handsome and strong and promised to take care of her. This is the woman whose life was turned upside down when one day her father went to pick up a ball and dropped it because his hand felt weak.

He had Multiple Sclerosis, and it spent twenty-five years eating its way through his body until finally it killed him. And while all that was happening, her mother was changing. She had to get a job; she had to learn to balance a checkbook; she had to learn to drive; she had to grow up. And in the process she became independent – but angry, too. She became the woman she is today.

'So what?' Byron is saying. 'They're going to get married and live happily ever after?'

Dorothy harrumphs at that – Dorothy with the Q-Tip of white hair, Dorothy who would seem to form a natural bond with Byron. Now she is shaking her head, but Ginger goes on.

'They might!' Ginger replies, and with that Alice raises her hand, Dark Alice, who sneaks into class like a whisper and has a cloud of misery around her. 'I have a lover,' she says, 'and I'm sixty-three.'

The class is silent for a moment as everyone ingests that tidbit. Bonita wipes some invisible dirt off her red leather jacket. Then Justin stands up. He is clutching his collection of Hemingway short stories to his chest as though the old man's heart might bond with his own. 'I just want to tell everyone,' he mumbles, 'that I've quit my job and decided to devote myself full-time to being a writer. I know Arabella has doubts, and I appreciate that she's trying to protect me, but I guess I feel I just have to do it. It's now or never, and I don't want to spend the rest of my life second-guessing myself. So I hope you'll all wish me the best.'

Ginger starts to clap and gets to her feet, leading all the others in applause. 'Bravo,' she cries out, clapping her hands.

The rest of the class goes by smoothly, and together they plot out a story for Pussy. They decide to stay with Ginger's idea, and so Pussy's story begins to take shape. She wants to go home to Buffalo because she longs to come to terms with the memory of her mother (Arabella got that part in). She has saved to buy a ticket for the flight, and it is the day before she is to leave when she meets Taylor (Ginger's choice of name). A strapping six-foot two, he seems much younger than his seventy years (this from Chuck Jones, no surprise) and his penis tilts sideways (this from Byron), but Pussy is swept off her feet. She has always had a problem saying no (this from Bonita) because her father was a transsexual (thank you, Conrad), but in this case Taylor really is too good to be true. 'He is the real deal,' Ginger says.

The problem comes in the shape of her daughter. Sheila. No one likes this daughter. Everyone senses she's a pain in the neck, and, sure enough, Sheila is trying to persuade her mother to go back to Buffalo. Sheila is planning to move there herself. She is planning to have a baby there, and she needs her mother.

'There must be conflict in a story,' Arabella has told them, and so they've imagined disagreements between Pussy and Sheila, and Taylor and Sheila, and even Pussy and Taylor.

'And in the end, in the climactic scene, Pussy has to find out if she is going to wind up with Taylor in Las Vegas or with Sheila in Buffalo.'

It's no contest. Only Arabella thinks that Pussy should go home to Buffalo, and she only says this to be contrary. Everyone else thinks that in the end Pussy is going to choose Taylor. She should choose Taylor. It is Ginger who gets the last word: 'Why don't they all go to Buffalo? Why can't they all get everything they want?'

'Now that's a happy ending,' Chuck says, and Arabella, who has an inborn suspicion of happy endings, finds herself going along with it, too. She is too tired to argue for the purity of an unhappy ending right now, and there is not much time left in the class, just a few minutes to go over the take-home assignment.

'Who did you write about?' she asks the class. 'Which historical figure?'

It turns out that Alice wrote about the Central Park jogger and Byron about Abraham Lincoln ('I wanted to stretch myself'). Dorothy chose Marie Antoinette, Justin chose Hemingway, and Conrad went with Jenny Lind. 'She was an opera singer,' he explains to the class. 'She lived a long time ago.' Bonita wrote about Mother Teresa, and Chuck wrote about nothing at all.

'Sorry,' he says after class. He has a trace of a southern accent, someone who was born in the South but moved to New York a long time ago. 'I didn't have the time. You won't fail me, will you?'

Arabella is not in the mood to laugh at his jokes. She doesn't mind when students have trouble with the exercises or when they have no talent at all, but it irritates her when they don't try. 'It's up to you. You'll get out of this class what you put into it.'

'Yes, teacher,' he replies.

She is putting her papers into her satchel, but he doesn't move away. From the corner of her eye he is a blur of yellow. What does he want? She is no good at flirting. She is not much good at friendly banter, either. The men she has gone out with have been serious men who were looking for a partner. In fact, she has always imagined herself married to a politician or a doctor or someone who needed support. What is the man doing?

'I have a present for you,' he says.

'A present?' She looks up at him, incredulous. 'Why?'

He hands over a brown bag; she looks into it and sees an apple – but not just any apple. 'It's so perfect,' she says. 'Is it real?'

He leans toward her. For a moment she thinks he's going to kiss her, but he is just whispering: 'Try it and see.'

She looks up into his face, into his serene gray eyes. He looks as if he is waiting for her to do something. She suspects he is hoping she will bite into the apple and dribble the juices over his body or some such thing. She should probably sign up for the class in romance writing.

'Well, thank you,' she says. 'I'll eat it tonight.'

He looks as though he will say something more, but she stops him. 'I have to go.'

On the way to the nursing home Arabella thinks of the apple again; if he had time to buy the apple, he had time to do his exercises. Maybe she should ask him to write about the apple. But, still, it was a nice gesture. She decides she will stop off at the Carvel in Port Chester and get her mother a vanilla ice cream sundae with chocolate sauce; she will also go to the deli in Rye and get her a pastrami sandwich. It's a foolish gesture. The woman is dying, and she gets her a different type of fast food. Yet Arabella hopes that her mother will take it as the token it is, that she will see it as a goodwill gesture.

Writing Assignment

ARABELLA HICKS – THE FICTION CLASS

This is an exercise in learning how to write a climactic scene.

A boat sinks during a storm, and only ten of its passengers make it onto the lifeboat. One by one the survivors are knocked off until, after a month at sea, only two survivors are left. There is not enough food for both of them, and one of them is going to have to get rid of the other. One of them is a teenage girl who is very strong for her age, but she is blind. The other is a musician from a successful boys' band. He is twenty-six years old and smaller than the girl. Who will survive? Write the final scene.

Chapter Four

ARABELLA CAN HEAR the sound of her mother's laughter even before she gets to her room. It is a brittle, cawing sound, and without even being in the room with her, Arabella can see her mother's face: lips wide apart, head thrown back, eyes welded closed, and her whole body stuttering with the force of the merriment that whips through her. Arabella is confident that her mother is laughing about something to do with her. What else could strike her so funny? She must be chatting with one of the aides, swapping stories. Clearly this visit is not going to be the emotional breakthrough that Marvel was hoping for.

Arabella considers walking out of the nursing home and driving home; it's an appealing notion, but she can't do it. 'Never run from trouble' is one of the Hicks family's golden rules, along with 'Always learn the name of the nurses' and

'Things are most likely to go wrong when you're feeling relaxed.' Still, even if she can't run from trouble, it is probably all right to avoid it for a little bit. She can stand in the hallway for a few minutes and wait for her mother to settle down. And while she's standing in the hallway waiting, she can think about Chuck's apple. That apple resonates in so many ways that Arabella could probably write a novel about it. There would be a Garden of Eden, an old Adam, an anxious Eve, and a snake – a laughing snake.

The nurses and aides are all busy getting the residents ready for dinner. Arabella can hear the sound of wheelchairs being rolled back and forth, water running, and the singsong voices of the aides coaxing their charges to put on their dinner clothes and put in their teeth. The hallways smell of paint because one of the residents has died and they are repainting her room. It is odd how people are always so concerned about the smell of bodily functions when they go to a nursing home, Arabella thinks. It should be the smell of paint that is terrifying to them.

This particular death took place three doors down from her mother's room. The yellow DO NOT DISTURB sign is still in the doorway. A bit of tarp lies over it, and she knows by the pink paint that it was a woman who died. The colors of a nursing home revert to the colors of childhood – pink for a girl and blue for a boy. The name tag will be gone; that's the first thing they throw away. Arabella automatically looks over at her mother's name tag: Mrs Vera Hicks. They would have kept the residents in their rooms today so that they would not be disturbed by the commotion of death, not that there is much commotion here: no weeping or wailing, no hysterical relatives, just sadness.

It occurs to Arabella that the nursing home is a little like the exercise she just gave her students. There is a boat filled with people who are being tossed off one by one, except in this case the boat is always being replenished. She wonders what her mother would make of the exercise. She feels confident that her mother's sympathies would be with the blind girl. Her mother has a passionate attachment to anyone who is handicapped. She feels camaraderie with them in the same way that men who fought in the same war or people who survived the same hurricane feel an automatic sympathy for one another. It is one of her redeeming features; it is actually her great redeeming feature, this courageousness her mother has in the face of adversity.

'There she is,' Sade says when Arabella finally walks through the door to her mother's room. 'We were wondering where you were.'

Sade is a soft-spoken woman from Jamaica who has been in some stage of pregnancy for the four years Vera Hicks has been in the nursing home. At the moment she is brushing Vera's hair, dragging a heavy brush across her soft curls. Her head is snapping back and forth with each movement of the brush.

Her mother is not laughing anymore, but her face is flushed

and she is wheezing slightly. 'We were just laughing about you,' she says.

'Well, that's nice. Thank you.'

'I was telling Sade about that time you went to the dentist.'

This launches her mother into a new spasm of laughter. She is laughing so hard that she begins to cough. Sade lifts a glass of water to her lips, which her mother drinks greedily, though it makes her cough all the more. Now she is dribbling water onto her blouse, an innocuous floral thing.

'Now, now,' Sade says. She rubs her mother's back. 'Drink slow.'

'You were ten years old,' her mother says, still coughing, although she obviously doesn't care. She is so determined to tell this story that she will choke to death if that is what is required.

'Yes, I remember.' Arabella sags down onto her mother's bed and rests her hand on the red and white afghan that once covered her father. He dealt with so many awful things with grace; she can deal with her mother. 'I remember it very well.'

'His name was Dr Fixell,' her mother explains to Sade, 'a good name for a dentist.'

He lived a few houses away from their house, Arabella remembers, in one of the few split-levels in their neighborhood. Most of the houses were ranches, set neatly side by side on the same size rectangles of land, with the same fencing, the same forsythia, and the same stunted mimosas. The smallest difference in layout, such as a second story, signified a major

Susan Breen

step up in status. This dentist had a small brick wall on his property because the house was on a corner, and Arabella remembers being transfixed by that curving brick wall, which was, in the end, nothing more than a barrier to prevent cars from careening off North Jerusalem Road and crashing into his lawn. But she remembers that there were always geraniums planted around the wall, and the number of his house, fifteen, was set into the brick with ceramic tiles. It had seemed to her the very height of elegance.

'Arabella had an appointment with Dr Fixell. She had to go by herself because I was at the hospital visiting her father. She was such a tiny little girl. Everyone always thought she was five years younger than she was. Plus she never brushed her hair and would not let me cut it. Such a nebbish. Anyway, it turned out she had a cavity, and the dentist had to fill it.'

She stops and looks at Arabella. 'Did I tell you that Dr Fixell wound up having cancer of the spine and moved to Florida?'

'Yes, you did.'

Arabella can hear the sound of her mother's roommate wheezing into the ventilator. She hopes it's her anyway and not herself having an anxiety attack. She imagines what would happen if she went running out of this room the way Pam went running out of the classroom. Probably nothing at all. Pam proved that much. It turns out that no one really worries about a woman running from her fears.

Her mother turns toward Sade and puts a bony hand on the aide's knee, making sure she is paying attention. 'The doctor wanted to give Arabella novocaine, but she said she didn't want it. And this is what my crazy daughter said.' Her mother is gearing up now for maximum effect, locking eyes with Sade, going in for the kill. From a plotting point of view no one would ever need to teach her mother anything about the narrative arc, Arabella thinks. She is a natural storyteller. 'My daughter said that Jesus had died on a cross without pain medicine, so she could get her teeth drilled without it.'

Her mother is laughing once again, and the floral pattern of her blouse is bobbing up and down with her exertion, flowers tossing as though in a hurricane. She is laughing heartily, and Sade is laughing, too. 'She was such a strange child,' her mother is saying.

Arabella closes her eyes. Oddly enough, she remembers that day quite well. She knew it was a strange thing to say, and she knew from the way the dentist's mouth slipped open that he would call and report her to her mother. She had actually thought the dentist might be romantically involved with her mother; she had fantasized that he might marry her, although she had not quite figured out what that would mean for her father. She had been trying to be honest with him, thinking her honesty would be winsome and that he would come to rescue her family, forgetting what she later learned as a writer: that to be honest is to open yourself up to people thinking you're crazy.

'Oh, I've got her mad.'

Arabella opens her eyes. 'I'm not mad.'

'She's very sensitive,' her mother says to Sade, speaking loudly as though, on top of everything else, she is suggesting that Arabella is deaf.

'I'm not mad.'

'That's why she became a writer, I guess, because she's so sensitive.'

'Are you a writer?' Sade asks. Clearly she has spent enough time with arguing families that she knows not to fan the flames. 'I didn't know that.'

'She teaches writing,' her mother chimes in, her voice raspy from all the laughter. Arabella wonders what Chuck's mother is like. She pictures a long-legged woman with a great tan and a big smile. She plays tennis and drinks martinis. She has a firm handshake. Her name is something southern. Bobbie? Amanda?

'She teaches writing in the city to adults,' her mother goes on.

'I've always wanted to write a story, but I just don't have the time.' Sade has begun moving around the room, cleaning up the mess – all the tissues lying around and the crumpled papers. It's actually odd how messy her mother is, given that she has only this small room and few possessions.

'You don't need that much time,' Arabella says, standing up so that she can help Sade pick up some empty cups and toss them in the garbage. 'You just have to do it consistently. You could probably write a story in ten minutes a day if you did it for enough days.'

'She never told me that,' her mother says. 'Of course, she doesn't think I have the talent.'

'I never said any such thing. You never asked.'

An old man wanders into the room, and her mother shoos him away. 'Wrong room, Mr Biedermeyer. Your wife is two doors down.'

Sade is straightening up the bureau, pushing the drawers closed and scooping up empty water cups. There is a marble composition book that she moves over to the nightstand, and there are pencils on the floor.

'My daughter has always thought I was an idiot.'

'That's not so,' Arabella cries out.

'I didn't go to college, you see. I was a foolish young woman, concerned only with fashion and fun. I could have gone to college, but I decided I'd rather work at Lord & Taylor. I think I spent every single paycheck on clothes. What a great wardrobe I had. There was a discount, you see.' She breathes in deeply and then picks at the crease in her pants with her fingers. 'Didn't save anything,' she goes on, 'All I wanted was to have fun.'

Sade clucks her tongue at that. In her line of work she must hear a lot of sad things. She rubs Arabella's back and scans the room one more time. 'I'll leave you two to your dinner,' she says. Arabella, horrified, realizes that the bag of ice cream has been sitting near the heater all this time. It will be soup. She could cry out with vexation. Can she do nothing right?

Fortunately, her mother is too tired to care. All the laughing and tension has worn her out, and now she leans against the wheelchair, slumped backward, almost a parody of a drunk. Even the flowers on her blouse seem wilted. Arabella wraps a napkin around her mother's neck, tells her they are going to start with the ice cream, and puts a spoonful to her lips. But she is almost too tired to lick it. Arabella is tempted to call Sade back and ask her to put her mother to bed, but the old lady still has fight in her.

'How was class today?' her mother rasps out.

'Fine. no disasters.'

'No one ran out of the room?' Her eyebrow is raised, and there is a stirring of life.

'No, they all stayed put.'

She puts some more ice cream in her mother's mouth. It is only six o'clock, although it seems so much later because it is dark outside. The room has the strange weightless feel of the middle of the night, the sensation of being dislodged in space and time.

'I talked about plotting today,' Arabella says. 'Would you like to hear the exercise?'

Her mother nods.

Arabella tells her about the young blind girl who is stuck on a boat with a member of a boy band. She sets up the scene, explaining to her mother how one by one each of the passengers has died or been killed – thrown overboard or perhaps eaten by passengers desperate for food. 'Just the two of them are left, and the point is to write the final scene, just the final scene. Show how one defeats the other. Decide which one is going to win.'

Arabella watches her mother. Before, she was sure her mother would choose the blind girl, but now that she is sitting across from her, she suspects she will go for the boy singer, just because her mother hates to be predictable. Arabella is not sure, and something in her uncertainty surprises and excites her. There is a mystery here; perhaps she doesn't know her mother as well as she thinks she does. Perhaps her mother can still surprise her.

In any event, her mother is thinking about the question. She has closed her eyes and is chewing absentmindedly at her gums. Her fingers are twitching slightly.

'What do you think, Mom?' Arabella asks, curious. 'Who do you think is going to make it? The blind girl or the boy singer?'

Her mother opens her eyes. They are wet. 'They're both going to die,' she says. 'Neither one of them stands a chance.'

Arabella feels her heart seize, feels her heart break.

'It is a foolish question,' her mother says.

FORTUNE
by Vera Hicks
(First draft)

Oh, to hug this waiter. To squeeze his slight body, so like a boy's, really, except for the muscles that swell his arms. When Joan looks at him, she sees the boy going down to his basement, lifting weights, trying to build himself up to normalcy and coming close, maybe even succeeding in everyone else's eyes but hers, of course, because she has trained herself to see. To hug him and to let him know she loves him, which she does, but, more important, to hug him because how else will she know if tonight is to be the night of her miracle?

On his sixtieth birthday. That's what the fortune-teller said. You are the miracle. That's what Joan's husband said. Says. He looks normal enough, this slight aging waiter with the slim build and ponderous arms. Could he be an angel? Is he of God? There is nothing magical about him, no hint of anything unseen. It is just a feeling Joan has, a sensation she couldn't begin to explain. If only she could touch the waiter. Touch seems a much more difficult sense to manipulate.

Now her husband, you know by his touch that he's sick. His hands are cold and rigid. Right now they are folded neatly on his lap, and they will remain so unless Joan chooses to move them. He is so vulnerable, it makes her cry. Once their dog leapt on the wheelchair, meaning to give Danny a kiss. Joan had forgotten to put the brakes on, and the dog pushed Danny to the other end of the room. They had all laughed, Annie, Michael, even Danny. Only Joan had cried.

She was the only one who remembered how strong her husband had been.

'Sauce, madam?' The waiter bows before her as if she were some sort of goddess, as if she were the angel and not him. She looks at him carefully, sees him sniff slightly with impatience, stretch his chest forward proudly. Not a nice man, she thinks, but then there is something not nice about miracles. Isn't it unfair to single out some when everyone suffers? Doesn't God our Father know about sibling rivalry?

'Would you tell me your name?'

'My name is Joseph, madam.'

'Joseph.' A biblical name. That's encouraging. It could be him, this waiter, this solemn man. He stirs the sauce a little with his spoon, loosening up the lumps. Joan suspects she is being foolish, and yet she plunges on. If there is no miracle, it will not be because

Susan Breen

she didn't try. Hers will not be the sin of omission.

She must touch him. She so wants to know if he is real, and yet how do you touch a waiter? Isn't that the point? They are barriers. There is the cook in the kitchen; there are patrons at the table. The waiter is the go-between, the procurer. But there is to be no intercourse with the waiter, surely. Joan catches Danny's eye. He has wet, warm, brown eyes, like a dog or God.

'Joseph, I want to taste some sauce first.'

'Of course, madam.'

He dips the spoon in the serving platter and then holds it out toward Joan's plate. She stretches out her hand somewhat faster than she had intended, meaning to guide his hand with the spoon toward her mouth, but last-minute timidity has made her awkward, and she knocks the spoon, dropping a puddle of brown liquid onto her lap. She looks at the waiter who is, in turn, looking at her, into her eyes, with an emotion she cannot read. What is it?

'What is it?' she asks and puts out her hand to grab him. 'What do you see?' But he steps back as soon as she touches him and then turns around and walks back into the kitchen. He has a surprisingly studied walk, as though he were a ballet dancer. The door slams behind him, and he is gone. Then Joan turns her attention to the obscene blotch on her lap. Her clothes, which are always spotless because she must always be ready, are ruined. She dips her napkin into Annie's scotch and soda and begins dabbing at her lap, trying to lift the stain.

'Mom, you just put your napkin in my drink.'

Joan pictures herself, a refined-looking, middle-aged woman, frantically rubbing at her groin in an upscale Italian restaurant. When Bad Things Happen at Good Restaurants. *She is giddy. She is insane. She has felt on the verge of a sneeze all evening. Or an orgasm. It has been so long, she's not sure of the difference. Has she just touched an angel? It was too fast.*

The red wine she has drunk is giving Joan a sinus headache that is spreading down her neck. She can almost see its trajectory, just as she has watched dye drip through Danny's veins during an MRI. The gravy will stain her new satin dress, her new yellow dress that makes her look like the mother of the bride. She had spent years considering the dress, years focusing on the only detail of this whole religious experience that she might have any control over. And now it is dirty. Now she looks pitiful. Now she looks as if she should be married to a slightly overweight balding man in a wheelchair.

She should not have let Annie talk her into coming to this restaurant. This is not a holy place. This is a place for people who work hard and want to show they can afford it. It is a hardworking place. Order a Caesar salad, and they make it at your table. What's the point? To see them working. Wouldn't a miracle seem like an unacceptable shortcut to these people? Wouldn't they say that it is Joan's duty to suffer? That that will elevate her somehow, just as jogging elevates them?

'Spillages make us uncomfortable. They change the way we see ourselves. Suddenly we are dirty. We are soiled.' *Joan hears the words and becomes aware that her daughter, Annie, is talking to* her. 'And then for a woman there's the whole menstruation issue to take into account. It can be a very upsetting episode.'

Annie pulls what looks like a gold lipstick out of her handbag. 'This is a new product that I plan to mention in my next newsletter.'

She takes off the top and, holding it like a pencil, presses it into Joan's lap. Joan flinches. Annie raises an eyebrow and, head down in concentration, starts rubbing in slow, deliberate circles. The whole time she is rubbing, she is talking about the woman dentist who invented the product, a woman with whom she has become 'great, great friends.'

'What I especially appreciate about her is her willingness to try. She had an idea, and she went after it. Now I expect she'll make thousands.'

'Shoot for the stars.'

'Well, I don't suppose it seems like much to you, Mother, but it's important to her. We are all entitled to our own dreams . . . whether you approve of them or not.'

When Annie lifts her head, the stain is gone.

Fourth Class: Point of View

'ONCE YOU HAVE some idea of what your story is going to be about, you have to decide who is going to tell it. This is an important decision because it affects the tone of the whole story.'

The words drip out of Arabella's mouth, relentless and uninspired. She feels frustrated. Point of view is hard to get across, and she wants to teach it right. The problem is that she doesn't fully understand it herself, which is why everything she has ever written is in third person. Also, she is exhausted.

'The character you choose to narrate your story is going to influence the tone of your story,' Arabella says. *Drip, drip, drip.* The bunny is lapping at a little steel tube that directs water into his cage; his eyes drift lazily to the artwork on the walls: little cotton-ball snowmen pasted onto frozen lakes made out of aluminum foil. Would the bunny rather be scampering across a frozen lake? Arabella wonders. Or perhaps he would just like to close his eyes, to sleep.

'Let's go back to the story we've been discussing about Pussy of Las Vegas,' Arabella says. Dorothy groans, Byron pumps his fist, Mimi looks confused. She is back for the first time since the semester began. If she has been sick, she doesn't look it; she is wearing a tight wraparound sweater that shows off her figure, and her hair is shaped into a Cleopatra style.

'Pussy?' Mimi asks.

'It's a long story,' Arabella explains, 'but all you have to know is that we came up with a character who lives in Las Vegas. She is trying to decide whether to move in with her lover or her daughter.'

'Lover or her daughter,' Mimi repeats, still looking confused. Arabella feels herself getting aggravated. Who asked this girl to miss so many classes? Why does she have to spend valuable time discussing this when she is so damned tired? But before she has the chance to say something she'd regret, Bonita intervenes. She pushes a page of notes in front of Mimi and points her finger on the page.

Arabella is surprised to see that the notes go on for several pages. She hadn't realized Bonita was writing down so much. She hasn't participated very often in the discussions, which makes it hard to know what she is thinking. It also doesn't help that she has one of those inscrutable faces that come from too much exercise or Botox.

'So,' Arabella continues, 'if you were writing Pussy's story, you would probably consider using her as the point-of-view character. Everything that happens in the story would be filtered through Pussy's consciousness. But you don't have to go with the obvious choice. You could tell the story from the boyfriend's POV, or you might want the ghost of Pussy's grandmother to tell the story. That might be interesting, and you could get in information about heaven that way if you have something to say about heaven.' Arabella clears her throat; she pictures her poor mother sitting in a wheelchair with that terrible expression on her face. *They're both going to die. Neither one of them stands a chance.*

And what can you say in response when someone is speaking the truth? For that is the terrible thing about her mother: She does speak the truth. What has caused Arabella so much pain is that her mother has a knack for seeing what she is trying to conceal.

'You might write from the point of view of Pussy's dog,' Chuck throws out. 'That might be entertaining.'

'That's true,' Arabella says, coming to attention. 'Or you might prefer to have Sheila tell the story.' She looks at Mimi and elaborates for her benefit: 'Sheila is the daughter.'

'No,' Dorothy says. 'I wouldn't want to use the daughter's point of view. I didn't like her.'

Alice raises her hand. She speaks in a whisper, so they are all forced to lean forward. 'If you write about someone – a woman, say – who is unsympathetic, do you risk losing the reader? Do people want to read about characters they dislike?'

'Was Sheila that disagreeable?' Arabella asks. She can't remember discussing her that much. All she remembers is that Sheila wanted Pussy to come to Buffalo. She notices that Bonita is staring at her, looking at her so intensely that it makes Arabella think of spy movies when the hero can use only his eyes to get information across. There is something competent about Bonita, something military; Arabella wonders who she is. There is the look of a doctor in those serious eyes, and yet there is no way a doctor would be able to sign up for a Wednesday afternoon writing class. Perhaps she lost a malpractice suit?

'I thought that Sheila sounded very whiny,' Ginger says. She looks different today, Arabella thinks. Her Connecticut sweater set is gone, and she is wearing jeans, a tie-dyed shirt, and stiletto boots.

'She sounded tense,' Byron concurs.

'Well, it didn't appear that she took such good care of her mother,' Alice whispers. 'She doesn't live in the same city, and her mother is in trouble. Instead of yelling at her about Buffalo, she should go there and help her. In my humble opinion, she is just waiting to put her mother in a nursing home.'

Ginger nods. 'I know this woman who had six children, and they still put her in a nursing home.'

'What is it they say?' D'mon asks. 'A mother can watch over ten children, but ten children can't watch over one mother.'

The glinting aluminum foil on the wall, flickering under her gaze, catches Arabella's attention. She wipes her eyes, and

the little cotton-ball snowmen blur. She finds herself thinking
of a story her mother liked to tell about how she met Arabella's
father at an ice rink. Her mother was in her thirties at the time
– a flighty girl, as her mother liked to describe herself, a good-
time girl. So there she was, skating around, showing off, and
then she tripped and started to fall. She would have hurt
herself except that she was swept up in the strong arms of a
strange man.

'Who turned out to be your father!' she liked to cry out, as
though it were a surprise.

'What happened next?' Arabella would ask.

'He carried me off the ice and bought me hot chocolate.'

'What happened next?'

'He asked me to marry him.'

'What happened then?'

'We had a beautiful daughter, and we were very happy.'

'What happened then?'

'He got sick.'

There the story always ended.

'Some people are just selfish,' Dorothy is saying. 'My
mother just moved in with me. Is she driving me crazy?
Absolutely. But I couldn't live without her. I just don't see how
people can put their mother in a nursing home.'

Suddenly Arabella has to sit down. She cannot possibly
continue to stand in front of this class. There is no reason that
she can't teach from a sitting position. She has never noticed
there are drawers in the desk and pencils in the drawers. For a

moment there is quiet, and then Ginger asks if there is class the second week of February.

'Why wouldn't there be?' D'mon asks.

'Because of President's Day weekend.'

'But that's on a Monday, and we meet on Wednesday,' Mimi says.

'Sometimes schools give the week off,' Ginger says. She looks over at Justin who is sitting alongside her, seeking confirmation from him. He is not holding his Hemingway short stories today, but is instead clutching a copy of *Anna Karenina*.

Chuck looks to be on the verge of speaking. Arabella can feel his eyes on her, probing. What does he want her to do? Probably teach the class. If only she weren't so tired. Bonita is staring at her so intently that Arabella wonders if she is trying to hypnotize her. Her eyes are swollen, moist, and intent. Who is she? Arabella wonders.

'All right,' Arabella says, forcing herself to teach. There is still an hour to go. 'Let's assume that you've decided Pussy is going to be the one telling her story. Now what do you do? Maybe you should use the first person.' Arabella gestures at the blackboard. If she had the energy, she would stand up and write on the board, FIRST PERSON and then ADVANTAGES, but she is hoping the class will be able to imagine it. Justin has started to whisper to Ginger. Conrad has put his headphones on and is listening to a song with a galloping beat; a deep, sexy voice drips out of his headset. The smell of coconuts fills the room, and Arabella wonders if it's like the poppies in *The*

Wizard of Oz and that is what is making her sleepy. Her eyes flicker. She sees her mother staring at her with those hopeless eyes. *Everyone is going to die.*

Bonita suddenly stands up and walks over to the blackboard. 'Why don't I write this down?' she asks. 'I'll be the secretary.'

Arabella wonders if she is seeing a vision. She should do something. You're not supposed to let your students take over your class, are you? Dorothy looks appalled, but everyone else just looks puzzled. No one looks ready to yell, and the fact is that Arabella doesn't have the energy to fight. Bonita looks competent up there, all yoga and angles and red leather. Arabella perks up at the sight of her. It is like going to see a doctor and having him say there is something he can do. Maybe Bonita really is a doctor. Maybe she is the foremost neurologist in Manhattan. There is no way to know; the nature of a writing class is that people keep their ordinary lives to themselves. People come to a writing class to escape their ordinary lives.

'Just tell me what you want me to write,' Bonita says.

'All right then,' Arabella says, inspired. Something about seeing Bonita standing there holding the chalk is tremendously reassuring. 'One advantage of the first person is that it creates intimacy. If I write, "My name is Pussy, and I'd like to tell you my story," you can't help but lean forward a little to hear what I have to say. It is like getting a phone call in the middle of the night. It arouses your curiosity immediately.'

Bonita begins writing on the blackboard, smacking the chalk against the board, creating sharp, edgy letters that are easy to read. INTIMACY, she writes, and then she turns to Arabella, prompting her to go on.

'Another advantage of the first person is that it comes naturally and therefore feels easy to do. When we tell a story to our friends, we use the first person, and the process is similar when you go to write the story.'

NATURAL, Bonita writes.

'I've heard that publishers don't like stories in the first person,' Byron says. He looks at Bonita and then at Arabella and then back at Bonita. Evidently the person in charge of the blackboard is considered the person in charge of the class, but Arabella, feeling slightly more energetic, responds:

'Many first-time writers use the first person, and it can come across as self-indulgent. Think of a Thanksgiving dinner at which you sit next to your Uncle Frank and he natters on for an hour and a half about how he got into the jewelry business. That's what a bad first person can be like.'

DANGER, Bonita writes. SELF-INDULGENCE.

'One final advantage of the first person is that it can be a fun way to get across an interesting voice,' Arabella says. 'I think of Edgar Allan Poe and—' Suddenly there is a rush of movement behind her, and, turning, Arabella finds that Bonita has put down the chalk and raised her arms. Bonita then begins to declaim:

' "True! Nervous, very, very dreadfully nervous I had been and am; but why will you say that I am mad?" '

She is rolling her eyes and waving her arms, and it takes

Arabella a moment to realize that Bonita is reciting the opening line of 'The Tell-Tale Heart.' In fact, it is Justin who realizes it first, and he shouts out, 'Bravo,' which Bonita takes as encouragement, or perhaps by now she has gone too far to stop. ' "The disease had sharpened my senses – not destroyed – not dulled them." ' Arabella can see her teetering on that line of ridiculousness and genius on which all writers must balance. How do you put your heart out there without looking foolish? How can Arabella rescue her if she goes too far? ' "Above all was the sense of hearing acute. I heard all things in the heaven and in the earth. I heard many things in hell. How, then, am I mad? Harken! And observe how healthily – how calmly I can tell you the whole story." '

Bonita stops at that, and then everyone is on their feet clapping. Arabella can feel something warm settling over all of them, the gift of friendship, the gift of a writing class that is going well. She feels something uncurling inside her as she turns to Bonita and says, 'I think I speak for all of us when I say you did a wonderful job, and we're very glad you did not do "The Raven." '

Oddly enough, she feels more in control of the class than she ever has before, and this after surrendering all control. She looks at Bonita and sees something in the woman's eyes that she has not seen before. Is it compassion? Suddenly Arabella realizes it wasn't that Bonita was staring at her, it was that she was staring at Bonita. She must have sensed that Bonita would help her; maybe she really is a doctor.

'Thank you,' she whispers as Bonita, her mission over, goes back to her seat. 'That was very kind.'

Arabella walks back to the center of the room and retakes the chalk. Everything feels right now as she talks about the first person and then the benefits of the third person, which allows the writer to use a wider panorama than the first person and lends itself to more descriptive writing, which is liberating. After that, Arabella moves on to omniscient, which she feels compelled to mention, although it is very hard to do and few students do it.

'My last teacher said that a lot of commercial fiction is in omniscient,' Dorothy says, 'but I'm not sure what that is.'

'Omniscient is hard to explain,' Arabella says. They are all looking at her hopefully. She has built up a shallow reservoir of trust and can't let them down. 'What omniscient means is that you know everything everyone is thinking.'

The room is hushed, but from anticipation. She begins by saying, 'The class was restive as they waited for their teacher to tell them about omniscience. Bonita was thinking how good her impression was of Edgar Allan Poe and that she may have a whole new career in front of her as a literary mimic. What she doesn't know is that Justin can do literary imitations, too. In fact, Justin is thinking that right now he would love to imitate Hemingway because he admires his writing so much, but he's worried that everyone will laugh at him, especially Ginger, though what Ginger is thinking is that she hopes everyone likes her exercise this week because she has worked very hard on it. Dorothy is wishing that Arabella would hand out this week's exercise soon. Her teacher last year always handed out the exercise at the beginning of class. She is eager to get to work, but not Chuck, who is thinking about the dinner he had last night at a very expensive restaurant. His favorite part was the clams on the half shell. Alice is hoping that the teacher will get to description soon because that is the topic she most wants to learn about. Mimi wonders why she smells clams and whether she's going crazy or whether someone had clams last night. She looks over at D'mon, but he hasn't had clams in years and, in fact, is thinking about how to get an agent. He knows Arabella said they wouldn't discuss it, but he is hoping she will change her mind. And Conrad is thinking about his next story and wondering whether the victim should be a teacher or perhaps a bunny, and then he looks at the teacher who is thinking that it is time for her to hand out the take-home assignment and go to see her mother, and she is hoping that she didn't leave the papers at home.'

The class is grinning now, delighted with the performance, and Arabella can feel a sense of belonging settle over them, which is a rare and beautiful thing in a writing class. She knows they will begin to feel more confident now; they will start to take risks with their writing. They will get better. This is what she was talking to her mother about; this is the secret of teaching writing. If only she could figure out how to hold on to this moment. If only she could bottle it.

'So here is the take-home assignment,' she says. 'Think

about a family gathering, a holiday, a birthday, a funeral. Whatever you like. Write about that gathering from a child's point of view. In the first person.'

'Oooh,' they croon. They are so into this now. And Arabella happens to know this is a good exercise. There will be a lot of good stories coming out of this one.

It has been a good day's work.

They ask her if she'd like to go out for a drink afterward, but she apologizes. She can't; she has to visit her mother.

'You visit her every week?' Chuck asks, walking her out the door. They pause on the street, both of them blinking in the fading light. It is late afternoon in the first week of February. A girl goes by walking a dog with little booties on its four feet; she has on the same exact booties. Both dog and girl look to be about the same weight. Welcome to New York.

'She's in a nursing home,' Arabella says. She feels herself flinching, waiting for the look of disgust to appear on his face, but he just smiles gently.

'You're a good daughter.'

She looks at him, at his carefully brushed hair, at that straight, arrogant nose, at the heavy wool jacket that looks incredibly warm. 'How could you possibly know?'

He leans forward. A warm, spicy scent fills her senses. He kisses her on the cheek. 'I know.'

Writing Assignment

ARABELLA HICKS – THE FICTION CLASS

Think about a family gathering: a holiday, a birthday, a funeral. Write about that gathering in the first person from the point of view of a child.

Chapter Five

ARABELLA HAS NOT been kissed for a long time, not even on the cheek and by someone completely inappropriate, someone too old and vain and complacent, someone she doesn't really like. She does like Chuck, but not in any romantic sort of way. What would they even talk about on a date? He is the kind of man she has always avoided and resented. Every day she sees hordes of these men walking along the streets of Manhattan, proud, ambitious, rich, sure of themselves, and she can never look at them without thinking of her sweet father and how he was ten times the man any of them are. It bothers her that they have no idea how lucky they are or, even worse, they think they deserve their luck and their money. They think they deserve what they have and that her father deserved what he had.

It is always your fault. That is something the sick learn early on.

Still, Arabella is too much the writer not to spend the drive to the nursing home analyzing her emotions. She prides herself on her honesty in her writing, and it is only fair to acknowledge that she does feel something for this man. There is a sensation boiling inside her that she hasn't felt in a long time. And he did give her an apple, which was nice. She never did figure out what to do with it. She couldn't bring herself to eat it; that seemed too much of a surrender. She couldn't bring herself to throw it out, either. She wound up putting it in the refrigerator where it has been sitting for a week, rotting. Now there's an image.

He must be sixty. She has never dated anyone that old. (For God's sake, she whispers to herself as she pulls onto Route 684, the part of the trip where the speed limit goes up to sixty-five and her poor old car wheezes with exertion. He only kissed you on the cheek. He didn't get down on bended knee.) She can't help but spin out the thread of the story. She wonders what he is like, what it would be like to make love to him. Are the rules different with an older man? Do you have to wear a negligee? Is it more formal? Does it smell disgusting? His coat smelled nice when he kissed her on the cheek. It was a heavy black wool coat of the sort successful men wear when they pace up Park Avenue on their way to their offices.

But if he is that successful, what is he doing in her class? They meet on Wednesdays from 2:00p.m. to 5:00p.m. and those seem to be prime working hours. Perhaps he has been pushed out of his job by some whippersnapper, some sleek young woman, which would explain why he is not attracted to Bonita. He has not done his homework, which is intensely annoying to her, but the exercises he has written in class have been about office politics. He said that if he had done his homework, the famous person he would have written about would have been Julius Caesar, which suggests he is preoccupied with betrayal.

Arabella gets to the parking lot and pulls into her accustomed spot, gliding in gracefully. It is only then she realizes she has been so distracted that she forgot to pick up any dinner for her mother. It is too late to turn around and go to Wendy's. She tries to imagine telling her mother that she was late because she was thinking about a man who kissed her on the cheek. It sounds a little desperate even to her.

Arabella makes arrangements with one of the nurses to have two of the nursing home dinners delivered to her mother's room; one of the perks of putting a parent in a nursing home, or in this one, anyway, is that you can always get a free meal. Tonight's will be Salisbury steak, mashed potatoes, and carrots, and as she is turning to go, the nurse mentions that her mother is not in her room. She is in the library.

'There's a library here?' Arabella asks. Her mother has been here four years, and this is the first she has heard of it.

'It's next to the solarium.'

'There's a solarium?'

It turns out that both are on the ground floor. The nursing home is divided into sections, depending on how much care the patient needs, and the patients do not tend to stray from section to section, in part because there is a secret code (*123) on the doors that makes it impossible for them to leave one section and go to another, but mainly because this is not an adventurous crowd. They are seeking safety here; they are not looking for anything new, even if it is just a new section on the ground floor.

The library is surprisingly lovely. In the midst of so much pastel neutrality, the bright colors of the book jackets are a welcome explosion of color. Here is life; even a nursing home cannot deaden the joy of a book. As she looks at the books on the shelves, Arabella is reassured when she sees a number of old friends: the black spine of *To Kill a Mockingbird*, a book she loved so much as a child that she tried to copy it word for word into her notebook because she couldn't bear having to return it to the library; the bright yellow of *Humboldt's Gift*; and the dark earthy green of the collected Emily Dickinson. There are a lot of paperbacks, too: well-thumbed romances, mysteries, and Reader's Digest condensed books. Arabella has always had a special fondness for those condensed books; she can remember how wonderful it seemed to her that four books could be contained in one volume. There are a couple of medical books and, amazingly enough, the collected short stories of V. S. Pritchett, a collection she loves so much that she keeps it on her desk at home for inspiration. The bulk of the shelves are taken up with Danielle Steel's novels. These look as if someone has actually read them.

'You found me,' her mother says. She is sitting in the center of the room at a beautiful old mahogany table that must have been a donation, perhaps from the same person who donated all the books. Her hair is done nicely this week; soft white curls fluff off her head, and her expression is soft, too. There is a Georgette Heyer book propped open in front of her on a little lap table that balances on her wheelchair. She has been reading *Arabella*.

'How many times have you read that?'

'It never gets old,' her mother says, rubbing her finger against the pink cover showing Arabella standing with a plumed hat on her head and the dance going on behind her. It is an odd cover for a romance because the heroine is standing all by herself. There is no drawing of Robert Beaumaris, and Arabella has always wondered if the cover suggests that romance is all in the woman's head. It is not a notion Arabella wants to consider now since she has had such a pleasurable time imagining Chuck Jones by her side.

'You look happy,' her mother says.

'I had a good class.' Arabella pulls up a chair and sits down across from her mother. It occurs to her that this would be the perfect time to discuss with her mother what Marvel said, that she is dying, and yet it doesn't seem right to ruin the moment by bringing up bad news. There is little enough happiness in life, and if her mother is in the middle of a brief spasm of happiness now, why destroy it?

'There was a mutiny,' Arabella says, and she goes on to tell her mother about Bonita writing on the board and reciting Edgar Allan Poe. Then she tells her about Ginger's new wardrobe and the way she looked at Justin. Her mother does love a story. Sometimes Arabella thinks that is part of the reason she became a writer: She got used to telling stories to her mother – or gossiping, as the case may be.

'Why weren't you writing on the blackboard?' her mother asks, as always cutting to the heart of the matter.

'I was just tired, and I sat down.'

'Oh.' She waits for her mother to press her, to say that Arabella has no idea what it means to be tired. Try taking care of a sick man for twenty-five years and loving him and watching him suffer, and then you'll know the meaning of tired. But her mother is quiet.

The social worker pops into the room just then, a pretty young girl who, her mother has found out, went to boarding school and then to Columbia for her BA and Yale for her MA. She is genuinely well intentioned but seems to have trouble connecting with the patients. She tried to organize a book club, but the first book she chose was by Beckett. It was an inspired choice in one sense – who better to understand Beckett's insane world than the residents of a nursing home, and vice versa? The downside was that everyone kept saying: What's the story about? Now she is holding a book by Gabriel

García Márquez, which does not bode well for the next book club meeting.

'Well, hello, Vera,' Julie calls out. She comes over and kisses her and kisses Arabella, too. Quite the day for physical displays of affection, Arabella thinks. She really is a nice girl. Girl. She is about five years younger than Arabella.

'How nice to see the two of you together. What are you doing?'

'Planning an escape,' her mother says.

Julie laughs heartily at that, but Arabella catches her looking at the window.

'Getting ready for the next book club meeting?' Arabella asks.

'I am. Thank you for asking,' she replies with the sort of enthusiasm people use to greet their family at Thanksgiving; the tone is sincere but guarded.

'What are you reading, Vera?' Julie croons.

'*War and Peace.*'

'Really?' Again the gush of enthusiasm. She is so blond and bright and sparkly; she has huge diamonds, two in her ears and one on her ring finger.

'Is that an abridged version?' Julie asks as she bends over to read the title. At the sight of the book she does an almost comical double take. She looks like a vampire exposed to a cross. 'Is that a romance?' she asks, and Arabella meets her mother's eyes. Julie is not a girl who reads romances; she is probably not a girl who needs romances. She was undoubtedly besieged by boys from the time she went to the pool at the country club.

'You should use this for your book club,' her mother says – the best advice her mother has ever given. 'People will want to discuss this book.'

'I'll think about it,' Julie says, backing away and leaving the room. They can hear the quick step of her loafers on the linoleum floor and then the sound of her voice as she swoops down on another resident.

'Poor thing,' her mother says after Julie has gone.

'I don't know, Mom. She seems to have a lot going for her.'

But her mother shakes her head. 'She thinks she's safe. She thinks she's doing everything right, that nothing bad is going to happen to her, so it will be worse for her when something does happen. She'll be unprepared – not like you,' she says, looking at Arabella and giving her what she thinks is a compliment. Arabella decides to take it as one. They are quiet for a moment, both of them contemplating all the terrible things that might befall poor Julie. There are several possibilities when you get right down to it; there is so much in life that can go wrong.

The books lining the walls of this library would seem to bear witness to that. What is a book if not a record of things gone wrong – divorce and illness and murder? The only difference between books and real life is that the tragedy in books makes sense. When something terrible happens, it is because the author wants it to. It's the randomness of life that makes it particularly terrifying.

'So what lesson did you give your class today?' her mother asks. 'Something else about blind people.'

'No, no handicapped people involved in this one – or not intentionally.'

Her mother has leaned forward, curious; her hands grip the Georgette Heyer. There is a light in her eye that always springs on when she expects to hear something tantalizing, and Arabella automatically reaches into herself so as not to let her down.

'It's an exercise about point of view. You're supposed to write about a family occasion like a funeral or Thanksgiving or a wedding, but you're supposed to write about it from the point of view of a child.'

'Ah,' her mother says, nodding appreciatively.

'It's a good exercise,' Arabella says. 'People tend to feel passionately about things that happened to them as a child, and that translates into the writing. The result is that the writing is impassioned. It's almost impossible to write something bland about an important time in your childhood.'

Her mother is nodding, her eyes closed. Arabella wonders what she is thinking about, what episode from her childhood has sprung to mind. She has always loved hearing her mother's stories about her family because they were all so happy and well adjusted. Her grandmother worked in a bakery, and her grandfather ran a mail-order company. They were decent people who did everything they could to help Arabella's mother when her father got sick. When Arabella was young, visiting her grandparents was like going to a safe haven. Arabella is looking forward to hearing what her mother has to say when she suddenly asks her what she would write about.

'Me?'

'You're the writer.'

'I know. It's just that I don't usually do these exercises myself.' The fact is that Arabella feels vulnerable with these exercises because she thinks she should do them better than anyone else. But it seems like cowardice to back out; there are too few of these moments. Anyway, she knows exactly what she would write about.

'I guess it would be that Thanksgiving when I was eight,' Arabella says.

'Why that one?'

'Don't you remember?'

Her mother shakes her head. An old man walks into the room, swears at them, and then walks out.

'Dad was in the hospital?'

'I remember your father being in the hospital, of course.' Her mother fingers the chain around her neck, the one he gave her for their twenty-fifth anniversary, the one he designed himself.

'I hadn't seen him in more than a year,' Arabella says.

Her mother nods. 'Hospital regulations. You weren't allowed to visit until you were thirteen. I hated that. I was worried that you would forget who he was.'

'You kept asking the hospital to make an exception, and

somehow you managed to persuade Dr Watson to give me a special pass so I could visit Dad on Thanksgiving. You were so excited that you took me to Lord & Taylor and bought me a new dress, a blue one with white polka dots. I remember I worked for weeks on a poem that I planned to present to him. I printed it out on pink paper, and you bound it with ribbons.

'The hospital was more than an hour away, and you were frantic the whole drive there that we would be late and Dad would be disappointed. Your hair was red back then, and you were wearing a black coat with fur trim. You kept telling me how excited he was to be seeing me, that it had been so horrible for him not to be able to see me for a year. We found a parking spot and ran across the lot. We were both wheezing when we got to the check-in desk, and then the guard looked at the pass and said, "This isn't valid."'

Arabella can still remember the smell of the turkey in the hospital and the sight of hundreds of friendly-looking turkey cutouts on the walls, turkeys with Pilgrim hats, turkeys with bow ties and dresses and goofy grins. It all seemed strange given that the hospital did not allow children. Who was the projected audience? It is a question she often asks her students about their fiction, and it is a valid question in this context, too. It was a hospital, which wasn't in the business of being cruel, was it? Yet she will never forget the look on her mother's face when the guard would not accept her pass.

Her mother didn't get upset right away. First, she tried to flirt with him, and in some respect that was the worst part of the whole afternoon – her mother smiling and simpering before this man who would not budge. Then there was fear in her voice: 'Just page Dr Watson. Can't you do that for me?'

'He's not here today, ma'am. It's Thanksgiving.'

There was a line of people behind them, but her mother did not give up. Arabella would have slunk back home, but her mother was determined. She began to yell, and then all of a sudden she began to cry. There was a commotion, and someone new was on the scene – a social worker they must have had on-site for just that purpose, although Arabella was never able to figure out what the social worker was doing there on Thanksgiving. Maybe she was a nurse or someone from billing, but she brought them into her office and began to talk to her mother. She gave Arabella a book, *Little Women*. Arabella remembers devouring the book, concentrating on the words so as not to hear the words being spoken around her.

Then finally this strange woman was holding her hand. 'We have a plan,' she said, smiling at Arabella.

By now she was afraid to look at her mother's face and didn't even look back at her when this strange lady tugged Arabella out of the room. She was not going to say one word to her mother; she would not cry or make a scene. All she wanted to do was go home, and she found herself hating her father for putting her in this situation. What in God's name was he doing in the hospital so long anyway? Why wasn't he home like every other father on their street?

She could remember apologizing to this strange nurse. 'My

mother has problems,' she tried to explain, but the nurse just gripped her hand and led her outside. By then anything could have happened and Arabella would not have been surprised. She remembers how cold she felt. It was late afternoon in November. The sky was beginning to darken, and she followed the nurse to a concrete island in the parking lot. They seemed to stand there forever in the cold, with the nurse asking her questions about her mother's problems and Arabella answering as thoroughly as possible. Later she wondered if the nurse was planning to recommend removing her from an unsuitable home.

Eventually the nurse ran out of questions and Arabella ran out of answers, and they just stood there, watching the cars go by, watching the ambulances roar up. Then the nurse jolted to attention and pointed. 'Look there,' she said. Arabella followed the direction of her finger and looked up at one of the windows on the tenth floor. Two figures were standing there.

'Wave,' the nurse said, grabbing her hand. 'Wave to your father.'

It took Arabella years to figure out that her mother must have harangued some orderly into lifting her father out of his bed and propping him against that window. The worst of it was that she really couldn't see him at all, just a shadow.

'Well, that was a happy Thanksgiving,' her mother says, sinking back into her wheelchair, and Arabella is brought back to this library, to this beautiful place in this nursing home, to the comfort of the books that surround her, and to the tired old lady who is sitting across from her.

'You didn't really forget all that, did you, Mom?'

Her mother shakes her head. 'No, but I thought perhaps you'd want to tell me about it.'

'I never realized until just now how brave you were,' Arabella says. 'You know it never occurred to me that you would give in and go home. I knew even then that you'd find some way to get what you wanted.'

Her mother sags against her wheelchair, and Arabella can see how thin she has become and how sick she is. She puts her hand on her mother's hand. What is she going to do without this old lady?

FORTUNE
(CONTINUED)
BY VERA HICKS

Annie's voice grates on Joan's nerves. It is too calm, too well balanced. It is the voice of 911. It is the voice of the nurse who tells you, Sorry, it's not time for your pain medicine yet. *Against such a voice Joan feels like a shutter flapping in the wind. Joan prefers the voice of hysteria. She has never been hurt by a hysterical person. She is suspicious of all these bottled-up people smiling like jack-o'-lanterns. She is suspicious of the people who read Annie's newsletter, people who are looking for tips on how to do things better, people who think they actually have control over their lives and that they can improve it by matching their table settings to their wallpaper border. A well-balanced person is someone who has not fallen yet.*

'There, now, you'd never know you had an accident.'

Annie is right. Where there was a brown blotch, there is now only a slightly damp patch of satin.

'I feel like a used handkerchief,' Joan says.

'It will be dry soon,' Annie says. She waves away the waiter who has appeared with a napkin. 'It's over.'

This waiter is blond and has hair that floats. He looks like an angel, though Joan is sure he is not one. He is too perfect. There is no faith to be had in perfection; there is no hope in it. 'Aren't you the lady . . .' he asks and looks at Joan's lap.

'It is over,' Annie says and makes a chopping motion with her hand.

There is a hush in the restaurant, one of those sudden fluctuations in sound that flows like a wave over a public place. Everyone is silent. I am in a restaurant. I am in a restaurant. *Joan fights her doubts. She has gone too far to have doubts. She needs this miracle too much to start to doubt now. You believe in what you need to believe. You believe that you are beautiful or that your husband loves you or that you are ugly or that your husband hates you. Generally, believing makes it so. Seventy thousand people saw the sun spin in Fatima. Seventy thousand people in 1917 in Portugal watched the sun fall from the sky and twist above the tree. And yet the* New York Times *did not report it until two years later.*

Click, swish. The sound of Annie's eating breaks the silence. Joan thinks about how God appeared to her so many years ago in a Mexican restaurant.

*

God – God's messenger anyway – appeared to Joan and Danny in a Mexican restaurant twenty-five years earlier. They were on their honeymoon. They had gone to look at a hotel that had cracked in half during an earthquake, and afterward they went for a drink. It was a small bar, insignificant, and Joan was never sure what had drawn them there.

It might have been the sound of a Neil Diamond song playing on a jukebox. It was horrible to think that her bad taste in music had changed her life. The Pathology of Popular Culture. *The bar itself smelled of smoke and cleaning fluid. Everything in Mexico was like that, seeming to go off in two directions at the same time. It was as though some hidden battle was going on constantly.*

Danny's hands were rough then. He had been a carpenter. Joan remembers she started to cry. 'I'm so happy,' she had said. 'Are you?'

'Yes.'

'Are you happier than you've ever been?'

'Yes.' Then Danny took a paisley handkerchief out of his pocket and wiped her face. The handkerchief was a present she had bought him after their first date. He was not a paisley sort of person. If he had owned a handkerchief, it would have been white linen. But Joan had seen this one and had known that he would love it. She had thought, If I buy it and he loves it, we will get married. That will be the sign. *Years later she felt redeemed when he chose to upholster his wheelchair in a zebra-striped fabric.*

'It's scary being so happy,' she had said. 'All I can think about is when it will end.'

There was a spray of bougainvillea in a vase in front of him. Danny traced a petal with his finger. 'You should enjoy it while you have it,' he said.

'Then you think it will end?'

He hadn't laughed at her. She loved him for that.

'No, I don't.'

'May I join you?'

Joan was surprised to see a thin, dark-haired man standing by their table. His eyes were hooded like an eagle's. His second button was in his third buttonhole, and yet he did not strike Joan as a sloppy man. She thought he might have dressed hastily, and she could almost see the unmade bed. The hand extended to hold him back. He held a comb in one hand.

'You're on your honeymoon,' he said.

'How do you know?'

He parted his hair with his comb, shook the comb over the table, and then carefully swept something onto the floor. 'I would not have to be a great fortune-teller to spot an American couple on their honeymoon.' He put out his hand and said to Joan, 'Let me see your palm.'

She had laughed. 'I don't believe in that.'

'In what?'

'In palm reading.'

'Then nothing I have to say will disturb you . . . Now let me see your palm.'

Danny had frowned then. 'Maybe you should take your business elsewhere, friend.'

But Joan had put her hand on Danny's leg. 'No. It's all right. Now I'm curious.' She looked at her palm. She saw a line in the shape of an M. 'You will be a mommy' – a fortune-teller had told her that at Katie Frank's sixteenth birthday party, Joan and every other girl there. She held out her palm. 'So how many children will I have?'

She had expected the fortune-teller to hold her hand in his, but he just leaned forward and examined it. He stared at a spot near her thumb. Then he looked at her and seemed to nod his head. 'It is a special palm, but I suspect it will upset you.'

'Am I going to die?'

He shook his head. 'We do not discuss things like that.'

'Is it something bad?'

Fifth class: Description

'HERE'S A DIRTY LITTLE secret about description: A lot of writers hold off putting it in until the last minute. They write out all the big stuff such as character and dialogue and plot, and then when that's all done, they go back and drop in the adjectives. It's like watching a Polaroid picture develop – first come the blurry shadows of the central forms, and then the details emerge slowly.

'Chuck, I can see you nodding,' Arabella says. The man doesn't take notes, but he is a veritable font of approval. 'I hope you're still going to be nodding when I ask if you've done that homework.'

'Oooh,' Byron says. 'Busted.'

But Chuck just smiles softly. He seems somewhat distracted. Arabella hopes she didn't overstep her bounds. She was just teasing. He looks much more serious today. He is wearing a shiny button-down black shirt and sleek gray pants; he looks like someone in one of those cell phone commercials, someone professional and cool. But he was the one who kissed her, wasn't he? He is the one who gave her the apple that is rotting in the center of Arabella's refrigerator. She remembers the warm touch of his lips against her cheek; clearly it has been too long since she was on a date.

'The fact is that many writers are intimidated by description,' she goes on, 'and many are bored by it – those long clumps of words that clog up the flow of the story. Somehow it seems as if you need to be a poet to do it well, and yet if you look at the best writing, it is not so much poetry that is required for great description, as precision.'

She forces herself to look away from Chuck to Justin, who is clutching *Pride and Prejudice*, which seems so sweet to her. His intentions toward Ginger must be honorable. She looks happy enough, sitting alongside him, tapping his foot every so often with her sneaker. Their romance is in the details, Arabella realizes. It would be a good observation for the class, although she refrains because she has no desire to embarrass them. They are probably not aware of how cute a picture they make.

Arabella has always been surprised that more singles don't come to her classes. A writing class is the perfect place to meet someone because everyone is honest, whether they realize it or not. It is impossible to stop your personality from coming through in your writing, and even people somewhat outside the norm, such as Byron and Conrad, are forced to reveal their preoccupations in their writing. In this class you cannot disguise who you are, and the odd thing is that even people who might be repellent in another context, such as Byron or Conrad at a bar, are oddly appealing here. There is something seductive about honesty. How else to explain the fact that she has come to feel quite fond of D'mon even though his last take-home assignment dealt with the pleasure he felt beating up someone who had trespassed at the building where he works as a security guard? 'His stomach felt like pizza dough when I punched it.'

'Tell me the difference between these two sentences,' Arabella says to the class. 'First: The woman drove her car into town. Now this one: June drove her Pontiac Firebird to Vegas. Or what about this one: Mildred drove her Cadillac to Boca Raton. You're not changing that many words in the sentence, but those small details make all the difference to the story. Right?'

Everyone is nodding except Dorothy, who is still scribbling notes, literally growling as she struggles to understand. Everything is hard for her. She holds up her hand. 'In my last class the teacher said that you should try not to use adverbs,' she says.

'That's true,' Arabella replies. 'Adverbs weaken writing because they are not specific. If you are describing a woman and you say: She dressed beautifully, what does that mean? You

129

and Mimi are both dressed beautifully today, but you are wearing a blue pants suit and Mimi is wearing a velour track suit.'

'A Juicy velour track suit,' Byron throws in. 'Just in the interest of being specific.'

Mimi doesn't even look his way. She is so far out of his league that she doesn't even despise him. Poor Byron. Honesty doesn't work for everybody; sometimes you do have to fall back on charm and good looks. Against her will she finds herself turning to Chuck and catching his eye, as he is staring at her. Well, of course, she's the teacher. She is standing in the middle of the classroom alongside a bunny and a blackboard. Where else would the man be looking?

She has not kissed a man in two years, not since the breakup of her last engagement, not since Todd got transferred to London and invited her to go with him, and she said, 'I'll have to talk that over with my mother.' She wonders what her mother would have to say about Chuck. *Wonder* is the wrong word; she knows exactly what her mother would say if she told her she had taken up with an older man. She is just starting to blush when the door slams open.

Bonita screams. Arabella jumps. But there is no intruder. Instead, standing in the doorway is Pam, the very same Pam who went running out of the room in the second class. Pam with the goggly brown eyes, the manic expression, and the hair that is cut in the shape of one of the Three Musketeers, Pam who is panting as though she ran out of the second class and kept on running until she arrived back at this one, three weeks later.

'Well, hello,' Arabella says, amazed, delighted, and dumbfounded.

'I'm back,' Pam calls out as she grabs the nearest available seat, which happens to be next to Conrad. Arabella can almost see his next story: 'Transsexual Murders Middle-aged Woman.'

'New medicine,' Justin says in a very loud stage whisper. Ginger giggles and kicks his foot.

'Did I miss a lot?' Pam asks. She is speaking as though holding a megaphone. Perhaps the medicine is making her deaf.

'Nothing much,' Arabella says. Just plot and point of view, she thinks, but who cares? Her stray student has returned. Things like this never happen. There is something almost biblical in the return of this prodigal.

'I'll find you the handouts you missed,' Arabella says, her hands shaking with excitement as she goes through her satchel. There are now eleven people in her class. She is almost halfway through the semester, and the whole class is intact.

She finds the handouts and surveys the class. They are all looking at her as if they expect her to do something interesting, perhaps pull another student out of her hat, perhaps transform the rabbit. Arabella finds herself thinking that she can't wait to tell her mother. This is a story her mother will love. Her mother loves anything to do with miracles and transformations. How many doctor shows did she watch with her mother in which the patient was rescued by some miraculous twist of fate? How many times did her mother come up with some insane plan for curing her father? At one point she suggested they go to Lourdes, although that was ridiculous. They weren't even Catholic, and they had no money. And now she is dying.

Arabella feels the tears start to well up, and then Pam, who has been catching up with Alice, yells out: 'Whoa, details and description! Cool!'

Arabella manages to get the class back on track. She talks about the importance of keeping adjectives simple: It is almost always better to call something green than emerald because you write to explain, not to impress. She talks about how a character's mood affects what he sees: When you're happy, things don't look the same as when you're sad. When you're happy, the colors seem brighter, and you notice such things as flowers and bunnies and playful artwork. When you're depressed, you notice the grays of the carpet, the dirt on the window, and the angry shouts from the screen-writing class next door. Things are not going well for that teacher, she thinks.

Then Arabella moves on to talking about the importance of verbs in description. 'People ignore verbs,' she says, 'but a good verb is worth a dozen adjectives. Which sentence reads better: "He walked into the room and hit the wall and then hit the other wall," or "He staggered into the room?"'

Having made her point, she introduces one of her favorite exercises. She has the class think of verbs having to do with cooking and then asks them to write a romantic story in which they use only cooking verbs. Ginger, enthusiastic, starts off with, 'Her heart sizzled when she saw him.' Justin counters with, 'He marinated her hair with his fingers.' Dorothy looks up from her notebook long enough to say, 'They marinated meat together,' which sets Byron off into a seizure of laughter. 'Was that not right?' she asks.

'No, that was fine,' Arabella says. She is one of those people who just doesn't get it, she thinks, but that doesn't necessarily mean she won't be successful as a writer. Dorothy is persistent, and that counts for something; in fact, of Arabella's students who have been published, most of them are of the plodding variety. The ones who sparkle brightly at first tend to burn out.

D'mon offers up 'tenderize,' and Mimi suggests 'butter.' Pam screams out 'juiced,' and then it is Byron's turn.

'I'm afraid to ask,' Arabella says.

Byron looks as if he is going to explode with his verb, which is a good thing, actually. The whole point of the exercise is to learn to choose every word with care and to learn to love the words you choose. Byron puffs up his chest, runs his hands through his curly hair, and then purses his lips. 'Skewer,' he says, drawing out the word into three different syllables. 'He unzipped his pants and—'

'Got it,' Arabella says, moving on to Bonita ('smoked') and Conrad ('melted') and eventually Chuck, whom she has saved for last. 'What's your verb?' she asks, feeling the strangest flutter as she looks into those gray eyes. He gives her his nice, relaxed smile and says, 'He burned to kiss her.'

'Yes,' she says.

The class moves on surprisingly quickly. Everyone is involved now; everyone is talking, even Conrad who has offered one or two insights into how he chooses to describe the dresses his characters wear. Then Arabella is surprised to hear a knock at the door; the next teacher and her class are waiting for her to vacate the room. It is the Advanced Nonfiction Class, and they all smell of nicotine.

Arabella asks them to wait a minute because she has forgotten to tell the class about the midterm party. It's a tradition of the Fiction Class. On the fifth Friday of every term all the students and teachers gather at a well-known bar in the Village called the White Horse Tavern. Arabella passes on the information and says she hopes they will all come. Then she hands out the take-home assignments.

The students scoop up their materials and head for the door. Pam's drugs seem to be wearing off because she is subdued as she leaves, but Justin and Ginger have their heads together, planning their next date. Arabella is looking forward to walking out with Chuck, except that he rushes by her, waving and saying, 'See you next week.' She realizes that he must have a dinner date. That is why he's so dressed up.

She feels ridiculous and irritated at him. She hates to be misled and hates liars. Say what you will about her mother, she is always honest. As quickly as that, her good mood leaves her. Discouraged, Arabella heads in the direction of the elevator and finds Dorothy by her side.

'Can I talk to you for a minute?'

She is much bigger than Arabella realized, but, then, the dynamics of the class conspire to make the students look smaller because Arabella is standing and they are sitting. She motions to Dorothy to sit on a bench in the hallway, having the dispiriting sensation that this conversation is going to take a half hour. (Who is he meeting for dinner? she wonders. Probably his grown-up daughter. No, probably his girlfriend. A man like that is going to have a girlfriend.)

'How do you know if you have talent?' Dorothy asks.

This conversation is going to take an hour, Arabella thinks, and he is already ordering the white wine, and not just a glass. He'll order a bottle, and he'll know what year he wants. It is not going to be the house special.

'You can't worry about that,' she says to Dorothy. 'You just have to write the best you can and let other people decide if you have talent.'

But Dorothy is shaking her head and mashing her lips together. She has a hungry, greedy mouth, and she seems to be always swallowing or gulping, yet she does not look full. Perhaps that is why Arabella likes her the least of any of the students in this class. Because she seems so needy, she reminds her of her mother. She forces herself to put thoughts of Chuck out of her head (although he's probably ordering appetizers

135

now, something Mediterranean, something with grape leaves). She forces herself to pay attention.

'I just feel that everyone writes better than I do.'

'Everyone feels that way,' Arabella says. 'That's the hard thing about these classes, but the fact is that everyone has his or her own style of writing. You can't compare yourself to anyone else.'

'That piece that Mimi wrote about Christmas in Jerusalem was just incredible.'

'That was,' Arabella says. She always asks for volunteers to read their take-home assignments out loud, and Mimi always volunteers. This particular exercise could have been published just as it was. 'If it's any consolation, I couldn't have written that, either,' she says to Dorothy.

Dorothy wrings her hands. They are surprisingly smooth, and her nails have French tips.

'Do you think I have talent?'

Arabella pauses, trying to think of what to say. There is nothing really wrong with Dorothy's writing; it is just that it's bland.

'Oh,' Dorothy says.

'No,' Arabella says, realizing she has taken too long to answer the question. 'Listen to me. Your writing is fine, but it doesn't have passion in it. You have a lot of passion in you, and I suspect that is leaching the passion out of your writing. Forget about yourself and think about the story you want to tell. Don't worry if you have talent or don't have talent. Just whack out whatever comes into your head. Try it with the take-home exercise for today and see what happens.'

Dorothy looks at her dubiously. 'In my last class,' she starts to say, but Arabella interrupts; she can't help herself.

'What is it with you and the last class, Dorothy? Why didn't you stay with that teacher if you liked her so much?'

Dorothy bites down so hard on her lips that she presses them white. 'My last teacher?' she says. 'I hated my last teacher. I couldn't wait to get out of there. I like this class much better. I like you!' she adds.

Writing Assignment

Arabella Hicks – The Fiction Class

Write about a place that was important to you growing up, but don't put people in it. Just describe it as though you were painting the picture with words.

Chapter Six

DOROTHY'S WORDS STAY in Arabella's mind the whole drive up to Port Chester. 'I like you!' All right, she thinks, the woman's a lunatic, she's lonely, and she's sad. It is not like having Philip Roth say he likes you, but still. It means something. It means a surprising amount. Between that and Pam's resurrection, it means quite a lot indeed. Not only that, but Arabella is amazed to realize that the advice she gave Dorothy was good advice. Not only should Dorothy take it, but she should take it as well. She has to learn to hear the passion inside her; she has to stop critiquing herself so much and start writing. Perhaps if she approaches *Courting Disaster* in a new way, the novel will take on new life, and she'll be able to find an ending.

Chuck is probably done with his dinner by now.

Arabella wonders what Chuck would make of the meal of

Susan Breen

Wendy's hamburgers she has on the seat alongside her. She can imagine him describing it as a picnic; she can almost see him lifting the hamburger out of the bag with those long fingers of his, just the pads of his fingertips touching the greasy yellow paper, setting it out on a paper plate – not a cheap paper plate, mind you; probably something colorful and expensive, something you could wash and reuse. Not that he would. He is not the sort of person to reuse disposable products. She is going crazy. So what? Evaluating a man by how he approaches recycling is as good a method as any. The fact is that she can imagine him doing just about anything because she doesn't know him at all. He is essentially a character in her imagination. He is probably in bed with his date now, and why shouldn't he be? Why should that make her feel so sad? Why is she obsessing over this man?

She doesn't even like men like him. He is not serious. He doesn't do his assignments. He is good-looking and thinks that's enough. He flashes his wealth at her as though it is some sort of lure. He thinks all he has to do is extend his hand, and she will jump. Well, she won't. She wants a different kind of man, a man who lives a life that matters. She wants her life to matter. That's why she is a writer. She has no time for this, and she forces the image of him at dinner out of her mind.

Today her mother is sitting by her bed with a thermometer hanging out of her mouth. She is wearing faded gray sweat-

140

pants, a sweatshirt, and dirty white sneakers. She has a composition notebook on her lap.

'What's wrong?' Arabella asks, and at that moment an aide she does not recognize runs into the room, grabs the thermometer out of her mother's mouth, looks at the temperature, and then shakes it.

'Just a slight fever,' the aide says, and then she leaves.

Her mother has not said a word, and seeing her so subdued makes Arabella realize how animated her mother normally is. Bizarrely, she misses the glaring eyes, the grimacing smile, and the haughtiness of her expression.

'What's up, Mom?' Arabella speaks gently, puts the bag of food down on the table, and pulls a chair over to where her mother is sitting. The old lady has still not spoken but is instead looking wistfully at the picture of Arabella's father that is propped against the table.

'Mom, you're scaring me. Say something.'

Her mother sighs. 'Do you believe in heaven?' she asks.

This is one of those impossible questions. Arabella wants to be able to say yes, absolutely, no problem, yet she has doubts and doesn't want to lie. Though now would be a good time to lie. 'I want to believe in heaven,' Arabella says, taking the middle ground. 'I want to believe in God. I know I love God. I'm just hoping that's enough.'

Her mother spits. Literally. The spit lands on the floor in front of Arabella's feet. 'All those years of Sunday school, and that's the best you can come up with.'

Arabella is on her knees, wiping up the spit. She stares at the gray linoleum on the floor, squeezes the paper towel into a tight ball, and hurls it at the wastebasket.

'Why do I even ask you? Why do I think you'll know anything?'

'How can you think I'm going to have an answer to a question like that, Mom? The greatest thinkers of all time have pondered the existence of God and heaven and not come up with a definitive answer, and you think that I know? You think that I, Arabella Hicks, am going to settle for all time the question of whether heaven exists?'

Arabella runs her hands through her hair and then stops when she realizes she must look just like Dorothy. The notion slams her. She has been thinking that Dorothy reminds her of her mother, but in actuality Dorothy reminds her of herself, of what she fears she will be like in ten or fifteen years. She calms herself down and sits near her mother. She is close enough to the window that she can feel the gusts of cold air from outside.

Her mother turns toward her. 'Why am I so afraid to die?'

'Oh, Mom.' She should have known. 'You talked to Marvel.'

'It was more that she talked to me.'

There is a new calendar on the bathroom door. February has so many days to it; the big white squares seem to mock her. There is a big red X covering Valentine's Day, but Arabella imagines there is another X on that calendar – one that is invisible to her but is there all the same; the date her mother will die.

'I'm so sorry, Mom.'

'I always assumed when I got near to death that I'd have it figured out. Either that or I'd be tired and ready to go. That's how it is supposed to be when you're old, isn't it? So why don't I have any answers? Why am I still so scared?'

'I—'

Her mother cuts her off. 'I've done everything right. I looked after your father, and I went to church for years and years. I served on committees, I organized dinners, and I gave money. So why am I so afraid? What do other people know that I don't? How do other people do it?'

'Do you want me to call my minister? He's very kind. You'd like him.'

'No,' her mother yells. 'What is your minister going to tell me that I don't know? Is there some secret they tell you right before you die?'

'He could pray with you,' Arabella whispers.

Her mother shakes her head at that, and then Arabella remembers the last time her mother was inside a church, which was not long after her father died. The minister had preached a sermon on the mysteries of suffering, and her mother had clenched her hands through the whole service. She hadn't even joined in singing the hymns, which was her favorite part of going to church.

'Is it possible God hates me?' she had asked the minister

when the service was over and they were leaving the church.

'No, Vera,' he had said. 'God loves you.'

At which point her mother uttered the last words she ever said inside a church: 'Then maybe the problem is that I hate Him.'

Her mother's room is so quiet, Arabella could believe they were the last people left in the world. Her heart is swollen with a terrible pity. She has seen her mother cry only once, on that terrible Thanksgiving at the hospital. On every other occasion, including her father's funeral, she was dry-eyed, and the thought of her crying now is terrifying. But she doesn't. Instead, her mother throws back her shoulders and clicks her teeth into place.

'I want to go to the mall next week,' her mother says.

'Why?' Arabella feels dizzy. There has been too much movement today, people coming and going and dying.

'I want to buy a dress, something nice for the coffin.'

'Good Lord, Mother. What difference does it make?'

'It makes a difference to me, and if I leave it to you, you're likely to pick a dress I won't like or it will be wrinkled. Anyway, you're the one who said you believe in heaven. You wouldn't want me to show up poorly dressed.'

The roommate starts to cough, and Arabella glares at her. Sometimes she has the oddest sensation that Lily is faking this whole vegetative coma thing, that she is actually listening in on all their conversations.

'Are you sure you're feeling up to the trip?'

'Yes, missy,' her mother snaps. 'And I don't want any of your excuses. Don't tell me your back hurts or the weather's bad. You can do this for me.'

On September 12, when the city was reeling from the terrorist attack, Arabella called her mother to say she wouldn't be visiting that day, and ever since then her mother has accused her of looking for excuses not to visit.

'You know you're going to die, too,' her mother says.

'Yes, I know.' Arabella can hear the irritation in her voice. It is unbelievable to her that her mother is going to annoy her about dying. She wishes she could pause this moment so she could go and retrieve Marvel. Let her figure out what to do with this woman.

'Do you think you're brave?' her mother asks.

'I've never been tested. I don't know.'

Her mother shakes her head. 'You have an answer for everything. All that psychoanalysis has turned you into a wimp. There's a reason they call them shrinks, you know. They make people smaller.'

Arabella smacks her hands down on her thighs. This is too much. 'I went to a grief counselor for six months after Dad died, and that was years ago. I'm hardly Woody Allen.'

She has to fight back her temper, fight the urge to scream and run out of this room. So she sets the hamburger on the plate and gets the dinner ready. Her mother scoops it up with both hands. Her anger has made her strong, but the motion dislodges the composition notebook. It falls on the floor.

'What's this?' Arabella says, picking it up and setting it on the bed.

'I'm writing a story,' her mother says. 'I'd write a novel, but there's not enough time. You can read it after I die,' her mother adds.

'That will be a pleasure,' Arabella snaps back.

Her mother chuckles softly at that, and for just a moment Arabella sees something tentative in her eyes, something that might even be love, but then it's gone. 'But I don't want you reading it at the funeral. You'll cry, and you'll ruin everything. Just read it to yourself.'

'Okay.'

Her mother seems to acquire energy from insulting Arabella because the drained woman she found when she walked in is now animated. Even her color is better. It is impossible to believe that this wretched and lively woman has only weeks to live. Why should she think her mother is going to change just because she's dying? Probably because she has read too many books, she assumed that her mother would pass down some sort of legacy. *A Lesson Before Dying*.

'I don't want a big fuss at my funeral anyway, not that there are that many people left who will care.'

'I will care,' Arabella snaps again, and her mother nods, acknowledging receipt of this information. It seems to mollify her. Her fingers begin to tap against the composition book, and Arabella wonders what it is really for. She is probably writing instructions for what to do with her clothes. She can't really hold a pen, so she doubts her mother is writing anything much.

They are both silent, winded from the exertion of being with each other. It is like an ongoing wrestling match. Arabella would like to go home, but it is too early. She has been here only half an hour. Her mother keeps careful track of the time, yet there is nothing she wants to say to her, either. She finds herself looking at her mother's roommate. A faded white woman with faded white hair, she is covered from the top of her neck to her toes with a worn white blanket. No one ever visits her, but she does have a grandson who is a photographer. He sends her pictures, the ones taped on the wall, along with a map of the world that shows the places he's been. Right now he is in Nepal.

He seems like a dutiful grandson, beyond the fact that he never comes to visit her. But he writes her every week and sends her flowers for her birthday and holidays, and, in truth, even if he came every day, she wouldn't know it. She is deep into a coma and is likely to remain so for the rest of her life, certainly for the rest of her mother's life. They have been roommates for two years without having exchanged a word, although the one time Arabella suggested that she request a different roommate, her mother was adamant about staying. 'I like her,' she said. 'You can see that she was somebody.'

Her mother's querulous voice interrupts Arabella's thoughts. 'So, missy, what did you do in class today?'

She was going to tell her about Chuck and about how he

never does his homework, but now, oddly, she hesitates. As irritated as she is with him, Arabella doesn't feel like listening to her mother eviscerate Chuck. Instead, she tells her about the writing assignment she gave the class. 'I told them to write about a place that was important to them and to describe it as though they were painting a picture with words. What place would you pick?' she asks and is startled when her mother says, 'The Continental Hilton in Mexico City.'

For a moment Arabella thinks she is joking. 'When were you ever there?'

'We went there on our honeymoon,' she says, clutching at her necklace and fingering the muted diamonds on the V. 'It was a long time ago.'

'I thought you went to Far Rockaway. I thought you stayed at a cottage.'

'No, that was another trip. We went to Mexico City for our honeymoon.'

'What on earth possessed you to do that?'

It would be hard to imagine two more New York–bound people than her parents. Arabella went on only one trip as a child, and that was to Connecticut; as far as her parents were concerned, there was no point in going anywhere else if you were from New York. Her father watched every single televised Yankee game for the last two decades of his life, and at the end of every game he belted out, 'New York, New York.' Arabella believed them and went to college and graduate school in New York.

'Your father wanted to see some place exotic,' her mother is explaining. 'Well, he wanted to go to India because that was where he was stationed when he was in the army, but that was impossible to arrange. Mexico City seemed the next best thing.'

The lights in the hallway are dimming; Arabella feels drawn into the story in spite of herself.

'We stayed at the Continental Hilton, which was and probably still is in the middle of the city, on the Paseo de la Reforma. There was a crack in the middle of the building. Amazing, really. There had been an earthquake, and they could have torn the building down, but they didn't. Of course you might say they didn't because they were trying to save money,' she says. 'But I thought even then when I was young and foolish that they kept the crack because they admired the scar. It was a country that celebrated pain; revered it, you might say. Very Catholic,' her mother concludes, pressing her tongue against her teeth, causing them to clack.

'At the top of the building there was a restaurant, and we ate there every single night. It had windows all around so you could look out over the city while you ate, and it made me feel like I was God looking out over the world. And the people at the bar! A collection of sinners and scoundrels like you've never seen – flamenco dancers, bullfighters, and American traders. In fact, you had to be American to eat in the main restaurant. They prided themselves on the fact that they served no Mexican food, only beefsteak.

'Beefsteak,' she repeats, playing with the word, toying with it, licking it, and for some strange reason Arabella imagines Byron saying that word and taking pleasure in it also.

'There was a fortune-teller there, and he read my palm.' She taps her notebook as though she has written it down. 'He gave me a fortune.'

'Was it good?'

'And,' she concludes, raising her finger as though hailing a taxi, 'if you were looking in the right direction, from the restaurant, you could see the Angel of Independence, a statue. Oh, what a glorious sight that was. She was so beautiful and big and gold. You had the impression she was watching you as you ate. Do you know that that angel fell during the earthquake? She went crashing down onto Reforma, and not one person was hurt. What do you think of that, missy-who-doesn't-believe-in-miracles?'

It is on the tip of Arabella's tongue to say that she never said she didn't believe in miracles. She said she wasn't sure there was a heaven, and surely that's a different thing. But she bites back the words. Her mother's voice is too calm now, the expression in her eyes too happy. She will not interrupt her with an argument, so she just nods and smiles.

But then her mother resumes talking. She looks at Arabella and raises her eyebrow. She is imperious, she is a queen, she is her mother. 'You were conceived at that hotel,' her mother concludes, 'and that was another miracle.'

To all students of
the Fiction Class
You are invited to a midterm party
This Friday
at
White Horse Tavern
567 Hudson Street
Drinks and hors d'oeuvres served
5:30–7:30 p.m.

The Party

IT IS 5:00 ON FRIDAY evening, and Arabella is still not persuaded that she should go to the party. She hates these midterm parties. Her students never show up, so she is invariably pressed into a circle of people she barely knows, listening to writers who seem so much more successful than she is. Plus, she tends to put her foot in her mouth. At the last party she was talking to a tall, spindly woman who mentioned three separate competitions she had won. Arabella had placed third in each of those competitions, so, trying to be charming, she said, 'Well, it's nice to finally meet the person who keeps beating me.' The writer looked at her and said, 'I never thought of it as being about competition. Is that how you see it?'

No one will notice if she goes to this party or not, and if by some miracle someone does care, she can just lie and say she was there and he or she must have missed her. It is not as though they videotape it; it is not as though it matters. It's a way for the students to feel they are part of the literary world, and this happens to be the bar where Dylan Thomas drank himself to death. The story goes that he left the bar and tripped on the curb, hit his head, and died. Most of the students are oddly inspired by that.

There is something much more appealing about dying as a famous drunk, she supposes, than dying as an unknown, but Arabella does not buy into it. She has long since resigned herself to dying unknown; she is all right with that most of the time, especially when she is by herself. There is something holy about writing, and she is content to worship at this particular altar. She feels like a failure only when she is out with other people.

One hour later Arabella is walking into the bar.

The setup is exactly the same as it has been for the last sixteen times she has come to this party. There are large jugs of Gallo wine at the bar, and almost everybody is holding a paper cup. There are several large plates of Doritos and some bowls of salsa set out on the tables. The room smells of cigarette smoke although she doesn't see anyone smoking, but there is a bunch of the lad lit writers in the corner, and they have probably smuggled something in. The person who looks as though he has had the most to drink is the bartender; it takes

Arabella several attempts to persuade him that she is on the faculty and is therefore entitled to free drinks.

The room is crowded with people she does not know. She might think she has wandered into the wrong party except for the conversation: 'Her suggestions were good, but what a bitch.' 'How many dropped out of your class?' 'They said I would be short-listed if I made him a woman. A woman. Shit.'

Arabella smiles genially at everyone, checks her watch, and walks purposely to a corner by the ladies' room. There is a battered couch there that she has occupied at previous parties, and she has noticed that if you sit down somewhere, the people sitting next to you feel they have to talk to you. If nothing else, they have to ask you to move when they get up.

Miracle of miracles, there is a sliver of a crack of tweed. She will be able to fit herself in. She is so intent on reaching the safety of the couch that she does not notice she is sitting right next to Dark Alice from her class.

'Well, hello,' Arabella says, more heartily than she intended, although she is genuinely glad to see Alice. She is the member of the class with whom Arabella feels most comfortable; there is an aura of misery around Alice that she associates with her parents' friends. Even here in the middle of a bar, surrounded by people chatting and flirting, Alice manages to exude misery. It is not just the misery of not knowing anyone at a party, it's the misery reserved for people who have suffered terribly, who have lost children or lost the use of all their limbs. It is the sort of misery that grows so deeply inside you that it pulses.

'Oh, hello,' Alice says, stuttering slightly and moving over to make more room. 'I'm glad . . . that is, I was hoping . . . that is, I'm very glad you could make it.'

'Have you been here long?'

'I don't know,' she says. She is wearing long, dangly earrings that look handmade by Indians. They seem to giggle as she moves her head.

'Anyone else from the class here?'

Alice nods and then furrows her entire face in concentration. She has beautiful fingers, Arabella notices, an artist's fingers, but then Alice is more of an artist than anyone else in the class. Her approach to words is deliberate. She is a poet; nothing is wasted. Her exercises have been violent accounts of rape and incest; for the first exercise, about a famous person, she chose the Central Park jogger. Yet the words she chose to write about that assault were so riveting and true that you could not help but feel ennobled by the writing. There was bestiality, yes, but how bad could the world be when there was such intelligence and beauty in it?

'There was someone from class here?' Arabella asks, curious as to who it might be. She hopes it isn't Conrad. He did come to one party; she spent an hour trying to draw words out of his mouth, and then there was no getting rid of him. He followed her around the party and to the parking garage, where he shook her hand good-bye and bowed.

'Was it Conrad?' she asks, but Alice is shaking her head, trying to force memory forward.

'Maybe Byron?' Arabella tries. It seems this would be more his milieu, but then Alice looks up and smiles. She has a beautiful smile that transforms her face. 'Chuck,' she says, and Arabella, looking up, sees that Chuck is walking toward them. She is so glad to see him that she feels a smile burst out on her face until she gets control of herself and forces it back into a hopeful grin or what she hopes is something inviting and yet not desperate.

As usual he looks as if he is ready for a book jacket photo: light brown leather coat, black T-shirt, and soft blue jeans. He is older than anyone else in the room, yet he also seems most to belong here. He looks relaxed; he walks easily, lightly, like an athlete, and he is holding two cups of white wine. He hands one to Alice and one to Arabella.

'For you,' he says and kisses Arabella on the cheek, just a greeting, nothing more, yet she is conscious of the warmth of his skin and the scent of his soap. His hair is white but flops boyishly over his forehead. She has to stop herself from smoothing it into place. 'I was hoping you'd show up.'

'How much do I owe? Is there money? How much was it, Chuck?' Alice asks, but he just smiles and waves his hand. At that moment the person sitting next to Arabella gets up, forfeiting her seat in this crowded bar, and Chuck sits down. It is a tight squeeze. Arabella is achingly aware of the touch of his thigh against hers, while his hand rests lightly on the couch behind her. She drains the glass of wine, not that it matters because it is so watered down. She suspects she could swill the bottle and nothing much would happen. But she feels the need to take control of something, and the plastic cup is nearest to hand.

Alice, too, has gulped down her wine, though in her case it went down the wrong pipe and she begins to cough. Then she goes staggering off in the direction of the ladies' room. 'Back soon,' she stutters. 'Don't wait . . . that is to say, I may have to go . . . that is, I may be back.'

'Maybe I should go with her,' Arabella says. She hates to see someone go off in trouble, although she doesn't think white wine can kill you.

'Don't leave me,' Chuck says. 'Sit and talk to me awhile. You're always running away.'

'Me!' Arabella cries out, the force of the words surprising her. She looks into his eyes and sees no malice there. 'You're the one who ran away on Wednesday.'

'Wednesday?' he says. His voice is deep; she suspects he sings well. 'Oh.' He nods. 'I was going to finalize my divorce.'

'Oh.'

'I had to get to the judge's office, but I didn't want to miss your class, and then I had to run.'

The lad lit writers are on the prowl, going up to young women and asking if they are in their online class, which is a good technique because no one knows what the online students look like. The volume of conversation is getting louder, and the room is smokier. Someone is finding liquor; someone is finding cigarettes.

'Did the divorce go through all right?' Arabella asks in the tone she thinks is required for such a question, factual and yet hopeful, too.

'Just fine. We weren't married all that long; it was a mistake. I was on the rebound.'

'From what?'

He puts both hands on his thighs; he has big, competent hands, and there is a cut on the side of his right hand that surprises her. It makes her think he is not as effete as she thinks he is.

'From my first divorce.'

'You were divorced twice?' she spits out. She can almost hear what her mother would have to say about this one, she of the 'till death do us part' ideology. How she used to rant when couples they knew got divorced; she would say they were taking the easy way out.

'Almost three times,' he says, grinning. 'But one of them was an annulment, and that happened a long time ago. So,' he says, looking directly at her, gray eyes crinkled with merriment. 'Now you know the worst about me. What about you?'

He lifts up his hand and catches the bartender's eye, the same bartender who would not give Arabella her free glass of wine. The man nods at Chuck, pours two glasses, and comes walking through the crowd, smiling yet. Chuck hands him some money and takes the cups.

'What are your sins, Arabella?'

He is smiling at her. His body is close to her, and his hand is so close that she can almost feel it. She just doesn't know how to flirt and doesn't know what to say.

'I don't really have any sins,' she answers. 'Nothing fun, anyway. Just generalized whining and complaining.'

'Sins of omission, then, not commission.'

'I guess that's one way to put it.'

She steals a glance in the direction of the bathroom, wondering if Alice is all right. It would be a terrible thing if something happened to her while Arabella was sitting here and ignoring her.

'I really should check on her.'

'Can I tell you how much I like your name?' he whispers. His voice is developing a twang. Maybe the bartender hasn't watered down the drinks as much as she thought.

'It's a silly name.'

'It's a feminine name. It suits you.'

Arabella takes a sip of her wine. It does taste stronger. 'I tried so many ways to change it. I tried Bella, but then everyone thinks of that Disney movie, and they start humming the song. Then I thought it would be cool to shorten it to Arab, but that starts too many arguments. There was a girl named Julie in my class that term, and she started calling herself Jew. Things really went out of control.'

He laughs at that, a hearty, happy sound. 'Are you always so funny?' he asks. She mishears him at first and thinks he is asking her if she is always so frightened. 'Yes,' she replies. 'All the time.'

Alice comes back then with Byron and Dorothy in tow, and they all cluster together for a bit. Then Chuck says, 'Would anyone like to go out to get a bite to eat? I'll treat you starving writers, but I've got to have something more than Doritos and Gallo.'

They all troop in line and follow him to a restaurant that is not far away, a lovely French place that serves soups and fresh bread and is exactly what Arabella wanted.

'When I was in public relations, this was one of my favorite restaurants,' Chuck says as they all gulp down their food and drink the three bottles of a French table wine that he requested from a waiter who seems to know him by name.

The evening goes by quickly. Maybe it is the wine or maybe it is excitement, but everyone is charming and interesting. Dorothy turns out to have a PhD in Byzantine studies. She is new to New York, having moved here to be closer to her daughter who is in graduate school at NYU. 'Since you talked to me,' she says to Arabella, winking, 'I've gotten over my writer's block.'

Byron works in an insurance agency. Arabella has a very bad moment imagining him reviewing her mother's claims and watching porn at the same time. She was right about his living with his mother, though. He tells everyone with a straight face that she was a stripper in Las Vegas. Chuck gently taps her foot with his own, but she shrugs. If Byron is going to lift Pussy's story and make it his own, that's all right with her. Fiction writers are supposed to be liars; that is part of the fun of it.

Alice is the most surprising because she is nothing at all what she seems. She is the mother of two children, lives on the Upper East Side, and has had absolutely no tragedy in her life. She is divorced but has a lover to whom she is quite devoted. She has a wallet filled with pictures of him. He is a musician, and she calls him throughout the meal to tell him she will not be too late. In the stuttering, whispery half of the conversation that Arabella can overhear, Alice is telling him that no one is trying to pick her up. She is just out with some friends from her writing class. *Friends.* Again Arabella catches Chuck's eye and blushes.

Then somehow Alice, Byron, and Dorothy leave for home, and Arabella has to catch her train, which is leaving in less than an hour. But Chuck suggests they walk to Grand Central Station.

'That's a long way,' she says, but she is not protesting. She is in no hurry to get home; there is a later train.

It is one of those strange February nights in which the weather is so mild you think it is spring, and it is all the more poignant because you know you're going to be slammed back into winter the next morning. The air even smells of spring, floral and moist. Chuck asks her something about her childhood, but she dismisses his question. 'I'm really not that interesting,' she says. 'Tell me about you.'

So he tells her about how he grew up in Texas, went to college in the Northeast, and then went to work for a friend of his who was a kind of stock market genius.

161

'Maybe you've heard of him,' Chuck says. He has his arm linked with Arabella's, and every so often he pats her hand protectively. 'They called him the Prophet.'

'Why?' He has an awfully nice nose, she thinks. One of those straight noses you could run your finger right down.

'Because he said that God told him what stocks to pick.' She pauses for a moment. The Empire State Building looms before them, its top lights red and white in honor of Valentine's Day. 'God told your friend which stocks to buy?'

Chuck nods. 'That's what Desmond believed, anyway, and it worked out quite well for him.'

'Do you believe that?'

He puffs up his cheeks. 'I read once that if you throw darts at a board, you're as likely to come up with a good investment plan as anything else.'

'So you don't believe in it?'

He smells warm and clean and rich. She thinks of all the prayers her mother sent to God, praying for her father's health. Who knew that God was hoping she'd ask for stock advice?

'I made a lot of money, Arabella. That's what I believe.'

'Then why are you taking this class?' she asks. 'If you have all this money, why aren't you cruising around the Mediterranean or doing something more exciting?'

They're both quiet for a while. They pass an NYU student setting up a table of books, stacking up piles of colorful paperbacks.

'Maybe I'm looking for meaning,' Chuck says.

'If you're looking for meaning, why don't you do the exercises?'

'I'm not looking for that much meaning.'

He laughs so delightedly at his joke that Arabella laughs along. His face becomes boyish when he smiles, and she feels as if she could see him many years earlier, a tall, thin boy standing by a stream – an outdoor boy, the kind she steered clear of when she was a girl because she found their physical strength overpowering. They frightened her. She would watch them jogging on the beach, sturdy and strong, and she worried they would run her down; it seemed disloyal to favor physical perfection when she could see from her father how unimportant the physical was. It was the mind that made a man, wasn't it?

'You should do the exercises,' she says. Maybe it is the wine or the excitement or the warmth that radiates off him, but she can't hold back. 'You have to try. If you're going to do this, you have to give it your best shot. You can't live life in half measures.'

'No,' he says. 'I suppose I can't.'

By now they are at Grand Central Station. They walk past a rogue vendor still selling hot dogs and pretzels and barbecued chicken. It smells so good; Arabella is surprised to realize she is starving. Chuck buys her a pretzel. She gives him half, and he holds it before him as though he has never seen one before. Then they are at the door to the train. He is still clutching his half of the pretzel in a napkin.

'Do you feel up to going home by yourself?' Chuck asks. He is so close that she feels as though she is being absorbed into him. She has to force herself to step back. 'I'm fine,' she says.

'You are welcome to come to my apartment if you like.'

He looks so handsome and hopeful, yet she hesitates. She wants to go home with him; she wants that desperately. But she also feels frightened. She sees her mother in her mind, sitting by the window, staring out sadly, waiting for her to come, waiting for death.

'My mother is dying. I can't right now.'

The bells on the train begin to scream, and soon the doors will close. 'I know it seems ridiculous that I can't have sex because my mother is dying. It's just that I can't do two things at once.'

He has the strangest expression on his face. The conductor is waving at her, but she has her foot on the entryway and knows he won't close the doors on her. 'I'm sorry, Chuck. Have I been a tease?'

He leans forward and kisses her lightly on the lips.

'Get on the train,' he says. 'I'll see you next Wednesday.'

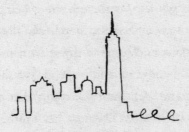

FORTUNE
(CONTINUED)
BY VERA HICKS

'*IS IT SOMETHING bad?*'

The words still echo in Joan's head. There was the fear, the absolute certainty that the fortune-teller was going to tell her something bad. Something that would change her life.

'*Is it something bad?*' *Joan asked.*

'*Listen, and I will tell you. I see a miracle here on your husband's sixtieth birthday.*'

'*But a miracle is something unforeseen, something unplanned.*'

'*Unforeseen by you perhaps.*'

Before she could say anything else, Danny stood up. That is the hardest part of the whole episode for Joan to remember. Danny standing. He has not stood in so long. He was tall, is tall, although stretched out on a bed is not the same thing.

'Friend,' he said, 'I don't like your attitude. It's time for you to go.'

Joan had thought the fortune-teller might argue, but he did not. He did not seem to want to stay and did not seem overawed by what he had forecast. That made sense. He was a charlatan. He told all Americans about their miracles to drive them crazy.

It was his own way of protesting the hegemony of God's country. And yet something about his words fit inside Joan like a piece of a jigsaw puzzle sliding into place. She could no more explain why any more than she could explain falling in love. She believed.

The very idea of it appealed to her. The suddenness of it, the violence of it. She read once about people who followed tornadoes, driving across the vastness of the Midwest waiting for the violence to erupt. She imagined the excitement and fear of spotting the twister. In the same way she expected the miracle to come with the sound of cracking and the smell of sulfur.

Danny's illness, when it came years later, only confirmed her belief. She did not talk to him about it. She felt that would jinx it. But as she watched the paralysis creep over him as steadily as a plant absorbing water, his strong hands curl up, and his alert gaze turn to one of befuddlement, it seemed to her that the prospect of the miracle was the only thing that kept her sane.

There is a steady rhythm to her daughter's eating that reminds Joan of a machine. Click, swish, click, swish. Joan has grown unused to such hard-edged sounds. It occurs to her that even the sounds of illness are different from those of real life. The sounds of illness are softer. They gurgle and suck and sink. Danny is sitting quietly, patiently, a polite smile on his face. A filet of sole lies in *front of him bathed in a smooth white sauce.*

Joan cuts a piece of the fish and puts it in Danny's mouth. He chews it neatly. She is glad he does not drool or spit. She knows others can't help it, but she finds it disgusting. She likes to think that Danny knows that and is making a real effort for her. She imagines he is trying to show her how much he still loves her, that every bit of spit he swallows is a sign of love.

'Did you read that fish isn't really good for you?' Annie asks. 'According to the paper it's all a statistical anomaly. You might as well eat beef.'

'You're kidding.'

Annie takes the last piece of bread and butters it. Joan looks at the basket. She can't believe it is empty; Annie has eaten the whole loaf. She finds Annie's hunger reassuring.

'No, it has to do with the way the Japanese measure cholesterol.'

'That's amazing,' Joan says, louder than she meant to. But it is amazing. It turns so many things upside down.

'It's certainly interesting,' Annie says, rubbing her hand against a napkin.

'No, really,' Joan says. 'Every time I hear something like that, I get all excited. It makes me think anything is possible. They – whoever they are – don't really know anything. It opens so many doors.'

'That's a novel way of looking at it, Mother.'

Annie opens up her pocketbook and takes out a hefty blue leather book. She opens it and begins to write. 'It does make me think that we should consider an issue on beef. I bet the beef council could supply some healthy recipes.'

Joan feels light-headed. She feels as if she is floating. 'Maybe that's the problem,' she says. 'Maybe you've been eating too much fish, Danny. Maybe you need to eat more beef.' She starts to laugh at that, then tries to fight it down because the sound of the laughter scares her. But she cannot. It is too ridiculous. Annie is rubbing the tip of her nose, rubbing a place where there used to be a pockmark. Joan is gasping for breath, her eyes are tearing, and her hands are shaking so much that she cannot cut Danny's fish.

And as she is laughing, as the noise from her mouth appears to be filling this shrine of a restaurant, it seems to Joan that the fish on Danny's plate is starting to shimmer. She quiets down and looks at the fish. Surely it is shimmering. Surely there is a light around it. Jesus fed five thousand with two fishes. Many people have reported a glimmering before seeing a miracle. Maybe this is it. Joan puts her hand out, looking fiercely at the fish that glows before her. She will look. She is so desperate for a clue, for help.

Joan leans forward just as Annie spears her father's fish with her fork. Four deep stigmata pucker its flesh. Joan screams. The kitchen doors squeak open. 'Good Lord, Mother, I was just trying to help.'

'Sorry,' Joan whispers. 'Sorry.'

'Joan.' Danny is looking at her. His legs are stiff with spasms and are sticking out in front of him. He is gulping, fighting back the spasm in his chest. 'Joan.'

He looks down at his hands, still neatly folded. She knows what he wants. She takes one of his hands and puts it around her shoulder. She leans against him. She rubs her cheek against the soft cashmere of his sweater. Gently she presses his arched fingers against her neck.

Sixth Class: Dialogue

'YOU THINK YOU know how to write dialogue because you know how to talk, right? You figure it's the same principle. You simply say what you want to say, but instead of speaking it, you write it down.

'But you're wrong,' Arabella says.

'Dialogue in fiction is not like dialogue in real life. Dialogue in fiction is better.'

Arabella waits for the rumble of laughter that always greets that remark, and sure enough it comes, mainly from Pam who finds everything she says hysterical. It is like having a laugh track in the class. Chuck is also nodding at her appreciatively. She is touched to see he has a pen and paper with him today and looks to be ready to take down notes. He is also wearing the most garish sweater she has ever seen a man wear – a sky blue and tan argyle that looks like a converted sock.

Mimi is sitting next to him, dressed in one of her slinky outfits, a tight black T-shirt covered with a skinny knit sweater. Every so often she leans over and whispers something into Chuck's ear. She would have gone home with Chuck, of that Arabella is sure. She would have known how to flirt with him. She's doing it even now. Not that Arabella thinks Mimi is interested in Chuck in any romantic way. She has a look of haughtiness on her face that suggests she only goes out with pro athletes. The problem for her in this class is that there is no one remotely in her range.

Byron is an assault case waiting to happen, and Conrad is of dubious sanity and sexuality. Justin would seem to be the best candidate, but Ginger has a tight grip on him. In fact, Ginger seems to be wearing him out. Today she is wearing black leather pants, and Justin is flopped against his chair in an exhausted manner that makes Arabella think of her mother – which reminds her, in turn, that today is the day they are going to the mall to buy what her mother refers to as her death dress.

She had hoped her mother would forget about it, but she has called Arabella three times to remind her: once at two in the morning, once at three, and once at four. Marvel asked her if she would like to put a block on her mother's outgoing calls; the idea of it is appealing, but there's no way Arabella can do that now. She can understand why her mother is having trouble sleeping; she can understand all her mother's problems. It is just that right now Arabella is so damned tired.

'Why is the dialogue in fiction better than real life?' Arabella asks, resuming the lecture. Then she answers herself: 'First of all, because it has a point. In real life we all tend to natter on about one thing or another.'

'Natter,' Pam screams out with a laugh.

'Say you want to ask someone for a favor. You want to ask your friend to take care of your cat, but you don't usually blurt that right out. Instead, you start off talking about the weather. Then you move on to politics and last night's dinner. After about twenty minutes you might say, 'By the way, could you take care of my cat?' In fiction we cut out all that dead stuff. In fiction you'd go right up to that friend and say, "About my cat." '

'About my cat,' Pam cries out. 'About my cat.'

Her laughter jerks a bottle of pills onto the floor from her purse, which she scoops right up with surprising alacrity. She has lost some weight over the course of this class; her face, which had been full and cozy, now seems haunted. Arabella wonders what she can do to help this poor woman. She is killing herself to be in this class, and Arabella is not sure she is getting anything out of it. Her assignments aren't really getting any better, which is unusual. Most people improve over the course of the ten weeks. You can't always get what you want – unless you're the Prophet, she supposes.

'So the thing to keep in mind about dialogue in fiction is that it is edited. You cut to the good stuff. The other thing to keep in mind is that it has to serve a point. You don't just put it into your manuscript when you've run out of other things to do. It has to serve a function.'

Arabella continues: 'You use dialogue when you want to show what your characters are like. Do they curse? Do they stutter? Do they whisper? Or you use it to get across a point about plot. 'The train is coming at nine o'clock.' Or you use it to talk about theme, and if you want to know how to do that, just read Dostoyevsky. He'll teach you everything you need to know. Yes, D'mon?'

'Just a craft point,' he says. 'My characters are terrorists, so should I have them speak Arabic?'

'If they're Arabic, you might want to sprinkle in some Arabic phrases. Why not?'

Phrases, he writes down. He always looks so spiffy in his ironed blue shirt.

'Do they have to be real,' he asks, 'or can I make them up?'

'The phrases or the terrorists?'

'The phrases.'

Arabella wonders if he is kidding, but he doesn't seem to be. There is no humor in his expression. 'They have to be real, D'mon. You cannot make up things that sound Arabic and put them in your book.'

He nods and writes that down. She notices that Byron is looking at Conrad and rolling his eyes, though Conrad does not give him any encouragement. His headset is on, and he is listening to something with a very strong beat.

'Just want to be sure,' D'mon says. 'Thought I might be able to get away with doing a little less research.'

'Arab terrorists,' Mimi mutters, rolling her eyes upward. 'That's a novel idea.'

But Arabella cuts her off. 'D'mon is right to ask questions even if they seem obvious. A lot of times you assume everybody knows something, and they don't. It's just they're too afraid to ask. That's what I'm paid for.' She feels a little pleasure at the way everyone responds so attentively. She is the teacher here; she is in control. She goes on:

'Another reason that dialogue in fiction is different from real life is that it's better because you have more time to think about it. We've all had the experience of having an argument with someone, possibly a mother, and having her say something hurtful. You respond with something lame, go home, and sit down at your computer. You work for a while, and then the perfect answer comes to you – the exact words that would have put her in her place.'

Arabella thinks of the day she told her mother she wasn't going to medical school because she wanted to be a writer. 'Just what the world needs, another writer,' her mother had replied. She should have said, 'The world needs . . .'

'I think Mimi's sick,' Pam screams out.

'What?'

Mimi has turned pale. She has her hands on her stomach. Chuck is handing her a handkerchief. 'I'm sorry,' she's moaning.

'What's happening?' Dorothy calls out, but Mimi is in motion. She has jumped up and is running for the door to the girls' bathroom. The facilities here are designed for nursery school children, so most of the students tend to avoid going to the bathroom until after the class is over when they can run to the diner across the street. But this is clearly an emergency. Arabella can hear the surging sound of Mimi's vomiting, and Byron starts to make a gagging noise; he is such a tough guy that the sound of someone vomiting makes him nauseated. Pam looks at her, terrified, and after a moment of uncertainty, Arabella gets up, knocks on the door, and then goes in.

There are finger paints everywhere; colors drip onto the floor. Mimi must have knocked them out of her way, and the poor thing is on her knees in front of the toilet. She has green patches of paint on her knees. Arabella grabs some paper towels and runs them under water.

'Please, I'll take care of it,' Mimi gasps.

'Don't worry about it,' Arabella whispers. 'You should see some of the messes I've cleaned up. I once took my mother out to the movies, and she had Chinese food. Well, let's not talk about it. Suffice it to say that I never did find out how *The Hunt for Red October* ends.'

She wipes the vomit off Mimi's face, noticing that even in this state Mimi is gorgeous. She has Cleopatra eyes and regal cheekbones. Arabella cleans off her chin and pushes the paper towel up against Mimi's forehead, and it's then that she realizes the girl has no hair. She is wearing a wig.

'Chemo,' Mimi says, her voice raspy from the vomiting.

'usually I have a few days before the nausea, but it hit me early this time.'

'Chemo,' Arabella says, crouching back on her heels. How old is this girl? No more than twenty-one, surely.

'I have breast cancer.'

'That's lousy,' Arabella says. She wishes she could say something better. All those years of her father being sick, dealing with people who wanted to apologize or help and feeling angry at them for being useless, and it turns out she can't think of anything comforting to say, either.

'You're going to tell me I shouldn't have come to class today, but I couldn't bear to miss it.'

'I'd be happy to e-mail you the lectures and the . . .'

But Mimi is shaking her head. 'I need to be here with other writers. That's the only way I can survive this thing.'

She grabs Arabella's arm, and the girl's hand is surprisingly cold. 'When I'm in this class, I don't feel sick. I feel part of something good. Then when I go home and write, I feel inspired.'

Arabella slumps back against the door to the bathroom; she is so touched. Why has she spent the semester disliking this girl? Why has she been so sure she was haughty? The poor thing was probably just afraid, brittle with fear. It is impossible to reach out to people when you think it is going to hurt you. Suddenly Arabella understands something about her mother, too, about the brittleness and edginess that has marked her.

'I feel as if I'm healing myself with my writing,' Mimi is

saying. 'I'm creating an alternative reality. If I can live in it, then I will be all right.'

Beautiful brown eyes blaze at Arabella, and she melts under their heat. 'Of course,' she whispers. 'I understand.' Then there is a soft tap on the door. Arabella, opening it, finds Chuck standing there, a worried expression on his face. She watches as he takes in the vomit and the colors, and she shakes her head. He is not a man designed for such a situation, but then he surprises her and puts out his hand to Mimi.

'Let's get you settled somewhere more comfortable.'

Dark Alice, standing slightly behind Chuck, says, 'I'll help clean up.' Two little pink patches glow on her pale skin.

The class spends the next few minutes getting everything ready: They pull out pillows in the story area so that Mimi will have a place to lie down. Dorothy finds a smock that Mimi can change into. Alice gets several glasses of water, which she spills all over the tiled floor. Bonita finds the mop, and Ginger and Justin head off in search of crackers. Conrad lunges for the bathroom, ready to clean it, which Arabella thinks is kind of weird but good-natured, too.

By the time they get Mimi settled, she looks like a fairy princess with her cushions, flowing smock, and courtiers. It doesn't seem right for the rest of them to sit around the table, so they all lower themselves onto cushions and form a semicircle around Arabella.

'Someone is going to have to help me back up,' Chuck says as he lowers himself onto a pink cushion and grimaces, but he is probably in the best shape of anyone in the room.

'Ready to continue?' Arabella says to her circle of students, thinking that this way of seating lends itself well to teaching. She also thinks that they really are a very nice group of people.

'Ready?' she asks Mimi, who nods drowsily. Pam is watching her fiercely, ready to lunge if Mimi needs help.

Arabella continues with her discussion about dialogue and gives them an exercise to do in which a nun and a convict get into an accident. They have to write about how different the two sound. When that is over, Arabella gives them the take-home assignment, which is to write an exchange of dialogue between any two people, but the first line of dialogue must be, 'Kiss me.'

Then the class is over, and Dorothy helps Mimi to her feet and says she will drive her home. 'I parked right out front,' she says as she puts her arm around the girl's waist. 'I'll take her home.'

'That's very kind of you,' Arabella says.

'We writers have to stick together, don't we?' Dorothy says. Her grin is so loopy that Arabella wonders if she has taken some of Pam's medicine. Arabella grabs Mimi's backpack while Chuck grabs the girl's other arm, and they make their way downstairs to the lobby and then out to the street.

Dorothy's Subaru is right in front of the writing center. Mimi is feeling stronger and is able to get in by herself, although Dorothy fusses with her and makes sure the seat belt is on tightly. She has a daughter Mimi's age, Arabella

Susan Breen

remembers. That would explain her intensity and why she seems to be gift-wrapping Mimi into place. After this goes on for a few more minutes, the car leaves and there is silence.

Arabella is standing with Chuck on the Upper West Side of Manhattan. She is conscious of the fact that there are people swarming around them and traffic and men selling peanuts and falafel. She wants to tell him that she thought he was kind to Mimi, but she is afraid if she says so, she'll start to cry. There is something about people being kind that always makes Arabella cry, so she looks up at Chuck and tries to think of what to say.

'Kiss me,' he says.

Arabella doesn't hesitate. She kisses him quickly and softly, only barely conscious of the cushion of his warm coat as he wraps his arms around her. She is briefly enveloped in his warmth, listening to the strong hammer of his heart.

'I can't wait for next week's assignment,' he says, rubbing his cheek against her hair.

'This is as racy as it gets, I'm afraid.'

'Too bad.'

He kisses her, and she has the strangest sensation of her body dissolving, melting into his, and then he whispers in her ear: 'My apartment isn't that far away.'

She laughs at that. He is so bold.

'I thought you were the generation that believed in waiting.'

'I'm not that old, thank you very much,' he says as he cups her face in his hands, almost crushing her cheeks with his grip.

Then he kisses her again, harder, and she can feel herself swelling, absorbing his passion, the city, the class, and her life. She feels tears, she feels Mimi, and she sees her mother. She pulls away slightly.

'You have to see your mother,' he says, but there is no impatience in his voice. He is a kind man. She reaches up and touches his hair.

'I'm available at other times,' she says. He laughs at that and hugs her tight, squeezing her to him. He is so warm to lean against. She catches a doorman's eyes, and he smiles at her. New York is such a romantic city, as everyone knows from all those movies with happy endings.

'You didn't ask to hear the exercises today,' Chuck says.

'I forgot. I got so caught up in the whole thing with Mimi.'

'I did it.'

'You did?' He looks so proud of himself, this elegant man with his boyish smile.

'You shamed me,' he says, 'and I didn't think that was possible. I wrote about a place that was important to me growing up.'

'I want to hear it.'

'Now?' He actually takes a step back, away from her. She moves forward and crushes herself back in his arms.

'Yes, unless you're lying.'

'Here?' She has never seen him look vulnerable before; there is something very appealing about it. He kisses her one more time, and she almost tips him over by kissing him hard. She can feel his lips turning into a smile even as she kisses him, and then she tugs him in the direction of a bench. It is that sort of day; she wants to sit down, and there is a bench right there.

'Go for it,' she says, sitting next to him and clasping her hands together automatically. Then she unclasps them. He takes a small notebook from his pocket. He licks his finger, then takes out a pair of glasses. He clears his throat. 'We were supposed to write about a place that was important to us growing up.'

'Yes,' she says, resting her head against his shoulder. 'I remember.'

'Now?'

'Yes,' she says. She closes her eyes and breathes in the clean smell of him.

He starts to read, squinting at the words in front of him. 'My tree house,' he says. He clears his throat again. 'It was a large space made of wooden planks, safe. There was a rope ladder you had to climb to get up to it, and there were knots in the rope for your feet to rest on. Inside there were beanbag chairs, a calendar, and some books and pictures from the *San Antonio Gazette* of when Neil Armstrong walked on the moon. There were binoculars that my father gave me so I could watch birds. I didn't use them much.

'There was a garbage pail, which was always filled with empty Dr Pepper cans. When it got full enough, I would toss them all down to the ground and make a pile. Then my mother would come to clean it up. To the north there was a forest, to the south a stream, and to the west was my father's church.'

Then he leans over and kisses Arabella. 'The end.'

'Your father's church?'

'My father was a minister.'

'You're kidding! You're a preacher's son?'

His eyes sparkle. She can see the boy inside him, the light that has not been extinguished.

'Not just any old preacher, a Methodist one, a strict one. I wasn't allowed to sing anything – except hymns – or dance or play cards. On Sundays I had to spend the whole day at church. I'm afraid I got into quite a bit of trouble when I was young. My mother laughs about it now, but I don't think they were sorry when I went east to college.'

'Are your parents back in Texas?' Arabella asks.

'No. They're in India, doing missionary work.' He shakes his head. 'They want to save the world.'

'But not you?' Arabella asks. 'You don't want to save the world?'

'No,' he says, his gaze now serious as he looks at her. 'I'm afraid I take a much more selfish view of things. If my little patch of the world is happy, then I think I've done my job.'

A church bell begins to chime. Startled, Arabella looks at her watch and then cries out. 'I have to go; I'm going to be late.'

'Cinderella,' he says, rising to his feet. He extends his hand to her, which she grabs onto.

'I'm lucky my mother doesn't go for fairy tales,' she says, scooping up her bag and all the assignments, trying to grab it all and hold on to his hand at the same time. 'Cinderella Hicks would really be too much.'

She can't remember where she parked, although she remembers it was not far. They start off toward West Ninety-third Street. Arabella is trying hard not to look anxious, but her mother is waiting to go to the mall. She will be all dressed up in her shopping outfit, ready to buy her death dress. You can't be late for something like that. But Chuck is strolling along, talking about a nice place they could go for dinner, admiring the wrought iron fence of a handsome brownstone.

'I'll just run ahead,' she says. 'We'll talk again next week.'

'Nonsense. now that I have you, I'm not going to let go so easily.'

She is beginning to feel panicked, trapped, but then, thankfully, she sees her car in the distance. 'Ah, there it is,' she cries out and tugs in the direction of her poor old Cadillac, which is squeezed between two gleaming red Audis. It does not look impressive. The roof sags slightly, the driver's side door has slid down so it is not completely latched into place, and the side-view mirror rattles with the wind.

'This is a death trap,' Chuck says, looking at it with horror. He is not used to such cars, she thinks; he is not used to any kind of suffering.

'It's lucky for you that I do like old things,' Arabella says. 'Don't be too critical.'

'How far do you drive in this?'

'It takes me an hour, but I do it only once a week.'

'I'm surprised it passed inspection.' He walks around it, and she feels irritated. Appearances to the contrary, she is not looking for a father, and it is her car. She has already said she is going to drive it, and she really has to get going. Her mother is waiting.

'Why don't I just get you a taxi?' he says, his eyes still on the car as though it might suddenly jump up and attack him. 'We could just have the car towed.'

'Chuck, that's ridiculous. This is my car. And, anyway, I'm going to Port Chester. It would cost a hundred dollars to take a taxi there.'

She yanks open the car door, no easy feat because the locks have a tendency to stick. She has to tug and tug. Her hands are now sweaty with anxiety. Why doesn't he stop talking?

'If the money's a problem—' he begins to say, but she cuts him off.

'The money is not the problem,' she says. 'You are.'

And before he can say anything else, Arabella has gotten into the car and slammed the door closed. Chuck looks distant, hard. This is what lies underneath that soft exterior, she thinks. now he looks like the man he really is: successful, bossy, cold. It is good to realize things like that early. It is good to realize that before you get hurt.

Writing Exercise

Arabella Hicks – The Fiction Class

Two people are having a conversation. It can be any two people you want, but this is the first line of dialogue: 'Kiss me.'

Chapter Seven

TWO MEN ARE digging a grave on the front lawn of the nursing home. That's what it looks like anyway, although Arabella is sure that is not right. This is not a place where death is discussed. When a resident dies, the other patients are restricted to their rooms until the body is taken away, and there is a separate door through which the bodies are carried out to the hearses. There is not even an announcement made of patients' deaths. There are no memorial services except monthly ones held in private for the staff, to give them an opportunity to mourn those whom they've come to care about.

Arabella doesn't blame them. She has no desire to think about death, either, and it's not as if it would make her feel any better to see the steady stream of corpses that must flow through these corridors. When her mother first moved here, her roommates died with such frequency that it got to be a joke. Her mother did in fact joke that she was poisoning her roommates, though that led to a very unpleasant conversation with the head of the nursing home and a warning to be more sensitive.

'Everyone's too sensitive if you ask me,' her mother had said. 'They should all be writers.'

'What are they doing out there?' Arabella asks Dotty, taking a cookie from the tray. She hasn't stopped off at Wendy's today because she and her mother are going to the mall, which means dinner at P. F. Chang's, which is her mother's favorite restaurant.

'They're putting in a butterfly garden,' Dotty says. 'It's going to be beautiful, you wait and see.'

'What is it?'

Dotty leans forward as though telling her a secret. She has the husky voice of a cigarette smoker. It looks as if the scar on her forehead is healing. 'Special plants that attract butterflies,' she says. 'It will be such a treat for the residents.'

Arabella nods. Dotty is so sincere that it does not seem like the right time to tell her that there is nothing her mother would like less than to be outside with butterflies swarming around her. It sounds more like torture than stimulation. It is like one of those crazy things her mother used to do with her father, such as the time she read that snake bites could cure MS, so she drove him to a special center in Florida where her father could be bitten by a snake. She was always so eager for a miracle, so desperate to do anything that would save him.

She finds her mother sitting by the window in her room. She is looking at the birch trees, but she has dressed up for their trip to the mall. She has on a pair of blue slacks, little matching socks, and a crisp white blouse with blue trim. The whole effect is quite nautical and jaunty and of another time. In fact, it makes Arabella think of pictures she has seen of the young Russian tsarinas before their execution – something perky and doomed.

'Hi, Mom,' Arabella says, 'and hello to you, too, Lily.'

There is a bouquet of flowers by Lily's bed and a balloon that reads, 'Happy Birthday, Mom.'

'Hi, Mom,' Arabella says again. Then she realizes that her mother is not looking out the window but at a picture of her wedding. It is Arabella's favorite photo of her parents because they both looked like movie stars – her father so trim and elegant in his black tuxedo, and her mother with her short white dress and flaming red hair. One of the things that has always amused Arabella about her parents' relationship, especially in the context of what was to come, was that her father was reluctant to get married. He had commitment issues, as her mother put it. He worked as a display animator, making figures move in store windows, and there was no time, no money.

They dated for four years, and every single Christmas her

mother expected an engagement ring, and every single Christmas he gave her a present that was thoughtful but not a diamond. By the fifth Christmas things were tense between them. Her mother had just turned forty; she was resigned to being an old maid.

That day he asked her to go for a drive with him. 'Just a ride,' he had said. 'We'll drive around Queens.'

He was a big man, and he drove a big car. They drove around Queens for a while, and then he pulled onto the Utopia Parkway. He looked at her mother then and said, 'Speaking of Utopia . . .'

He had put the engagement ring in the glove compartment. Arabella can see it sparkling on her mother's hand even now.

'Are you going deaf?' Arabella asks as she leans over to kiss her mother's cheek, the skin like paper and a scratch on her forehead. 'Can't you hear me?'

Her mother turns her head slightly and then holds up her hand, beckoning Arabella to lean forward, which she does. As soon as her face is in range, her mother punches her hard, right in the nose.

'Jesus Christ!' she yells out. The pain is intense. Who knew the old lady had such strength? She can taste blood on her lips.

'Mom!' she says, eyes hot with tears.

Then her mother opens her mouth wide and begins to laugh, a terrible cackling sound, the sound of madness and nightmares. Arabella goes running out of the room to the nurses' desk, to where Marvel is sitting, manning her space station of a desk. When she sees Arabella's face, she jumps up and runs toward her.

'My mother,' Arabella says. Marvel rushes past her, a breeze of lemon and soap. The night nurse comes, too, and the skinny little one who hands out the meds. Sade is there, too, and they surround her mother who is still cackling uncontrollably. There is an aria playing on the speakers. Arabella has no idea what it is, though she is sure her father would know. It is so terribly sad. The singer's voice is slow and sweet like maple syrup. Arabella stands back, next to Lily's bed, as she watches the nurses look after her mother.

They take her temperature, undress her, and give her a shot and some pills. Sade runs out to call the doctor and comes back with some different pills. All the while Arabella is watching her mother. Her notebook has fallen to the floor, but Marvel picks it up. They are careful and loving here; it is just that there's nothing much they can do. Lily's birthday flowers from last week smell ripe; next week they will be gone.

'She's had a seizure,' Marvel says after they've gotten her mother settled in bed.

'She punched me.'

'Your mother's disoriented,' Marvel explains. 'She has a kidney infection, and it's secreting poisons into her. We've given her medicine, and she should be all right. Let me get you some ice for that bruise.'

'Is she going to die?' Arabella asks, her voice tremulous.

'You know she's sick, Miss Bella.' Marvel's voice is soft and solemn as a dirge. 'Why don't you go home?'

'I think I'll just sit here for a while and keep her company.'

Marvel nods. There's a commotion in the hallway; some new crisis for her to deal with. To her credit, she looks as though she'd like to stay and talk, but there is so much for her to do.

'She's not going to wake up tonight,' Marvel warns her.

'I know, but I don't want to leave her.'

Arabella's nose is killing her. Her mother got off a good shot, and she was completely unprotected. She's not used to such sensations. She never played contact sports and had no siblings, no one to hit her. Certainly her parents did not believe in corporal punishment. She doubts her father even yelled at her over the course of her childhood, much less hit her. Oddly, the one time Arabella can remember physical pain was because of her writing. She had been sent to a sleepaway camp and wrote something unflattering in her journal about one of her bunkmates, not realizing that the whole cabin was reading her journal when she was out. When she came back to the cabin after pottery class, the bunkmate rammed her in the nose – in the same spot, actually.

But then her mother came and got her, and yelled at the camp and threatened a lawsuit. Arabella never went to sleepaway camp again. What a tiger she once was, this poor frail woman who lies like a corpse on her bed. She has never seen her with so little animation; she looks as if someone sucked the soul right out of her.

'You all right, Miss Arabella?' Sade calls out from the hallway.

'I'm fine,' Arabella says, although she's not. Her heart is breaking. The aria has finished, and now the radio station is playing something waltzlike. She wishes she could have that aria back.

'You want me to put the TV on?' Sade asks.

Arabella is tempted. It is so quiet in this room with only the sound of Lily's breathing breaking the stillness. Yet she doesn't want the sound of the TV, a sound she associates with hospitals, with killing time.

'No, thanks.'

She looks over at the table, at the piles of books and letters, and picks up the one book she knows her mother loves.

'Why don't I read to you, Mom? Why don't I read to you from *Arabella?*'

The very touch of the book comforts Arabella, and when she turns to the opening page and reads the opening line, she feels the warm sensation she always gets when she begins a new book, that sense of being swept up into a new world. ' "The schoolroom in the Parsonage at Heythram was not a large apartment, but on a bleak January day, in a household where the consumption of coals was a consideration, this was not felt by its occupants to be a disadvantage." ' The odd thing is that Arabella has never actually read this book before.

She associates such romances with lonely middle-aged women who have already made their choices and are not happy with them. She has always assumed that romances are for people who are not expecting to find any, and she supposes that she has also felt that if her mother liked it, it could not be all that good. Her mother has always leaned toward the type of commercial fiction that you find at the checkout counter, the type that she has always found manipulative, like Byron with his sex slave story. It is not that it is not a good story, but you just feel as though the author is secretly laughing at you on the way to the bank.

But now as she starts to read it, Arabella finds herself intrigued in spite of herself. She loves Georgette Heyer's voice, the playfulness and humor of it. The deeper into the book she goes, the more she feels that Heyer is right there with her, sitting by her side. She enjoys the clean authority with which Heyer writes, and she is amused by the way Heyer tosses in all her research, the names of the books Arabella and her sisters would be reading or the words they might use – 'fustian'.

It is all a little creaky and self-conscious, and yet, for all that, Arabella is entertained and finds herself wondering how her namesake is going to get herself to the London season, how she is going to hook up with the wealthy and desirable Robert Beaumaris. She flips forward until she gets to page 85, which is where he is introduced. There he is, vain and handsome in his Hessian boots and with the smile that could harden 'just for a moment' when he felt someone was taking advantage of him.

More than two hours have gone by. The music in the hallway is off, and the lights are dim. All the residents are in their beds, Marvel has gone home, and a whole other staff is here. Arabella knows that her remaining in the room is against regulations, and yet she cannot bring herself to go; she has a horror of her mother waking up and not knowing where she is.

She looks so small. It is strange to see her with her eyes closed; usually those pale blue eyes are blazing at her. Arabella puts her hand on her mother's hand and holds it, something she would never do if her mother were awake. The nails are neatly manicured, the polish a pretty pink. Her toes are pink, too, although Arabella can't see them because her mother is all covered up, like a mummy.

'You have to get better, Mom,' she whispers. 'I can't lose you just yet.'

Her voice is raspy in the silence of the room; there is no other sound but the roommate's breathing. How still this place is, how frightening; how different from the splash of color on the bathroom floor of the nursery school. Was that only a few hours ago? Was that still today?

'I've had a bad day,' she says. She can feel the track of a tear down her face, a warm, wet finger rubbing itself against her.

'I had a fight with this man who I like, and I thought things were going to go somewhere with him. He's sort of old – well, he's definitely old – but there's something about him that I like. There's a quality of gentleness in him. He's cultured, that's what he is.'

Arabella is still holding her mother's hand, and she tells her about the class and how she talked about dialogue. Then she backtracks and tells her about the party and how she felt a communion with Chuck. 'It's odd, but I felt we belonged together, and I thought other people thought that, too.' Then she goes back even further, to the first class, and then she jumps ahead and tells her mother – only because she is unconscious – about the way he kissed her. She draws out the scene, describing the street and the touch of his wool coat and the swirling sensation that gripped her. As she is telling this story, she feels as though she is telling her mother one of the romances she loves so well, with the exception that this really happened.

'It was nice,' Arabella says, remembering. 'It was easy. Isn't that silly? So much of life is hard, and yet kissing Chuck felt easy.'

The birch tree is swaying outside the window, its white ghostly shape seeming to nod encouragingly, and Arabella sees her own pale face reflected back to her. She looks like a ghost herself; her eyes look black, her hair is wild, and her nose is swollen. She half-expects to see Heathcliff tapping at the window.

'So what happened?'

The sound of her mother's voice is so startling that Arabella's heart actually lurches, as if she is being punched from the inside.

'Mom?'

Her mother clears her throat. 'What happened with this old man?'

What happened? The best words in the English language.

'I didn't know you could hear me.'

Holding her mother's hand now feels weird – they are not hand-holding people – but she doesn't let go because her mother is gripping hers tightly. Her eyes look tired, but her pointy chin is raised. She is paying attention, so Arabella tells her the rest of the story, about how she got irritated over his bossiness, the way she felt that they were just too far apart in experience, and that she just wasn't ready to have someone bossing her around. *Not on top of you* was the unspoken sentence, but she knew her mother understood.

'Do you love him?' her mother asks.

'I barely know him, Mom. It's not a question of loving him or not. This isn't some romance. I'm not the real Arabella.'

Her mother shuts her eyes and clears her throat again.

'My throat hurts,' she says. 'Did they do a tracheotomy?'

'No, but you were yelling, and you probably just hurt your throat. In fact, I should probably tell the nurses you're awake.'

Her mother sighs at that, and her eyes flicker. Arabella knows she must be exhausted, but she also knows that the nurses will come in now and do their tests and take care of her. The crisis has passed, and Arabella feels she has done the right thing. She senses that her mother feels that way, too. She is still clutching Arabella's hand.

'I should probably go now, Mom, and let them do their thing.'

Her mother nods. She can barely keep her eyes open. When she speaks, it's a mere whisper.

'What?' Arabella leans forward, next to her. She smells sweet, like the caramel candies she eats all the time.

Her mother whispers something again, but Arabella has to lean down even further to hear. She has to fight back the fear that her mother is going to hit her again.

'I can't hear you, Mom.'

Her mother speaks, and this time she hears what she says: 'Kiss me.'

Seventh Class: Pacing

'IF I COULD GIVE you one piece of advice about pacing, it would be this: never start a story with someone waking up. You might just as well stamp your manuscript in red ink with the word *Beginner* and wear a sign on your head saying REJECT ME.

'Instead, you want to start your story in the middle of the action. We call this *in medias res*, and we use the Latin to emphasize just how important it is. We will assume that when your character wakes up, she would rather stay in bed, that her room is chilly, that she brushes her teeth and combs her hair, and has breakfast. But we don't really need to know all that unless she eats five eggs and six sausages for breakfast, or some other thing that makes her stand apart. We want to see the character in action, and that brings up my next point.

'Do not leave your character alone in a room. You may

think your character's thoughts are interesting. You may think your thoughts are interesting. But trust me, they are only half as interesting as you think they are – maybe even a third. Of course, you can ignore both these bits of advice if you are Proust or Ian McEwan.

'Yes, Chuck?'

'If I've written a story in which the character wakes up and thinks, should I throw it out now?'

His voice is relaxed. There is no anguish there, and no pain, either. If he was upset by her anger last Wednesday, he is not showing it now. No sleepless nights for Chuck.

'You don't need to throw it out. You could probably find some nice writing teacher to browbeat, and she'll fix it for you.'

She purposely looks away from him toward D'mon, who is busy writing notes, his brow furrowed in concentration. Behind him is the bunny, and Arabella almost does a double take at the sight of it. Surely that is not the same bunny! Wasn't the other one angrier looking? This one has gained ten pounds and is curled up at the side of the cage.

'Seriously, what should you do if you have a story that begins that way?' Bonita asks. Her red leather jacket seems to weep under the fluorescent lights.

'You have to figure out a way to entice the reader into your story, and the best way to do that is with a scene that is intriguing. Instead of showing your character waking up, show the character going into a liquor store at nine o'clock on a Saturday morning and asking to buy a bottle of Chivas. Or, if you remember Pussy from our class on plotting, you might show her starting off at her desk at the MGM Grand, welcoming some interesting character into the hotel. Think of yourself as a carnival barker; you've got to do something to get the reader into the story.'

'What if your character wakes up, but instead of being alone, he has a prostitute with him?' Byron calls out.

She notices that Chuck is wearing the same outfit he wore on the first day of class: white shirt, white sweater, blue jacket, and jeans; she remembers how callow she thought he looked, and she was right.

'And for the record, Chuck, I don't believe you've written a story in which the main character is waking up. I don't believe you've written anything at all.'

'Oooh,' Byron says. 'Someone has pissed off teacher.'

'That's right,' she says to Byron, 'and you could well be next, so be quiet.'

The bunny is pregnant, she realizes. Why has she been thinking all along that it is a male bunny, and, more important, how did it get pregnant? It has been alone for the last seven weeks. Certain religious themes present themselves, but Arabella cannot believe that God would choose to involve a bunny in a miraculous birth. She doesn't know much about miracles and doesn't believe in them, although she wants to, but it seems to her that given a choice between impregnating a bunny or curing her mother, God would choose to cure her mother.

Again tears well up, threatening to spill out. She is having a nervous breakdown in front of eleven people, twelve if you count both of Conrad's personalities. Chuck is laughing about something, completely oblivious to her suffering, and everyone seems relaxed and happy. Even Mimi. Not that Arabella wants her class to suffer. She doesn't know what she wants except that she is tired of being sad and can't quite figure out how to cross over to this normal world, this happy world.

She notices Chuck's eyes on her, but she turns away from him. She just cannot deal with him, not today.

'The other thing you have to watch out for is flashbacks,' Arabella says. 'If there is one thing that leads beginning writers astray, it's getting bogged down in too many flashbacks. The fact is, your reader does not need to know as much about your characters' histories as you think he needs to know. The reader is quite content if you just entertain him with a good story.'

D'mon's hand is up.

'Just a craft question?' Byron asks, but there is no animosity in his voice.

D'mon nods. 'How many flashbacks should you have?'

'At least three,' Arabella says because it's as good a number as any. Three is one of those worthy numbers that always rings true; three good flashbacks will work.

She has decided that she won't wait around after class to talk to Chuck. She doesn't want to talk to him, to hash things over. She is going to walk right out the door, go to visit her mother, and take her to the mall. Strangely enough, they are going to be able to go to the mall today. Her mother has recovered from the illness that trapped her last week, and although her health is still in a downward trend, as Marvel put it, there is no reason she can't try to enjoy herself. Fortunately, her mother no longer wants to buy a dress. Last week's brush with death was intense enough to scare her out of that plan; now she just wants to go to the Chinese restaurant and have a nice meal.

'Another thing you should know about flashbacks is that it's good if they are triggered by something specific,' Arabella explains. 'Maybe a photograph or a book.'

She hears the distinct sound of a vial of pills shaking. She looks over at Pam who stares back at her, implacable, and then swallows. Now there's another person who's suffering, Arabella thinks. There's a person who would probably understand what she's going through because it is obvious that this class is putting Pam through torture. It is always the housewives who have the hardest time with these classes because their hopes are so high. Someone like Pam doesn't have a lot of options. It's late in the day for her to take up international law or neuro-surgery. Those eager eyes pulse with ambition, but Arabella is not sure what she can do to help her. She is not doing such a great job helping herself.

'Of course, if you want to try something that is different from a flashback, you can use description to get across someone's history,' Arabella says. She is looking at Pam as she speaks, finding courage in looking into those popping brown eyes. 'For example, every room tells a story. Look at your own living room and try to see it as a stranger might. What does it tell about you and your history? Do your books tend to be of a particular genre? Do you have a Ming vase? Do you have certificates on the wall?'

'How did you know?' Chuck calls out, always making jokes. Irritated, she decides on the next thing she's going to say, determined to see shock or anger in his eyes – or even pity.

'I can give you a good example because I happened to be sitting in my mother's bedroom for a couple of hours last week because—' Arabella rubs her nose, which still hurts. She is tempted to blurt out the whole ugly story. She feels a sudden click of understanding with those people who bare their souls on talk shows. She wants to be understood. She wants the class to know that she is not who she seems to be. She is both better and worse. She wants their complete attention.

'—because my mother is dying,' she goes on. She is not proud of herself, and yet she can't stop. This sort of self-revelation is addictive. 'Actually, a nursing home is a good place to do this type of observation because people keep only the things that are important to them. When you are allowed only one drawer and one small piece of board on which to tack your things, you are not going to bring along those issues of *National Geographic* that you have been saving for the last thirty-five years. So every item in my mother's room resonates with meaning.'

The class has quieted down. She can feel their attention warming her, and it occurs to her that she is doing exactly what her mother has always done: making a big deal out of her suffering. Well, why not? She is suffering.

'There is a small table in my mother's room, and on this table there are several objects. There is a little papier-mâché angel that my mother bought at some arts and crafts fair. She used to have a collection of them, but this one was her favorite. She used to keep it next to my father's bed.

'He was sick for most of my life,' she throws in. 'Everyone I've ever loved has suffered.'

Arabella clears her throat. She feels as if she is doing an emotional striptease. At this point she feels as if she would say anything, would tell about losing her virginity, would tell about the book she stole from the library in the seventh grade, would say or do anything to get their sympathy.

'There's a family Bible on that table, although it's no heirloom. My family did not come over on the *Mayflower*; they just seemed to drift over here over the course of the twentieth century. There's also a book on that table by Georgette Heyer; it's called *Arabella*. And there is a bunch of framed photos, most of them of me or my parents and a few of their friends, all of them dead. The largest one is of my parents sitting at their anniversary dinner. It's not a great picture of my father, but then he never took a great picture – and not just because he was in a wheelchair and had a tendency to list. His nose was too big, his lips were too red, his face was too pale, and his hair was black against it. He just didn't look right. In person he was quite appealing, but that was because there was something warm about him that came across. But in photos he was not so good.

'The last thing on the table is a dried rose. My father held that rose in his coffin, and somehow my mother snatched it away, though quite honestly I'm not sure how she did it. It's a fragile thing and has not held up well, except that you can still smell the aroma of it very slightly. I think so, anyway. Of course, my mother was convinced that it would never go bad; for some reason she thought my father's soul was in that rose, and as it began to crumble, as everyone knew that it would, she grew more and more bitter. I used to think she kept that rose there because it reminded her of my father, but when I was sitting there the other night, I realized that for her that rose was a sign of disillusionment. It was the sign that she gave up.'

The class is completely still now. The room smells very slightly of popcorn; it must have been some child's birthday.

'Were you with your mother when she died?' Pam asks.

'What?'

'Were you with her when she died?' Pam asks again. Suddenly all the drama is over, and Arabella feels ridiculous. She is taking her mother to the mall today, not going to her funeral; she has lathered on all this drama for nothing.

'No,' she says. 'She did not die – not yet.'

She can feel herself blushing. 'But she's going to die.'

Things are going from bad to worse, although no one seems annoyed with her. If anything, they are looking at her with the acceptance that she has been craving. She is surprised to realize that she is more honest with this class than with any other group. Normally, she is concerned with putting on a good front, but with this class she has been bitchy and tawdry and confused, and for some reason they are still following her, even Chuck. She feels strange. She finds herself thinking of a quote from John Wesley that her minister is quite fond of: 'I felt my heart strangely warmed.'

It is time to do the in-class exercise, and yet when she looks down at her notebook, the exercise she planned seems boring. She feels she owes this group something better than that, something more exciting. She looks at the walls, at the pictures of the children's families on vacation. There are handsome families skiing and handsome families in front of large hotels, getting onto airplanes, and lying on Caribbean beaches.

'Here's the exercise,' Arabella says. 'Imagine that your name is Danika, and you live on an island where there is a volcano that explodes every ten years on October 4, which just happens to be your birthday.'

Arabella surveys the room. Everyone's expression is kind, interested. 'Dorothy, you will be Danika at ten. Mimi, you will be Danika at twenty; D'mon at thirty, Pam at forty.' Pam groans at that and says, 'I'm always the middle-aged woman.'

'Hold on. It gets worse. Alice, you can be Danika at fifty, Byron at sixty – and don't give me that look. We've already established that sixty-year-old women can have exciting sex lives; that is particularly so when a volcano is about to explode. Conrad, you are Danika at seventy; Ginger, eighty; Justin, ninety; Bonita, a hundred; and Chuck, you can be the oldest. You can be Danika at one hundred and ten.'

'Thank you, my dear.'

'You are most welcome. Now, this is what you do,' Arabella says, looking into eleven pairs of eyes, all of them quizzical and faintly excited. 'Write a few paragraphs about Danika at the age that I gave you, and then we will put it all together.'

They tear into their assignment. Is there a better sound than the scratching of pens on paper; a better sight than heads bent over and shoulders hunched? Is there a better feeling than to be a teacher with your class excited by something you've said? They write for ten, fifteen minutes. Arabella keeps watching them, waiting for the energy to flag before she tells them that their time is up, but the energy doesn't seem to wane. They keep writing and writing, and finally it is almost time for the class to end, so she says, 'That's enough. Let's read them now.'

They start with Dorothy, who is Danika at ten. She tells a touching story about a girl who is excited by the drama of the eruption. Then it's on to Danika at twenty, old enough to know fear; Danika at thirty, worried for her children; Danika at forty, blasé about the whole thing. She will survive, but she loses one of her children. And so it goes, the story gathering steam, the pieces of Danika's life coming together into this beautiful quilt, not always connecting exactly right. Somehow Danika has three husbands and four divorces, but by the time they get to the end of her story, and Chuck is preparing to read his section, they have all been swept up in this woman's life.

They all seem sad when Chuck reads the final portion in which Danika decides to stop fighting her fate. 'She hurls herself into the yawning mouth of the volcano,' he reads.

'That's so neat,' Ginger says.

'It's a great exercise, isn't it?' Arabella says. 'It's a good thing to do if you ever get stuck. Just think of some recurring event and plant someone in the middle of it. It could be anything from an erupting volcano to a weekly class.'

There is some general rustling now as the class prepares to leave. Ginger and Justin have their heads together. Byron is gathering up his things, and Alice is carefully straightening up her papers. Pam is chewing on something and trying to swallow. Suddenly another idea occurs to Arabella. She has been wanting to do something to help Pam.

'Before you go,' Arabella says, holding up her index finger.

They look at her, alarmed. It is hard to build trust with a bunch of New Yorkers; they always think you're going to ask them for money. 'I just wanted to tell you that I've enjoyed reading the take-home assignments from this week, and if Pam doesn't mind, I thought I'd ask her to read hers aloud. Not to make anyone else feel bad, but I think you'll enjoy Pam's.

'Or I could read it if you'd rather,' Arabella says to Pam, though Pam is already on her feet. For a terrible minute she thinks Pam is going to run out the door again, but she is walking toward Arabella to get her paper. She has a big smile on her face, and her voice is steady as she starts to read:

'Kiss me.'

'I can't. Not while everyone is looking.'

'But you said you loved me.'

'I do.'

'Then it's silly to be afraid.'

'We're at church. It's not a place for kissing.'

'Church is a place for love. Where better to show it?'

'Not this type of love.'

'I want us to get married. I want everyone to know how much we love each other. You want that, too, I know it. You don't want the lies any more than I do. Anyway, what does it matter if people don't understand? We understand, don't we? Kiss me, Doris.'

'All right, Lois. I will.'

The class erupts in applause the moment she's done, and Arabella is struck by how generous they are. It is as though the writing is so exciting and empowering for them that they don't feel jealous that she hasn't called on anyone else to read.

'Wow,' Ginger says.

They all stop by on the way out of class, each one with some little tidbit or question. Pam stops by to say thank-you for choosing her work. Only Chuck goes out without saying anything to her. He is not a man who is looking for aggravation, she thinks. It is better to find out now – better than her first fiancé who waited until a month before the wedding to tell her that she was going to have to make a choice between him and her mother.

Why did she have to make a choice? Why couldn't she have both? Better yet, why couldn't she have just lied and told him that she would choose him? He would hardly have asked for an annulment afterward if she continued visiting her mother. She had this insane idea that a relationship should be built on honesty, but that wasn't taking into account the realities of being a single woman in New York City.

Now, instead of Chuck, it is Alice who seems to want to walk with her. She walks as slowly as she talks, each step labored. 'I'm sorry about your mother,' she says.

'Thank you.'

'You sound like a devoted daughter.'

'Obsessive, more likely.'

'I have something that you may want to give her. She can put it on her table.'

She can't be a Jehovah's Witness, Arabella thinks. They're a smiling lot, and there's nothing cheerful about Alice. Of course, Alice cannot find what she is looking for, so they stand for ten minutes on the corner of Ninety-second Street and Columbus Avenue as Alice searches through her handbag. She is a tall woman with cropped black hair that looks as if she cuts it herself. Her skin looks soft, though she is in her sixties and wears no makeup. She is not beautiful, but she has an aura.

'Here it is,' she calls out and withdraws from her bag what seems to be a pebble.

'It's a healing stone,' she says. 'It may comfort your mother. She should put it on whatever spot causes her pain.'

'Are you a doctor?' Arabella asks, puzzled.

'No,' she says, shaking her head. Her earrings twinkle in the sunlight. 'I'm a witch.'

'Are you a good witch or a bad witch?' Arabella asks.

'A good witch, dear,' Alice says, and then she is off, walking slowly down Columbus Avenue, leaving Arabella with her pebble. Arabella does not believe in witches or fortune-tellers or miracles or anything outside the bounds of regular science. She has this idea that there is a set of rules, and you are supposed to play by them. However, she can hardly throw the pebble on the street. It is possible it will help. At the place where her mother is, it certainly can't hurt. Anyway, it will be a story her mother will enjoy, so she tucks it into her pocketbook and heads in the direction of her car, which, fortunately, is just around the block.

The weather has gotten cold again, and she remembers how warm she felt last week when she kissed Chuck and he wrapped her up in his coat. Son of a bitch. What type of man kisses you four times in public and then deserts you? What sort of woman kisses a man four times and then harangues him in front of her class?

There is no point in fretting about it now. Arabella has to get up to Port Chester and get her mother to the mall. She hopes this is not a disaster. Her mother assured her that she is up for this, but it is hard for Arabella to believe that a week ago she was in a coma and today she's ready for the mall. She hopes her mother doesn't pass out in the mall the way she did a couple of months ago, right in the women's department at Nordstrom's. The saleswoman was so sweet and ran to Customer Service to get help, but it was embarrassing. Arabella would rather not go through that again.

She reaches West Ninety-third street and begins looking around for her car, which is generally easy to spot because it is usually the ugliest one parked on the road. Sure enough, there it is between a Bentley and a Mercedes. There is a man in the Mercedes. She hadn't realized she had parked right in front of a doorman building, and she cringes as she walks by the elegant doorway and the doorman dressed in blue and red. Then, as Arabella gets closer, she realizes that the man is not in the Mercedes but in her car. Then she sees it's Chuck.

'What are you doing in my car?'

'I considered standing outside, but the door was open.'

The doorman is talking into a radio, and several people are walking up and down the street. This is not the place for an argument, so Arabella goes around to the driver's side door and tugs it open. She gets into the driver's seat, which sags hopelessly when she sits on it. 'What are you doing?' she asks him.

'I'm apologizing, and I can't guarantee it's going to happen more than once or twice in our relationship, so I would enjoy it while you have it.'

He is not a man who shows his desperation, not like

Arabella, anyway, who stands in front of a class and pleads for pity. Yet she senses that he really has made an effort. For one thing, he is inside the car, and for another thing, he is in the passenger seat. And then there is the vulnerable look in his eyes. This could go either way.

'How did you find my car?' she whispers.

He laughs at that. 'It's not that hard to find in this neighborhood, Arabella.'

Chuck puts his hand over hers. 'Let me come with you,' he says.

He looks so neat and protected in his outfit, which has four different layers to it. So much preparation went into creating the effect that is Chuck.

'It's not exactly like *Tuesdays with Morrie*.'

Chuck breathes in deeply. 'Would you like me to come with you, Arabella?'

She stares into those gray eyes. He will leave her, he will break her heart, he's probably stubborn, and he won't like her friends. But she likes him. She thinks of Danika and her volcano, and she thinks that life goes by too quickly.

'I'm falling apart,' she says. 'I feel as if there's a giant hole opening up in front of me. I'm close to falling into it, and I'm scared.'

She looks at his face, praying that she will see in it what she needs to see, and she sees a tear at the corner of his eye. She starts to cry, and he wraps his arms around her and holds her close. 'Let me catch you,' he whispers.

Writing Exercise

ARABELLA HICKS – THE FICTION CLASS

Imagine a moment of crisis: someone shooting a bullet into you, someone about to be hung, someone going under anesthesia, someone falling in love at first sight across a crowded room. Write a few paragraphs describing the crisis, trying to expand time as you write so that the moment becomes as tense as possible.

Chapter Eight

IN HONOR OF Chuck's presence, Arabella does not pull into her regular parking spot alongside the Dodge Caravan; instead, she eases into a prime spot next to a gold Jaguar. The occasion seems to call for something special – plus, she doesn't want Chuck to pity her. She has been begging for pity all day, yet now, when she might legitimately troll for it, she feels it is time to put on a brave front. It takes a few minutes to get the door open, but Chuck jiggles at it and the latch eventually pops and he is out. She thinks, as she looks at him, how handsome he is. All those men she's gone out with because they reminded her of Atticus Finch, and now it turns out she's with Atticus's father.

'You ready for this?' he asks.

'There are so many things that could go wrong; I don't know what to worry about first.'

'It will be all right,' he says, which she does not find reassuring. In fact, she considers that particular set of words the worst in the English language, the words that invariably follow some horrible diagnosis and mean absolutely nothing.

'I know,' she says as she clasps his arm.

The nursing home seems to have been spruced up for Chuck's arrival. The dead sprigs of holly have been weeded out of the urns by the front door, and pansies have been planted in their place, although it is much too early in the season. They will be dead in a week, but they look great now.

Dotty is almost out of her mind with excitement at the sight of Chuck, and Arabella realizes she has never been to the home with anyone else. There is no other family to speak of, and it is not the sort of place you bring your friends. For the four years her mother has been here, Arabella has always been alone. Now Dotty is fluttering excitedly around Chuck. He takes three cookies and a cup of coffee, and he compliments Dotty on her white headband. 'Very chic,' he says.

'I got it in Greenwich,' she whispers, winking broadly at Arabella as she speaks, as though they are sharing a secret.

Even the dogs are well behaved. They do not bark or whimper but lie down next to Chuck and sigh.

The loudspeaker is playing a song from *Oklahoma*, and some of the residents are actually whistling cheerfully as they walk through the hallway. Marvel smiles and waves at her, and Arabella realizes, to her relief, that although Chuck is old to her, in this crowd he looks quite young. A surge of hopefulness goes through her, and then they are at her mother's room, right in front of the little paper name tag with her mother's name. Arabella has stood here many times, catching her breath.

'I just want to thank you in advance,' she says. 'This means a lot to me.'

She notes the crooked smile and the pulse that beats under his jaw. She longs to touch it, to kiss it, but now is not the time for that.

'Come on,' he says. 'Let's do this.'

Her mother is sitting by the window, and for a terrible moment Arabella thinks this is going to be a repeat of the last visit. She automatically brings her hand to her nose, but then her mother turns to her and smiles. She looks lovely today, and Arabella feels a sudden gust of pride that her mother has not let herself go, that after all her years of carping about manicures, facials, pedicures, and so on, she actually looks pretty good. Her hair flows softly around her face, her eyebrows are just right, and her lipstick is a soft pink that brings color to her pale face.

'This is Chuck,' Arabella says. 'I told you about him when you were in that coma.'

'I remember,' her mother says.

'How do you do, Vera?' Chuck goes toward her, bends down, and kisses her on the cheek. Arabella feels proud of him, too. He is a gentleman.

'He's going to come with us to the mall.'

'How nice,' her mother says. She looks so genuinely pleased that Arabella can't help but grin. She has never seen her mother so pleasant. 'I do love to go to the mall, but it's hard for Arabella to cart me around. You, however, look quite strong.'

Arabella thinks of a movie that her parents used to love to watch called *The Enchanted Cottage*. It was about a homely girl who falls in love with a handsome RAF pilot, who was, coincidentally, Robert Young who in later years her mother watched in countless episodes of *Marcus Welby, M.D.* In the movie his face has been scarred by the war, but because they love each other so much, they seem beautiful to each other. She remembers how her parents watched that movie, holding hands, both of them crying at the end when they realized that love is the enchantment.

Her mother is not going to carp about his age, she realizes with relief. Her mother doesn't care.

Meanwhile, Chuck's attention is on the table next to her mother, and he gives a cry of delight when he sees Georgette Heyer's book. '*Arabella*,' he says. 'This is the book that started it all.'

'It's my favorite book,' her mother says. 'It has everything.'

'May I tell you how much I love your daughter's name?'

She looks at Arabella then and fixes her with that rooster look of hers. 'You see?'

Getting Arabella's mother into the car is so much easier with Chuck's help, as is getting the wheelchair into the trunk. They are going to The Westchester, a mall about twenty minutes away from the nursing home. The Westchester is a lavish mall with bathrooms everywhere, which is a great selling point for Arabella. Her mother is like a dog when she gets to a new place: She needs to mark her territory immediately by peeing.

'Yes, he was a mass murderer,' her mother is saying to Chuck as Arabella pulls into the parking lot at the mall. She has launched into a story about Joel Rifkin, who happened to live not far from Arabella when she was growing up. 'And yet,' her mother says, 'it might surprise you to know that he was quite helpful to me.'

'Really?' Chuck says. He is sitting in the backseat, and all Arabella can see is his smooth white hair, floating like a cloud in the back of her mirror.

'We were at the video store one day, me and Arabella's father, Benjamin, and, of course, Arabella. She wanted to rent *Black Beauty*. She did so love anything to do with animals, but it was on a high shelf and we couldn't reach it. Well, my husband was a tall man, taller than you, I think, but you understand that if you are in a wheelchair, you are quite short. It keeps you at the height of a child. People treat you that way. The salesgirl was busy, but Joel Rifkin was there.'

'Joel Rifkin was there,' Arabella whispers to herself. She wishes she could see Chuck's face. Fortunately, he can't run away because the doors to the car don't open.

'He came right over and got that tape for us. He was quite tall,' her mother concludes. Arabella finds the perfect parking spot and pulls into it – two empty spaces, big enough for a van.

'I know he was not a good man,' her mother is saying, nodding her head sagely as she speaks. 'But he was kind to us, and that counts for something, doesn't it?'

'Yes, it does,' Chuck says, his voice sounding much more southern. Arabella looks at her mother and is swamped with the familiar feeling of pity and love. Wouldn't anyone else be relieved that a man who murdered more than thirty women did not think to murder her daughter? Or herself? Only her mother focuses on the fact that he helped her husband.

Chuck manages to get out the door, the trunk springs open, and he sets the wheelchair down. As they help her mother into the chair, she looks up at Chuck, concerned. 'Not that anything excuses murder, you understand.'

They stroll up and down the aisles of the mall. They stop in front of Brooks Brothers, and her mother points out a suit in the window that she thinks would look very nice on Chuck. Then they go by Ann Taylor, Eileen Fisher, and The Gap. Her mother looks in the windows and admires the clothes, but she doesn't want to go in anywhere. 'I don't need anything,' she says. The Godiva store is handing out free chocolates, and Chuck snags three. Her mother pops hers into her mouth and her eyes roll with pleasure.

'This would cost you twenty dollars,' she says, 'just this one piece.'

Toward the center of the first floor of the mall is a bench, and after spending half an hour wandering around, they sit down on it. There is a sculpture near the bench that Arabella has always liked – a bronze sculpture of a woman holding her daughter's hand. There's nothing sentimental about it, but Arabella has always been touched by it. It looks so normal.

Suddenly Chuck taps her knee, and Arabella comes to attention. 'What?'

'Look over there,' he whispers. 'Do you see what I see?'

She looks in the direction he is indicating. There is a shoe store, and an elderly man is trying on shoes. A salesman is putting a shoe on his foot. The salesman, smiling and ingratiating, is wearing a thin brown suit. For all those reasons it takes Arabella a minute to realize it is Conrad.

'Good God, he's a shoe salesman.' It is hard to imagine Conrad in a service industry. It is also hard to imagine Conrad smiling, although he is smiling away, not twenty feet from her, on bended knee. Arabella looks down at her own shoes, comfortable black pumps that she has owned for years.

'Here I thought his big secret was that he was a transsexual.'

'This is New York,' Chuck says. 'No one cares about your sexual orientation. They care about how much money you make.'

Conrad is gesturing and laughing, and when he smiles, he looks so different. The sad fact is that he looks ordinary. The only reason she paid much attention to him was that she thought he was a transsexual.

'Should we say hello?' Chuck asks.

'No,' Arabella says, getting to her feet and tugging Chuck away from the bench. She pushes her mother away from the shoe store before Conrad can turn his head. 'The poor thing doesn't want anyone to know. It would ruin everything for him.'

They are now racing down the corridors of The Westchester, and Arabella is feeling something rise in her that is part joy, part sexual, and then almost all sexual. Her mother says, 'Did you say something?' and Arabella realizes the poor woman has no idea what's happening.

'Sorry, Mom. I thought I saw one of my students. Are you all right?'

Her mother nods, but Arabella can see she is getting tired; she's listing to the right of the wheelchair, and her feet are flopping between the guards of the footrest.

'Do you want to go back to the home now, Mom?'

'What about dinner?' she croaks.

Arabella is surprised to realize it is almost 7:00. So they head over to P. F. Chang's, which is on the lower level of the mall and is her mother's favorite restaurant. Normally there is a long wait, and they give you a little walkie-talkie and beep you when it's your turn, but Chuck goes up to the maître d' and talks to him for a minute. They get a great table, right in the center. The restaurant is soothing with its murals and wide windows, and Arabella thinks of the story her mother told her about the restaurant in Mexico City and how important that was to her. She tries to imagine what her mother was like back then, a pretty newlywed in a flounced skirt and high heels.

Arabella gets her mother a cup of tea, puts some ice in it, and then holds it up to her lips so she can drink it. Her mother perks up under its warmth. Arabella can almost see the tea making its way through her mother's body, like one of those science experiments in which dye is absorbed by a plant. Her eyes begin to sparkle again, and she looks around appreciatively. 'Have you eaten here before?' she asks Chuck.

'No, I haven't had the pleasure.' His accent has become a twang. Arabella imagines him drawing on all his southern resources.

'You must get the shrimp with orange sauce. It's their specialty.'

He puts down his menu and smiles at her. 'Thank you for the recommendation.'

A young woman sits across from them with a little baby in a carrying seat, accompanied by what must be the grandmother. They are both fussing over the baby and making him smile. So much love.

Chuck leans back slightly and rests his arm around the back of Arabella's chair. He is not touching her, but she is so conscious of his hand that it seems to burn her.

'So, is my daughter a good teacher?'

'Yes,' Chuck says. 'You would be very proud of her.'

'And she is teaching you to write?'

'She's trying to. She says I should try harder,' Chuck says.

'She's right. It's never good to take the easy way out.'

Arabella can feel his hand against the back of her shoulder, his fingers touching her lightly. Her mother is not bothering him; she is not being insulting. He is not going to go storming out of here the way one of her boyfriends did, though that was because her mother told him his grandparents were Nazis: 'They were in Germany during the war. What do you think they were doing?'

'I may not be Jewish,' her mother had said to her then in the brief quiet that followed her boyfriend's escape, 'but I feel that I'm an honorary Jew because I've suffered so much.'

A different waiter appears now with a bowl of crispy noodles, a cruet with mustard, and another one with oil. He has a napkin over his arm, and Arabella feels certain that he has graduated from some fancy cooking school. He is so sincere, it is sort of sad, but her mother loves it. She gazes at him as enthralled as if he were making complicated French cuisine. When he is done, they order their meals, all of them getting shrimp with orange sauce. Then her mother turns her full attention to Chuck.

'What made you want to write?' she asks, and Arabella leans toward him, curious. She remembers that night weeks earlier when they walked to Grand Central, and he said he was looking for meaning. She had assumed he was joking, that he was really just looking to meet women.

'I've always wanted to write,' he says to her mother. 'I've traveled a lot with my business, and I've often jotted down notes on people I've met. In fact, I have shoeboxes full of those

223

notes. When I retired recently, I thought I should see if there was anything I could do with those boxes.'

'You seem young to be retired,' her mother says. 'Were you forced out?' She glares at him fiercely, ready to go to war. Her mother was always protesting something during Arabella's childhood. She went on countless marches protesting against architectural barriers, or agitating in favor of civil rights or job equality.

'No, I was in a position where I had what I needed, so I could stop working.'

'Oh-ho!' her mother cries out. 'So you're rich.'

'I'm comfortable,' Chuck says.

Her mother laughs at that. 'Remember that joke your father used to tell, Arabella? A man finds another man lying in the street. He's been hit by a car, and he's on the street. The man says, "Are you comfortable?" and the man lying there says, "Eh, I make a living."'

She caws with laughter. Chuck smiles, too, not exactly laughing but not angry, either. His hand still rests on the back of her chair, and Arabella can't help herself: She leans against him, softly. Her mother catches her eye; she sees everything. Really, the old lady should have been a writer. As though reading her mind, her mother says, 'Arabella has been teaching me how to write. You might say she's been giving me my own private fiction class, a free one.'

'That's very nice,' Chuck says. His hand presses lightly yet insistently on Arabella's back. She imagines the touch of his hand on her bare skin and feels something warm bubbling inside her.

'I've written a story,' her mother says. She tips her chin up, something she does when she's nervous, something Arabella has seen her do with countless doctors – the head back, the chin up, those marble blue eyes haughty and direct.

'Have you really written a story?' Arabella asks.

'You're not the only writer in this family. Who knows? Maybe I'll get published before you do.'

'It's entirely possible,' Arabella says, leaning back into Chuck's arms. It would be just her luck: Her mother will have a best seller, and it will be all about how lousy a daughter Arabella is. She tucks herself more closely into him and presses her leg against his. If she could burrow her way into him, she would do that. There is such comfort in his presence.

Her mother picks up one of the noodles and holds it in her shaking fingers. 'Actually, it's harder to do than I thought it would be. I'll give it to you when I'm done, and you can fix it up for me.'

The statement stuns Arabella, the acknowledgment of weakness. It is the central tenet of her mother's life that you do not acknowledge weakness because if you do, people will pity you, and there is nothing worse than pity. Pity takes away your humanity, reduces you to a pulsating need, reduces you to someone who people feel they can come up to, as they used to come up to her father, and say terrible, thoughtless things. 'How do you do it?' someone once said to him as they waited on line at a Home Depot. Arabella thought they were asking how to hang a shower rod. 'You must have to get on top.'

Her mother, eyes blazing, said 'You are a pig.'

But now her eyes are soft, questioning, even hopeful. 'I'd be happy to,' Arabella says, touched, sad, and frightened – all the sensations she normally feels with her mother. What if she really did write a story about how terrible a daughter she is? 'I'd like to help you.'

The food arrives then, and it is beautifully prepared, with neat little dabs of crispy shrimp dancing in a bed of soft brown rice. Arabella's mother croons with delight. It is the same meal she always gets when they go there, and she is always delighted by it.

'I think I can do this,' she says and picks up the fork. Very slowly she inserts it into the shrimp and then raises it awkwardly, as though there is a ten-pound weight on her arm. Arabella forces herself to eat slowly so that she will not be done before her mother has finished the first bite of shrimp.

The rest of the meal goes by fast. Her mother does not eat much more of her food. Her hands start to shake too much for her to hold the fork, and she is clearly too tired to eat much anyway. Chuck gets the bill, and then they get her in the car. She is weak and tired; Arabella has to force herself not to speed. The nursing home is safety, and she wants to get her mother there. When she pulls into the circular driveway, Dotty calls over some of the orderlies, and they help her mother out of the car. Dotty tells her not to worry – the nurses will get her to bed. She'll be fine.

For just a moment they all stand in the lobby, her mother listing against her wheelchair. Chuck kisses her good-bye and tells her it was nice to meet her. She has a happy glow on her face, and she turns to Arabella and smiles. 'Thank you,' she says. 'That was fun.'

'Thank you,' Arabella says when they get back to her car. 'I don't know when I've seen her so happy.'

'I liked her.'

'She's one of a kind.'

'Would you like me to drive?'

'Yes,' she says, feeling exhausted all of a sudden. 'That would be very nice.' But suddenly reality hits her. 'How are you going to get home? We'll have to go back to the city, or maybe we can find a train station. I didn't think about it, but I guess I've kidnapped you.'

She looks at him, at those gray eyes, at those hands she's been so conscious of all night. 'We could always go to your place,' she says.

'We could, couldn't we?'

FORTUNE
(CONTINUED)
BY VERA HICKS

Over the next few years Joan got to know the fortune-teller. It turned out that his name was Guillermo, and he was the oldest of eight. He had inherited from his mother the gift of sight; from his father he inherited his homosexuality. He said to Joan that he hoped it would not be a problem. She said no, a little flustered; she wasn't sure what he meant. She was looking for information, not sex. Even in her dreams she could not betray Danny. There had been opportunities; men had even propositioned her. The druggist had been quite insistent. But every time she thought about it, she started to cry.

She did not mind that the fortune-teller did not seem to like her. She suspected she was too middle-class for him — she in her small house on Long Island, her two children, her sick husband,

and her mundane concerns. What had she to say to a fortune-teller? But she found solace in his coldness. She was surrounded by pernicious good humor. 'He's looking very well.' 'You're making strides.' Against the sucking swamp of other people's good intentions, the fortune- teller's irritability was like a strong board that she could bang her head against.

They would oftentimes say nothing at all to each other. He would simply sit in her bedroom, in Danny's bedroom, and watch TV with her. It comforted her to see him there, in that cold room. She should have decorated it. God knows Annie had offered to do it enough times. But she felt that to do so would be to surrender, and she was not ready to do that yet. And so the walls were a bright white, often shaded blue by the light of the TV. The windows were bare. What was there to hide? The only decoration was a calendar marked with appointments with physical therapists, doctors, and ministers. There were pictures on the wall of Annie and Michael, then Michael in college, and then Michael and his wife, Rochelle, and the house in Alaska they had built.

Guillermo liked to sit on a metal chair between the telephone and her bed, while she perched at the end of the bed, alert, on guard. At first she asked him many questions. Should she pray more? Should she become a Catholic? But every time it was the same: 'How should I know? I am not God.'

'Well, what do other people do? Lucia knew there would be a miracle in Fatima. What did she do?'

'She seemed to me a headstrong girl. I did not know her.'

'Who do you know who had a miracle?'

'I am not People magazine. It does not matter what anybody else did.'

'But there are others, aren't there? I'm not the only one.'

'You worry about ridiculous things.'

'Well, you tell me what to worry about then.'

When Guillermo appeared to Joan in a dream last night, his manner was different. For one thing, he smiled, and she realized she had never really seen his teeth. They were very nice, which surprised her. She would have expected them to be yellow from cigarette smoke. 'You're different,' she had said.

'No, I'm not.'

She had to smile at that. 'Well, maybe not so different.'

He leaned forward. 'Tomorrow is the day.'

'Will I see you again?'

'See me?' He hit the side of the chair with his hand. The chair seemed to ring like a gong. 'What do you care if you see me if you have a miracle?'

'I've known you for twenty-five years . . .'

He looked at the TV, which seemed to stare back at him with the impassiveness of a blind man. 'You get caught up in these side issues.'

She sat next to him, closer to him than she had ever been before. He smelled of licorice. She was surprised to notice that he had aged. He was still a handsome man, but you could see he had crossed a line of no return. She touched his cheek. It occurred to her that in some ways she was more married to this man than her *husband. They had aged together. They had grown together. 'You do like me a little, don't you?'*

He looked at the ceiling. 'You are an annoying woman.'

'I know, but I will see you afterward, won't I?'

He had said nothing then, but she read acquiescence into his silence.

Eighth Class: Theme

'WHAT ARE YOU going to talk about in class today?'

'I'm not going to tell you,' Arabella says, kissing softly the only flaw she has been able to find on Chuck's body: a slight bump on his chest from an old broken collarbone. It turns out he played football in college, although he was cut the first season. He didn't exercise enough, didn't go to the weight room, and went to too many parties. 'If I tell you, you'll cut class,' she adds. 'I know your kind.'

The pale morning sunlight shines through the slats on his bedroom windows; pale yellow light envelops the room. Everything is clean and fresh, just what she expected, except for the bookcases that fill his bedroom. They are filled with the collected writings of Winston Churchill. Arabella is not persuaded that he has read them all because they are bound in white leather and make a cracking sound when she opens them – and they are shelved according to height. But, still, there are books here in his bedroom. It is like finding out they are related. She loves it.

He has been reading to her from Churchill's wartime memoirs. Who ever thought that the story of Britain finding its soul could be so romantic? But there it is. She has spent the morning listening to Churchill hector his populace. She has spent the morning with her head burrowed against Chuck's chest, listening as the warm drip of his voice falls over her. She has spent most of the last week like this and would cheerfully spend the rest of the day like this, but class is in two hours. She has to talk about theme, which she enjoys talking about. Arabella's opinion is that writing should mean something.

'You know my kind?' Chuck whispers. 'That sounds frightening.'

'I'm not a slut if that's what you're implying.'

He laughs at that, a big-hearted sound. 'No one could accuse you of being easy, Arabella.'

His sheets are paisley. Sleeping with him is like being in a forest, with patterns everywhere – unfamiliar, foreign, and yet lovely. Chuck runs his hand gently over the curves of her body, and under his fingertips she can see her body through his eyes. She feels how soft her skin is to him, how thin her waist, how long her legs, how healthy she is, and how desirable. Generally she has tried to ignore her body and doesn't even do those breast self-exams because she is scared of what she might find.

It seems so strange to her that it can actually be a source of joy.

A grandfather clock chimes. It is an antique, a genuine antique handed down from generations of his family, not bought at some store somewhere.

'Are you happy?' he asks.

'Why, is something wrong?'

'No,' he whispers, kissing her neck and tugging the sheets back over them. 'Nothing's wrong.'

'Here's a question for you,' Arabella says to her class a few hours later. 'A man and a woman fall in love, get married, and are happy, but then he gets sick and their whole world changes. He can no longer work; he can no longer stand or sit or hold her or make love to her. What if I write a story about this couple and say they go through hard times but never think of getting divorced. Why?'

Arabella looks at Chuck as she speaks. He is wearing jeans today, though they are the most formal jeans she has ever seen. They are pressed, dark blue, and cost $395, which she knows because the price tag was still on when he took them out of the closet. Such a closet it was, with built-in shelves and a separate wing for shoes. She loved looking at them all. She had spent so much time observing his shoes over the course of the class that seeing them together was like visiting with old friends. There were those strange leather saddle shoes and the red and gray walking shoes. Such abundance. It makes her feel strange, drunk even.

'Maybe we can go shopping,' he had said. 'You should own something that isn't black.'

'Don't you think that's patronizing?' she had snapped. 'What are you going to do next? Set me up in my own apartment?'

'Maybe we'll just go to a museum,' he had said, unflustered, untroubled.

A nervous thought frets her: What happens when trouble comes? What will he do?

She pulls herself back to her hypothetical couple who refuse to get divorced.

'Why?' she asks. 'Because there's nothing stronger than true love,' she says.

'It's almost impossible to say that and not raise your eyebrow because we live in an ironic age. We live in an age where to say something like that you have to automatically sneer to show you don't really mean it. But if you believe that, and I do, you are going to write a story that is very different from one by someone who does not believe in true love. A writer who believes that true love is possible is going to write a story that is very different from one who believes all men are slime.

'That's what it means to have a theme in your writing. Your theme is how you interpret the world.'

Arabella pauses to catch her breath. She knows she is speaking fast. Poor Dorothy is writing so fast, her hand is going to come off. 'Your theme is how you explain what people do. If you believe that all people are basically good, your theme will be very different than if you believe all people are basically bad.

'Do you see what I mean?' she asks.

They all nod, and she can't help grinning at them. She loves this class, and not just Chuck. She loves Dorothy and her Q-Tip hair, and Bonita and Justin with his book, which today is *Of Mice and Men*, an interesting choice. She hopes he is not planning to shoot Ginger. She even loves Conrad and his fancy sneakers. How has she never noticed before how unusual it is for a man who dresses in sweatpants to be always wearing expensive sneakers? She grins at Conrad, and his shadowed eyes widen. She can't believe that the class is almost over, that they will disappear from her life, and that she will never see them again, except for Chuck.

Except for Chuck.

'One thing you should do, if you don't think you have a theme in your writing, is look at what your characters do and see if you can explain it. For example, think of *The Wizard of Oz*. Think of Dorothy and how she spends most of that movie trying to find her way to Oz so that she can get home. Why? Because there is no place like home. That's the theme.

'Or what about *To Kill a Mockingbird*? That's a novel in which the theme is written right into the title. It's wrong to hurt the innocent, and keep in mind here just how simple that theme is and how true. No one would argue that it's right to hurt the innocent. Your theme does not mean you have to come up with some revelation about human behavior.

'But what you do have to do is find a way to connect with your readers, and the theme will pull them in. The theme makes *To Kill a Mockingbird* more than a story about a young girl growing up in the South. The theme gives it extra resonance.'

D'mon's hand is up. 'Just a craft question,' he says. 'Do you have to have a theme?'

'No, but you probably do whether you know it or not. I mean, you have a reason for writing, don't you? And that reason probably ties in with your theme.'

She looks around the room at what seems to be twenty flowerpots sprouting shamrocks. Saint Patrick's Day is on Friday. Then it will be spring, and then the class will be over. Arabella thinks how much she is going to miss these people. Her boss called her yesterday to tell her that he had been getting good reports from this class, and he asked if she would be interested in teaching the Advanced Fiction class next semester, assuming someone signs up for it.

'I'm sure at least one person will,' she had said, looking over at Chuck who at that moment was asleep next to her.

'Well, try to encourage them.'

Now she looks at the class and thinks about the themes they write about. 'Byron, you're easy,' she says. 'Your theme would be the way that sex affects people's lives.'

'Absolutely,' he says, beaming.

'D'mon, you often write about African-American men and

the way they deal with their family responsibilities, so that seems to be the theme you want to explore. Dorothy, you often write science fiction, and yet the themes you are exploring have to do with isolation versus adaptation. A great thing about science fiction is that it can give you alternative ways to approach your themes.'

She goes around the class, and it is surprising how easily each student's theme comes to her because, in fact, people do tend to write about the same subjects over and over again. Then she gets to Justin, and she draws a blank. She knows he has done the exercises, but she doesn't have any strong recollection of what he has written. There was something about a man who worked in a delicatessen, and she thinks there was something about a woman learning to use a computer. But she can't find any unifying thread unless it is that they both involve human beings. She decides to fall back on that old teacher standby. 'Well, what would you say, Justin? How would you describe your theme?'

He is clutching *Of Mice and Men* tightly, and she recalls that John Steinbeck said that if he couldn't put his theme into a sentence, he couldn't write.

'I want to write about ordinary people,' Justin says.

This sort of statement always strikes Arabella as being condescending because it is usually uttered by people who are convinced they are anything but ordinary.

'Ordinary as opposed to what?' she asks. She is not trying to bait him, but she would like him to think.

'People who work in delis and barbershops and toll-booths.'

'Why?'

'I feel they're overlooked,' he says.

He is a nice boy and very sincere, and she suspects he comes from a good home and that his mother loves him and went to all his soccer games. 'I notice that you refer to your characters as *they*, and yet I think you should be thinking of them as *we*.'

He frowns. She considers backing away. She doesn't get any pleasure out of criticizing her students, and she doesn't want him to feel bad. He is not looking very well anyway. There are dark circles under his eyes, and his skin, normally pale, has become translucent. She can see the veins beating under his skin. The thing is that she knows he aspires to be a great writer. Why else would he be carrying books around all the time?

'Do you know any ordinary people?' she presses.

He grimaces and looks at Ginger, who smiles at him reassuringly. Then he shakes his head and looks away. 'I've met some.'

'You might want to think about it a little more,' Arabella says, keeping her voice gentle and trying to smile away the anger that she sees flare up in his eyes.

The next part of the class is when they do their in-class writing, and Arabella has brought along one of her favorite exercises. She pulls out a brown bag, holds it up in front of the class, and then withdraws from it a handful of fortune cookies. They all *ooh* at that. It is funny how people are always hungry. Someone always asks if it's okay to eat the cookie, which, of course, it is. But the point of the exercise is to look at the fortunes and write a story in which the fortune is the theme.

Justin gets 'Left to themselves, things tend to go from bad to worse.' Alice gets 'Words are better than stones.' Dorothy gets 'It is they whose ideas we should ponder.'

'What does that mean?' she wails. 'What am I going to do with that?' Her hair is standing up in electric currents. 'It's not English. It doesn't mean anything.'

'Take mine,' Chuck says. He leans over and hands her his, which is 'A smooth, long journey. Great expectations!'

'Thank you,' Dorothy gushes. Arabella grins. She takes such pleasure in everything he does. Every time she looks at him, it is like getting a present, and her face must be expressing this thought because he looks up at her and smiles.

The exercise takes most of the rest of the class, and then they read them out loud. Arabella is struck, as always, by how well people are able to write in such brief periods of time. In fact, she has noticed that people often do better writing these short exercises than the longer pieces. She supposes it is easier to stay focused. So much of bad writing has to do with losing track of what you are writing about.

When they are all done writing and going over the exercise, Bonita raises her hand and asks if there are any exercises from last week that Arabella would like to read. 'Like you did last week,' she says. 'Do any stand out?' Bonita's hair is slicked back, and her eyes are made up, but there's the same hopefulness as in everyone else's eyes. We all want approval, Arabella thinks.

'Why don't we read yours?' Arabella says, and Bonita assents so quickly that Arabella knows she has been sitting through the whole class waiting for just this moment.

The exercise had been about drawing out time in a moment of crisis. She hands the paper to Bonita, remembering as she does so the day that seems like years ago when Bonita seized control of the class. That was the day the whole dynamic seemed to change, the day the class started to gel.

Now Bonita stands before everyone in her bright red leather jacket and makes a big show of clearing her throat and taking out her reading glasses. 'My first public reading,' she says to the class, grinning at them all, although for all her confidence, Arabella can see her hands shaking. She nods at Bonita encouragingly.

'The Surgeon,' Bonita reads.

Damn him. Damn him for his arrogance. Damn him for his strong good looks and his hands that look as if they could play me like a cello and thighs that look as if they should be covered with riding boots, and his strong, firm buttocks. I long to grab hold of him and pull him on top of me, but I cannot move because I am confined to this stretcher. I am paralyzed. He walks toward me. His gait is as cumbersome as a giant, and that is because he is master of this domain.

241

He is the head of surgery at Mount Sinai. He is all powerful. He leans toward me, and his devilish eyes meet my own. I want to cry out, and even as the words break against my teeth, desperate to free themselves, I can feel sweet consciousness departing and my plastic surgery begins.

'Wow,' Byron says. 'That's hot.'

'Bravo,' Dorothy calls out. 'Such passion.'

'Thank you, my fans,' Bonita calls out, blowing kisses to everyone and bowing. 'Thank you, my readers.'

The reading over, it is time to hand out the assignment for next week, which is to think of a book you like and try to figure out what its theme is and how the author gets that across. No one seems to be in a hurry to go, however. They are still pumped up from Bonita's reading and the fortune cookies, and Arabella notices that Conrad is talking to Mimi. She sees a little dimple forming on his cheek and sees him fighting to stay serious. Eventually, they all wave good-bye, and she can hear them laughing as they head for the elevator. She knows that Chuck is waiting for her outside. No one will care that they are going out. She is not a schoolteacher, after all, and he is not a fragile teenager, but it still seems better to keep it quiet.

She has just about packed up all her things when Justin reappears. She hasn't seen him without Ginger on his arm for a long time, and by the way he is panting, she has the feeling that he left her somewhere and came running back to talk.

'Is everything all right?' she asks.

During class he is so well hidden with his hats, his tucked-down chin, and his mannerisms that she forgets how young he is, but up close she can see that he must be no more than twenty-three or twenty-four. Now he rubs his hands through his hair. He smells of smoke, and his eyes are unfocused, though he seems alert enough to talk to.

'I'm thinking maybe I should quit this writing,' he says. 'What do you think?'

'Justin, the last time you talked to me, you were planning to quit your job and devote yourself to writing.'

'Yeah, I know.'

Arabella starts walking toward the elevator, Justin trailing alongside her like a dog.

'You were right,' he says, his voice a mixture of despair and whine. 'I don't have a theme.'

The doors to the elevator open, and they get in. Arabella does not believe in talking in elevators. She has spent so much time eavesdropping on other people's conversations that it embarrasses her to think of someone listening to hers, and so she doesn't speak her mind until they are in the lobby.

'Justin, I have been working on my novel for seven years. Before that I spent five years writing short stories. But if I were to stop writing today, there is not one person in the world who would care, not even my mother. The sad fact is that the world does not need one more writer. In fact, if you drop out, you just leave room for one more potential writer to claw his way forward. So if you are going to run this race, you have to do it because you want to, because you have something you have to say or because it means more to you than anything in the world.

'But I can't give that to you. That's a decision you have to come to yourself. You hear me?'

He stands there, looking as though she has slapped him, as perhaps she has. She leaves him behind and walks toward her car. As she expected, Chuck is waiting for her. She runs toward him, throws her arms around him, kisses him, and then leans her head against his shoulder.

'Do you want me to play you like a cello?'

She starts to laugh and then stops. She has promised herself never to laugh at anything one of her students writes, and she is not about to start now, particularly with Bonita who has, in a way, saved her life.

'Now, now,' she says, 'don't be cruel.'

'Yes, teacher.' Her body pulses with the pleasure of sensation: his lips on hers, the warmth of his touch, the happiness she feels in his arms.

'You're sure you don't want me to go with you today?'

'No. She'll be bursting to talk about you, but she wouldn't be able to do that with you there. I don't want her to have an aneurysm on top of everything else.'

'But you'll meet me later? We'll go to dinner.'

'Of course,' she says, and then she gets into her car.

Writing Assignment

ARABELLA HICKS – THE FICTION CLASS

Choose a novel or short story that you like and try to discover its theme. How does the author get the theme across? Title? Plot? Names of characters?

Chapter Nine

THE SUN IS still out. The days are getting longer, and, amazingly enough, the pansies in the urn in front of the nursing home are still alive. Or else last week's pansies have died, and someone has planted new ones. Arabella's mother used to do something similar. She would buy pots of hostas and other green plants and then arrange them near her father's bed so that he would see some greenery. But the room was not nourishing to plants and her mother never watered them, so after a week of air-conditioning and no light and no water, the plants would dry out and die, and then her mother would buy new ones. That should have been a sign, Arabella thinks now, that her mother needed help. But who was there to help her? All she had by way of support was one hypersensitive little girl and a husband who was so exhausted from keeping his own battered resources together that he had nothing left to give his wife.

But at least for today, at least for right now, Arabella feels as if she has what her mother needs. She knows what to do to make her happy. She will talk to her about Chuck. She'll tell her about the fortune cookies and Justin, and they can discuss whether or not he will really stop writing. (Arabella thinks he will; she is of the view that anytime you ask someone if you should quit, that's a sign you should quit.) She has brought chicken nuggets from McDonald's as a change of pace, and she has also brought a fortune cookie because she thought her mother might like to do that theme exercise with her.

She is not even that tense, she thinks, as she walks through the front door, waves to Dotty, and stoops to pat the little white dogs that stare mournfully at her bag of chicken. Arabella is almost certain this visit will go well, which is a bad sign, of course. She has read enough fiction and seen enough movies to know that it is when you let down your guard that things go wrong. One of her favorite movies is *The Great Escape*, and one of her favorite scenes is when Richard Attenborough says how happy he is. The minute the words have left his mouth, he hears the click of a machine gun being cocked.

In a way it is inevitable that when Arabella gets to her mother's room, she finds her not sitting by the window, as she had expected, but lying in bed.

'What's wrong? Why are you lying down?'

'The fever's back,' her mother answers. 'They said it would be better for me to take it easy.'

Arabella sits down on the chair next to the bed and sets the bag of chicken nuggets on the nightstand. Now is obviously not the time to eat.

'Has the doctor looked at you?'

'Yes. He said I'm old and sick.'

'Nothing serious then,' Arabella says with a smile, although something sharp twists inside her. Her mother looks so pale. She has lost more weight, which makes her cheekbones look higher and her patrician nose sharper. The necklace that her father gave her rests against her chest, but the diamonds look blurred.

'I want you to take this necklace,' her mother says, catching her glance. There has never been much that she's been able to get past her mother.

'I don't want it.'

'It's your only inheritance. You might as well take it unless you're going to count on that rich boyfriend of yours to take care of everything.'

'I'll take it when the time comes, but the time's not here yet, is it?'

The words come out harsher than Arabella intended. She wants to comfort her mother, not yell at her.

'Are you comfortable?'

Her mother laughs. 'I make a living.'

Just last week they were out to lunch. This is the part of life

Arabella can't deal with. One minute you're happy, and the next minute you're on the verge of death.

Her mother covers the necklace with her hand. She hasn't had a manicure, and her nails are ragged, which is shocking. Arabella has never seen her mother look anything less than perfect. She notices then that her father's picture has been moved; it now sits on the nightstand directly across from her mother's pillow. Someone has tidied up the table, too. Most of the books and papers are gone; there is just a composition book and *Arabella*. The calendar on the bathroom door is also gone; no more photocopy of the month of March with all the little shamrocks on it.

'I had them take all that stuff away. It will save you some trouble after I'm gone.'

'You're killing me, Mom. Why don't you just crawl into the coffin and be done with it?'

Lily's wheezing breath seems to stop for a moment. Through the window Arabella can see a family out on the lawn; the children are playing on the grass. It is chilly out, but warm enough for a child who is running around and happy.

'I'm sorry,' Arabella says. 'I don't want to argue. I don't know how to do this. I don't know what to do for you.'

'There's nothing you can do.' A tear seeps onto her mother's cheek, a sad, little tear that breaks Arabella's heart. She grabs her mother's warm hand.

'I don't want you to feel as if you have to be brave with me, Mom. You've been so brave all your life, and if you want to be scared about this, I think that's okay. We can do it together.'

That sets her mother to laughing. Her thin body fairly bobs with merriment. 'It's a good thing you didn't go into medicine,' she says. 'You would have been a disaster.' She's quiet then, her sharp blue eyes scanning Arabella, taking her in, memorizing her.

'You're happy with him, aren't you?'

Arabella thinks of Chuck waiting for her even now, preparing her dinner, getting ready to love her, and she feels her heart break. This was what her mother should have had. It's so unfair.

'It's hard to think about right now.'

'No.' Her mother shakes her head. 'Be happy while you can. I didn't have a lot of happiness with your father, but the happy times we did have, I enjoyed. They kept me going for a long time after that.'

Her eyes flicker closed, and she smiles. Arabella wonders what memory she is drawing on to comfort her. She imagines her parents on the parkway and her father saying, 'Speaking of Utopia . . .'

Sade comes in then, all bustle and cheerfulness, which is a bad sign. They are never so cheerful in a nursing home as when they think something is really wrong. She goes up to Arabella's mother and pops a thermometer in her mouth.

'Just a moment, Miss Vera, and then you can finish up your conversation.'

'How's she doing?' Arabella asks.

'She's good, isn't she?' Sade touches her hand to her mother's forehead and clucks when she feels the dry skin there. She reaches into her pocket, pulls out some cream, and smoothes it on. When she's done with the thermometer, she takes some pills, mashes them into a bit of applesauce, and spoons them into her mother's mouth.

'These are going to make you sleepy, Miss Vera, but you need your rest.'

Her mother nods, which surprises Arabella. She was expecting some crack about how she doesn't need her rest, how she's on the verge of getting all the rest she'll ever need. She wonders how many pills her mother has had. She suspects there are worse ways of dealing with death than with serial medication.

The room seems quiet, intimate, after Sade leaves. 'Are you hungry?' Arabella asks. 'I brought you some chicken nuggets.' But her mother just smiles and shakes her head.

'I did bring you something from class that I thought you'd like. You're probably too tired to do it right now.' She pulls out the fortune cookie and explains about the exercise. She tells her mother about the class, and although her mother's eyes are closed, she can see she is paying attention. Her hand seems to twitch every time she says something interesting. When she goes to snap the cookie open, her mother's eyes open as well.

'What does it say?'

'It says, "Every journey begins with a hop." Well, that's encouraging, I guess.'

Arabella is not sure what to do. Her mother looks as though she's sleeping, but she doesn't think she really is, and she doesn't want to go. What she wants to do is figure out what to say to her mother, something that isn't foolish or pitiful, something that doesn't make her mother laugh.

'Do you believe in fortune-tellers?' her mother asks, startling her back to attention.

'I thought you were asleep.'

'Not yet,' she says, her thin lips turning into a grimace.

'Do you believe in them?' she asks again.

'I've never met one, but I guess I would believe in one. I think I believe in everything, actually, or maybe I don't believe in anything.'

Her mother sighs.

'I'm sorry, Mom. I don't know. Do you believe in fortune-tellers?'

She shakes her head, irritated now, and Arabella's heart sinks. How is it possible to annoy someone who is dying? Chuck would know what to say. She should have had him come with her. He would have held her mother's hand, whispered to her, comforted her. All she can ever do is irritate her, and the worst is that the more she wants to please her, the more she says the wrong thing. Even Arabella knows it's the wrong thing.

'I've written a story,' her mother says, 'I want you to read it.'

'Yes, of course, you mentioned that.'

'It's in that book,' she says, pointing to the composition

252

book on the table, and Arabella suddenly realizes that her mother actually has written a story. The next thing she realizes is that she does not want to read it. It is certain to be about her; it is certain to be hurtful. She picks up the composition book and puts it in the satchel.

'I'll read it tonight.'

'I can't think of an ending,' her mother says. 'I want you to think of one.'

Arabella can't help but laugh. 'You're asking the wrong person. I've been trying to end my novel for the last seven years.'

'Well, unfortunately you're the only writer I know.'

Arabella clutches the satchel against her chest. She can feel her jaw click into place, can feel raw panic sweep through her and, worst of all, irritation. She cannot do this. Why is her mother asking her to do something that is beyond her?

'Make sure you come up with something good,' her mother snaps. 'Don't dawdle with this.'

But Arabella does dawdle with it. She leaves the nursing home and drives straight to Chuck's apartment building where the parking valet, after a week's acquaintance, knows who she is, takes her car keys, and says not to worry about anything. There is a bench in the elevator, which seems to Arabella the height of elegance, and when the doors open, Chuck is there waiting for her, a glass of wine in his hand. The wine hits her immediately; she sinks into his leather couch, curls herself up against him, and watches the fireplace that he has clicked on. The flames glow with an unnatural color. He had taken her satchel and set it down in a corner. She was tempted to protest that she needed to look at it, but it was so much more pleasant to lean against him, to kiss those soft lips of his, and to enclose herself in his warm arms.

'What can I do for you?' he whispers. 'How can I love you?'

She spends the next few days in a haze. She finds a beautiful old edition of *Middlemarch* in his library. When she is not reading, she is eating one of the meals he has cooked for her or going out to a restaurant or making love to him or just lying in his bed and listening to the sounds of the city.

Even without being able to see what is going on in the streets below, there is an amazing amount of noise and excitement that rises up, but Arabella's favorite sound is the *clip-clop* of the horses as they make their way around the park. It makes her feel as though she is Georgette Heyer's Arabella, as though there ought to be a maid scurrying around, getting ready to dress her in muslin. (There is actually a maid who scurries around, but she mainly sweeps and vacuums and takes Chuck's clothes to the dry cleaner.)

On Monday morning, after close to an entire week of this pampering, Arabella is sitting in Chuck's kitchen, watching him cook. It's a warm, cozy room with tiles from Tuscany and every gadget imaginable: a coffee grinder, a machine for squeezing oranges, and a Sub-Zero refrigerator that is housed in built-in drawers. A few times Arabella has opened a drawer expecting to find silverware or linens, only to find a pile of eggs instead.

Now he is cooking a Spanish omelet for her. He has a special pan just for omelets, and his tomatoes are ripe, which is the most amazing thing of all. It has been years since Arabella has eaten a tomato that wasn't the consistency of a tennis ball.

'I have to go home today,' she says.

He looks up from the stove. His hair is messed up, but the rest of him is neat. Wearing faded jeans and a gray T-shirt, he looks as if he should be on a sailboat. 'Why?'

'I have to get ready for class on Wednesday, and I have to read my mother's story. I have to have something to say to her about it. I have to figure out a way of ending it, and that's not my strong point.'

'You still have a day,' he says, his voice soft and melodious. 'There's a new restaurant I thought we could try tonight. It's French,' he says, flipping the omelet up into the air. She loves to watch his hands. He could have been a musician in a past life; there's something so coordinated about those long fingers. 'Then I'll take you back tomorrow, first thing.'

'I think you're trying to seduce me.' His kisses taste of coffee.

'Yes, I am.'

Now he flips the omelet onto a plate, which is also from Tuscany and is a gorgeous shade of green. Then he brings it over to her. He just eats toast and coffee, but he likes feeding her. 'No one has ever liked my cooking quite so much.'

She does love his cooking. Everything is delicious, and she wolfs it down, finishing the omelet in ten bites. She has never been one to eat slowly.

'So will you stay? Another day?'

Then it is Tuesday morning, and she is eating his breakfast again, this time German pancakes that are the consistency of butter. He suggests he drive her home after lunch. There is no need to rush. He wraps her in his arms, and she drinks the warmth of him and the strong, steady beat of his heart.

'I really have to get back, Chuck. I have people's exercises to read, and I haven't written anything in almost a week. And I have to read my mother's story. I'm going to be seeing her tomorrow, and, believe me, she won't be happy if I haven't read it.'

But now it's late Tuesday afternoon. They are sitting in his library. There's a fire burning in the fireplace, and the late-afternoon sun is streaming in through the window. She can see her satchel still in the hallway and can almost feel the composition book pulsating, calling for her to read it.

Chuck catches her glance and puts his arms around her. His couch makes her think of bars and restaurants. It's a convivial couch; it's a convivial room. 'I thought you were worried that the story was going to upset you.'

'I'm sure it's going to upset me, but I still have to read it.'

He laughs a little at that. This laughter is the only awkward sound she has ever heard him make. She feels herself sinking into the softness of the couch. 'I don't see why,' he says. 'Not if it's painful. This whole situation with your mother is painful enough, I would think. You need to protect yourself.'

She shakes her head. 'That would be cowardly.'

He grins at that. Again there is that boyish look: Tom Sawyer trying to talk his way out of trouble. 'I think cowardice is underrated as a virtue,' he says. 'It's always worked for me.'

'I think I owe her more than that.' She is gripping the leather of the couch. It is so rich and old, and she imagines that it belonged to generations of Chuck's family, one handsome, wealthy man passing it on to the next generation of handsome, wealthy men.

'From the way you spoke, I didn't think you owed her anything.'

The room is airless. Arabella sees her legs curled up on the couch, sees her hand resting in Chuck's, sees the glass of merlot she was drinking resting on the table, and yet none of it appears to belong to her. Everything looks unfamiliar.

'You've done so much for her, Arabella. Surely there are limits.'

She looks into his eyes, gentle gray eyes with nothing in them but humor, and tender concern. They remind Arabella of one of the doctors her mother went to later in life. She had wanted a prescription for something to calm her nerves. She was explaining to the doctor that she couldn't seem to relax, that she was always jumping up, always expecting something to happen. The doctor looked at her with the same humor in his eyes. 'I'll give you a prescription for some pills,' he said, 'but you might do better to find a hobby.'

A fire siren goes off in the distance – or maybe it's an ambulance fighting its way up Central Park West. Startled, she looks toward the window and then back at Chuck.

Behind him is a painting of a Golden Retriever. It is a beautiful pedigree, standing at attention, his nose pointing authoritatively in the direction of a duck. She wonders if he ever owned a dog or if he just bought the painting from someone. She wonders what about him is real. She looks into his eyes and then down toward his chest, to that one small scar of a bruise that healed.

'You need to understand how hard their life was. I don't even know if you can imagine it if you didn't see it firsthand. He couldn't move. I don't mean he limped or he staggered or even that he sat in a wheelchair. I mean that man could not move. He could not do anything. Everything that makes a man a man – a job, sex, money, power – he lost. But this is the amazing thing: neither he nor my mother was bitter. You see what she's like now, but she became that way after he died. She changed after he died. But when he was alive, she loved him so.

'I don't know if I'll ever find that type of love myself,' Arabella says, rising to her feet and grabbing up the satchel, 'but I do know I won't find it looking for the easy way out.'

*

Arabella drives back to Yonkers, walks to her apartment, and settles herself at her desk. Then she takes out her mother's composition book. It is late, but she is not tired, so she starts to read 'Fortune.' She flies past the opening pages, past the woman who is wondering if the waiter is going to bring her a miracle, on through that terrible dinner and the daughter, Annie, who seems so self-concerned and so annoying, and then there is the scene with the fortune-teller, which Arabella finds heartbreaking, and now they are back at the restaurant.

'I'm thinking of changing my name,' Annie is saying.

'Oh.' Joan looks over at Danny, hoping to catch his eye and smile, but he is not looking at her. He is looking instead at a crystal candleholder mounted against the red wall, and then his eyes become unfocused. His eyes flicker twice, and then he sighs and closes them. Joan closes her eyes. Her head feels stuffed. She feels like a piñata that is waiting to be smacked. She has been unable to sleep these last few weeks. She has not really wanted to; she has been afraid of missing something.

'D'Ann,' Annie says. 'Of course, you could still call me Annie, but we would change the name of the newspaper to "Details from D'Ann."'

Danny's eyes are still closed. Joan knows what is happening. It is happening more and more often. His kidneys are wearing down, emitting noxious chemicals into his body, causing him to pass out every so often. He will sleep for a few hours. There is no way to wake him. She rushed him to the emergency room the first few times it happened, but they told her the best thing to do was wait it out. She tastes something bitter, as though she has swallowed sour milk.

'Do you like it, Mom? I combined Ann with Diane, which has always been my favorite name.'

'I didn't know that.'

'Don't you remember that doll I had? I called her Diane? No, you probably don't remember. I think that was the year Dad was in the hospital with bedsores.'

'That year,' Joan says. That year. Danny was in the hospital for a whole year. He went in a man and came out like a prisoner of war, with stubble on his cheeks and surrender in his eyes. A year suspended in a contraption so that he would not lie on his back, swaying in the air like a manic circus act. And Joan in hysterics, crying, screaming, fighting. Reading to him, singing to him, anything to stop him from fading. 'I was crazy that year.'

'Just that year,' Annie says, and Joan notices something strange about her voice, the way a violin sounds if you leave it out in the rain. There is a pile of paper shreds in front of Annie. It is a high pile, an hour's worth of shredding. Joan looks from the pile to the girl, the woman. Surely there are smudges under her eyes that were not there before. And what happened to that necklace she always wore, a string of blue and white beads that looked like chewed-up Chiclets?

Joan forces her mind toward the doll; she pushes herself to remember a ratty little cloth doll whose hands moved because

Danny, who still had the use of his hands at the time, put in a motor.

'I remember,' Joan says. 'It had yellow hair.'

Annie smiles. 'Yes, that's it.'

'What happened to it?'

'It got lost.'

Joan is quiet. It got lost. And how much else? What else has she done? She catches sight of the plate in front of Danny and the fish, now cold, that remains before him. She cuts off a piece of the fish and puts it in her mouth. It tastes terrible, but she feels a need to chew, to do anything that will make her feel like a normal member of the human race.

'Would it be too late to buy you a new one?' She raises her eyes to Annie and finds her looking at Danny's plate, too, looking at the fish as if fascinated. 'It's better than it looks,' Joan says. 'Would you like some?'

Annie takes a napkin from another table, puts it on her lap, and begins smoothing it. 'You know, I am absolutely famished.' She cuts a piece of fish for herself and rams it into her mouth. Even as she chews she is cutting herself another piece.

'I'm sorry, Annie. D'Ann,' Joan mumbles. Some bread crumbs fall on her lap, and she sweeps them off. 'I am so sorry.'

Annie's cheeks are puffed out with fish. 'That's okay,' she says, her words spewing Joan with some spit. She starts to laugh then, and so does Joan.

A ridiculous feeling of joy settles over Joan's body, the type of joy you can actually feel, warm and wet. All things are possible to those who believe. Everything is possible. Nothing is impossible. She looks at her daughter shoveling food into her mouth and laughing. She feels like a fist unclenching.

There the writing ends except for some words jotted on the bottom.

Dear Arabella,
I've tried and tried, but I can't figure out how this story should end. Can you help me?
Love,
Mom

Ninth Class: Revision

'NONWRITERS ARE ALWAYS curious about how fiction differs from real life. They want to know who you based your characters on or if something in the story really happened. And often stories do have their beginnings in something that happened to the writer.

'But there's one way in which fiction is completely different from real life, and that is revision. Writers get a chance to do it over. It sounds like a bumper sticker, doesn't it? You can picture something like that on the back of a pink Volkswagen: "Divers do it deeper." "Musicians duet better." "Writers do it over." Writers do it over and over again. Writers do it until they get it right.

'That's a gift, isn't it?' Arabella says, picturing in her mind the old lady who is waiting for her, hoping that she will get it right.

'But in order to get it right, you have to figure out what you were trying to do in the first place, and that's the tricky thing,' Arabella says, purposely looking away from Chuck because it hurts too much to look at him. He looks so perfect. If his world fell apart yesterday, if his girlfriend walked out on him, if he is feeling sad, Chuck is not the man to show it. In fact, he is wearing a brown woolen sweater that Arabella has never seen before, and she spent a lot of time admiring his closet. She wonders if it is possible that he went shopping yesterday.

'I just read a story,' she tells them, fighting back the tears that well inside her, 'and it seemed at first to be about a woman who was waiting for her husband to have a miracle. The woman's husband was sick and had been for many years, and the only thing keeping her going was the fact that a fortune-teller had promised her a miracle on her husband's sixtieth birthday. She wasn't sure if she believed in this miracle, but that didn't matter because it was all she had left to believe in. In effect, if she wanted to keep living, she had to believe.'

The class is paying close attention. There is nothing quite like a story. It fulfills a basic human need. What happened? What happened next? These are the words that keep us going. Arabella suspects this is what is keeping her mother alive, the desire to see what happens next.

'This woman is at a restaurant, and her daughter is there. I believe that when this author began to write this story, she imagined that the daughter would be no more than a minor figure. After all, the story was about the woman and her husband.

'But as she began to write, the daughter began to capture more and more of her imagination, and the daughter's story became much more important. The woman and her daughter did not get along. The mother was preoccupied with the husband, and the daughter was sensitive and needy. But I think that as this author began to write, as she tried to make her daughter come alive on the page, she had to try to understand her, and as she did, she began to know her better. The shape of the story shifted because the better she understood her daughter, the more she realized that her daughter did have something to be upset about.'

The class is hushed, and she can feel Chuck's eyes on her, though she will not look at him. The Saint Patrick's Day decorations are gone; as soon as the holiday is over, all mementoes of its existence are swept away – similar to a nursing home and its residents. We don't like to linger. The latest artwork is paintings of pussy willows, which reminds her of Pussy of Las Vegas, and this makes her wonder how many times over the course of this semester she will have occasion to use the word *pussy*.

'But here's the strange thing,' Arabella says. 'The mother came to understand the daughter, but reading the story, because it was honest, I came to understand the mother as well. I realized that I, or the daughter, had not been fair to the mother – not that either of us was cruel, but up until my mother wrote this story, neither of us understood what the other was talking about.'

Arabella still cannot believe the courage it took for her mother to write what she wrote, to bare her soul like that. She never knew that was how her mother thought. She is glad she found out before it was too late, that she pulled herself away from Chuck just in time. She looks at her watch automatically, praying that this will not be one of those terrible jokes that God sometimes plays, that she will not get to the nursing home to find out that her mother died.

She feels her voice catch and remembers the wash of emotion she felt last night after she read the story again and again. It was like watching her mother forgive her. It was like finding out her mother loved her, and she never would have known it if her mother had not written the story. And she might never have done that without this fiction class. She thinks about how much she loves these people and how sad she's going to be when this class is over.

Just one more week to go, and then she'll never see them again. She'll never find out if Mimi gets better and if Byron writes his great American porn novel. Will Ginger and Justin stay together? Will Justin get his act together? Will Dorothy and Pam have nervous breakdowns? Will she ever figure out what Bonita does for a living? Will she ever see Alice again? Is Chuck worth the heartbreak he is certain to give her, and will she ever see him again? She senses that she does not have much time left with her mother, either. Everything seems to be winding toward a close, just as when you near the final pages in a book, and know that everything has to end.

'I would suggest to you that one measure of whether your story works is when you wind up at the end of the first draft in a place you didn't expect to be.'

She is testing her words as she speaks, not certain of what she's going to say next. She has that odd, cloudy feeling she gets when she writes. Something is stuck in the dense wool of her brain, but she knows she can't chip it out. She can only try to unravel it and hope that something will appear. It is a slow process.

'Writing is about surprising yourself,' Arabella continues. 'I don't just mean the reader here; I mean the writer, too. You should be on a journey yourself when you are writing, and, hopefully, you will wind up in a new place.'

She looks toward D'mon as she finishes speaking because she feels confident his hand is going to be up. 'A craft question?' she asks.

His uniform is starched and clean, as always. She wonders if he ever relaxes. 'Just one question,' D'mon says. 'Do you have this story with you? Could we hear it?'

'Yes,' Pam shouts out, her voice a slash in the quiet of the classroom. 'I was thinking that, too.'

Arabella feels embarrassed, as though she has been caught asking for a favor. She's always hated asking for favors. When you spend your childhood with a father in a wheelchair, waiting for people to open doors for you and lift packages for you and help you, it creates in you an intense desire to never ask for help again.

'It's not necessary,' she says. 'I don't want to take up your time by reading the story, which is twenty pages long. Then we wouldn't be able to get to much revision.'

'I'd like to hear it.' The words come from Chuck, although she has to look over at him to be sure. His voice sounds so much deeper, he could be someone else entirely. All heads are bobbing in agreement; at this point it would be ungracious to say no.

'Well, thank you,' Arabella says. 'That would be a help because in fact the story is missing an ending, and the author, my mother, wanted me to help her with that. But, quite honestly, I don't know what to tell her.'

She picks up her satchel and goes through it, pulling out the typed sheets. She typed them last night after she had read the story several times. Somehow she can never analyze something unless it is in twelve-point type. Anything else doesn't seem official to her.

Arabella holds the text in front of her and looks out at the class one more time. She sees Conrad nodding his head, although in his case it is to the beat of music on his iPod. Justin and Ginger are holding hands. Pam is sitting there wild-eyed. And Chuck. She holds the papers in front of her and looks at her own scribbling that runs all over the margins. She spent hours last night trying to think of ideas.

'All right,' she says, 'but if you get bored, let me know.'

She starts reading the first lines: 'Oh, to hug this waiter. To squeeze his slight body, so like a boy's really, except for the muscles that swell his arms . . .'

The class tilts forward with attention. There is that focused hush you get when everything is going right. She reads her mother's words, forcing herself to continue to read loudly as she gets to the exchanges with Annie, feeling her face blush and wondering whether the class will think less of her. Even as she reads, she feels them absorbing her words. She always forgets how powerful honesty is, that people will accept any type of information if they feel you are being honest with them.

Then she gets to the part where Annie says she is going to change her name to D'Ann. She looks over to D'mon, thinking of the day she told her mother about his name and how incredulous she was.

'Isn't it hard to say?' her mother had asked.

'No, you just ignore the apostrophe.'

She wonders if D'mon notices the similarity in name, but his gaze is impassive and focused. He is swept up in the story.

Her favorite part of the story has to do with the fortune-teller and the way the 'Joan character' talks to him because she can hear the patterns of her mother's speech in the conversation. She finds herself acting it out as she reads, giving the fortune-teller a bit of a Mexican accent. The class is with her still, and she feels the warmth of this small room and its softness, even down to the pussy willows against the walls. She wonders how she never noticed before how like a cocoon this room is, how safe she has felt here.

She herself is swept up in the story, wondering what is going to happen, wondering what did happen. That is the mystery at the heart of this story: Her father did die on his sixtieth birthday. Arabella always assumed it was just one of those strange coincidences, one of God's jokes. Arabella was just eighteen at the time, home from college for the day to celebrate and then leaving early that night, eager to get back to her boyfriend. When her mother called the next day to tell her that her father was dead, she was sad, but she was also relieved that she had paid him this final visit. She was certainly not suspicious. There was no mystery to his death, no hint of fortune-tellers. There was nothing beyond the ordinary story of a man who suffered with a disease until his body wore out. The only thing that made it a little odd was that he died at home. Her mother said he had died quietly in his sleep, which was so in keeping with her father's personality that Arabella never questioned it – until now.

Standing here, she wonders what did happen that night with her mother and father, and she keeps on reading to her class:

Annie takes a napkin from another table, puts it on her lap, and begins smoothing it. 'You know, I am absolutely famished.' She cuts a piece of fish for herself and rams it into her mouth. Even as she chews she is cutting herself another piece.

'I'm sorry, Annie. D'Ann,' Joan mumbles. Some bread crumbs fall on her lap, and she sweeps them off. 'I am so sorry.'

The story is almost over. All that is left is for Joan to feel that moment of joy, that moment that anything is possible, and then the story ends and Arabella reads the last few words:

She looks at her daughter shoveling food into her mouth and laughing. She feels like a fist unclenching.

There the writing stops, and there is nothing more to say – except that Alice exhales sharply, as though she has been punched.

'What happens then?' Alice asks.

'I don't know,' Arabella says. 'That's the problem. The author doesn't know, either.'

'Is there a miracle?' Pam screams. She is fingering a cross she has pulled from underneath her blouse, tugging on it as though summoning Christ to give her an answer.

'It's impossible,' Arabella says, staring down at the pages, wishing the black ink would magically appear. 'She has written herself into a box. Normally that's a good thing because it forces you to come up with something creative, but this box is too tight. I can't see a way out of it.'

'Do you believe in miracles?' Alice whispers, Dark Alice so quiet that they all have to listen intently to hear her.

'I would like for this story to end in a miracle,' Arabella says.

'But we live in the twenty-first century, and this is not religious fiction. I just worry that having a miracle at the end will sink the story. It would be like my wearing a hat with a bowl of cherries to class. It might be beautiful but it would seem out of place.'

'I believe in miracles,' Pam yells. 'I want to believe.'

Mimi pulls at the little blue hat that sits on her bald head and grimaces. 'Faith isn't about what you want to have happen.'

Pam looks as if she is going to burst, but Arabella breaks in: 'This is not a class on religion, this is a class on revision, and what we need to do is figure out an ending. There are four ways we can go. We can give Joan what she wants. We can give her a miracle.'

Dorothy has stopped writing notes. Instead, she sits thoughtfully, chin on her hands, looking into space.

'Or,' Arabella says, picturing her mother's bitter face, the sour look that she has worn for the last two decades, 'we can say that she does not get what she wants. Her husband does not get a miracle, she drops out of church, she stops seeing her family, she becomes angry with her friends, she turns in on herself.'

'That's so sad,' Bonita says. She is wiping at her eyes, smearing her mascara. Arabella has to smile. Like most hard-nosed people, Bonita is much more of a mush than she lets on. 'Then she'll have to go her whole life being bitter.'

Arabella shrugs and looks at the pictures on the walls, at the drawings of happy families. 'That's real life, isn't it? Most of us don't get a miracle. Most of us do have to deal with the hand we're given.'

'But this is fiction,' Justin says. 'Can't we do what we want?'

He isn't wearing his hat today, and she is surprised to see that his hairline is receding. He is older than she realized. The book he has with him today is by Edgar Allan Poe. She feels reassured that he has gone back to the classics. Maybe he will get his act together. Maybe he'll be a writer yet.

'We could imagine another possibility, which is that she doesn't get what she wants but realizes that she never really wanted it.'

'So she doesn't get the miracle, but she realizes she didn't really want it?' Mimi asks. She looks puzzled, and the whole class looks confused.

'Yes,' Arabella says. 'I don't see how that plays out, either. And I don't see the fourth choice happening, either, which is when you get what you want but realize you don't want it. If she got a miracle, she would want it, wouldn't she?'

'Unless . . .' Mimi says.

There's a distant sound of traffic from the street four floors down. The class will be over soon, and then she will have to see her mother and help her find an ending, but Arabella has absolutely no idea what she is going to tell her.

'Yes?'

'Unless his death was the miracle,' Mimi concludes.

The class almost hisses at the thought. They are a romantic

bunch, this class, and it's cruel to think of that. Actually, it is something Arabella has thought about, but she doesn't think it's right. 'I don't think she would have changed the way she did if she thought of his death as a relief.'

They are all silent then. Even the bunny is silent. In fact, the bunny is no longer there. There is an empty cage. Another miracle? Or just the facts of life?

'Is it possible not to have an ending?' Chuck asks, ever the compromiser, always looking for the easy way out.

'No,' she fairly shouts. 'There has to be an ending even if it doesn't seem like one.'

Arabella can feel the class's concern, their puzzlement. She pictures her mother's face. She is depending on her. She has to come up with something.

D'mon's hand is up. 'I hope you don't think I'm being nosy, but how did it end in real life for your mother?'

That's the million-dollar question, isn't it? Arabella thinks. She shakes her head. 'I don't know what really happened.'

'You'll have to ask her,' D'mon says as though it's the easiest thing in the world. Probably he has one of those mothers you can ask questions of, one of those nurturing mothers, and yet Arabella knows he's right. The only thing to do is ask her.

Everyone files out after class is over except for Chuck, who stops by her desk. It has been less than a day since Arabella saw him, yet it feels like a lifetime. She aches to sink into his arms. She longs to surrender to his love or whatever it is that he is offering her, whatever sweet confection it might be. Maybe it is ridiculous to expect something more.

'That was a beautiful story,' he says.

Up close he looks more tired than she had realized. He is still neat and well groomed, but he looks older, or perhaps it is just that he looks his age. He looks like a well-dressed fifty-three-year-old man who was up late after a good time.

'Arabella,' he whispers, and the sound of her name on his lips is a kiss.

But she shakes her head no and clutches the satchel to her. 'I have to go.'

He turns down the corners of his lips, an expression she has never seen him make before, as though he is fighting something within himself, something that is giving him pain. Then he reaches out and takes hold of her hand. She almost cries out at his touch, how she wants him.

'Arabella,' he says, tugging her to him gently. She is so close to him that she is enveloped in his smell. She can feel the heat radiating off him.

He sighs. 'My father told me a story once about something he saw when he was a young man. He grew up in a small town in Texas, and one day a preacher came to hold a revival meeting. My father went because there was nothing else to do and because he was curious. This preacher had quite a big reputation.

'There was a lot of commotion going on. You know how these things are, or' – he looked at her, his gaze gentle – 'maybe you don't. But, anyway, my father and his friends were all having a pretty good time, and then a girl came forward. She was a beautiful girl, but she had a bad limp. My father used to say he remembered feeling pity for her. She went into the river, and the preacher prayed over her for some time, and when she came out, the limp was gone.

'My mother used to say that that pretty girl was probably a plant and that the whole thing was a lie, but my father believed it. He was sure he'd seen a miracle.'

He pauses. 'There are miracles, Arabella,' he says. 'It's not impossible.'

Writing Assignment

ARABELLA HICKS – THE FICTION CLASS

This is an exercise in learning to find creative solutions or how to write yourself out of a corner. There is a man sitting in a tree, and he is wearing a tutu. What happened?

Chapter Ten

WHEN ARABELLA GETS to the nursing home, she finds her mother in the lobby, having an argument with the director of the nursing home, which strikes her as a very bad move. Never argue with the people in charge is Arabella's motto – not when you are so vulnerable, not when you are dying and they can pull the plug. But her mother is fearless. She is aggrieved and has succeeded in backing the owner of the nursing home into a corner – literally.

The woman is standing in the corner of the lobby, hands held before her, pleading. She is not a bad woman, this Adela Fine. She runs a nice nursing home, and she is very sentimental. She bursts into tears at every Mother's Day and Fourth of July gathering, but she is used to being in charge and being deferred to. She is not used to being screamed at by a resident.

'Aha!' her mother cries out when Arabella walks through the doors.

The director is cowering in the corner of the lobby. The little dogs are watching with their ears flapped back, and Dotty is holding her head. It is all Arabella can do not to laugh out loud. Here she has been expecting some tender deathbed moment with her mother, and instead the old lady has picked one of her arguments. Arabella finds the sight of her angry mother reassuring. Maybe things aren't that bad quite yet.

'What's wrong?' she asks.

Her mother throws back her head. She is Queen Elizabeth facing down some snippy courtier. 'This woman has fired Sade.'

'Why?' There was nothing objectionable about her that Arabella can recall. She was a gentle woman who was always pregnant and laughing kindly at her mother's discourses.

'This woman says that Sade was a troublemaker.'

'Hiring decisions are made by the board of the home,' Adela says. 'They do not come under the purview of residents.'

'*Purview*,' her mother says. 'My daughter's a writer. She knows what that word means. And I'll tell you why she fired Sade – because her papers aren't in order.'

'That's true,' Adela says. She is a large woman, built like a ship; her head is her prow, and the rest of her body seems to follow. 'Sade is not legal. We could get in trouble with the government, and she knew from the start that her papers had to be in order. She lied.'

Immigration. That's one of those big issues, along with death and the economy, that makes Arabella feel completely hopeless. She sees lawyers and money and Congress, and she is tempted to push her mother right out of here. She could do it, too. The one virtue to having a parent in a wheelchair is that you can move them from room to room, and they can't stop you. And yet . . .

'You could help her get her papers in order,' her mother says. Arabella looks down at the bright pink skin of her mother's scalp. She is so much tougher than Arabella.

'You have a lawyer,' her mother continues. 'Can't your lawyer help her? It's not that easy to find good staff, and I'm sure if you helped Sade, she would reward you with her loyalty. You could help her, couldn't you?'

Adela says nothing. Dotty answers the phone, and the dogs tiptoe off in search of scraps. Her mother's scalp is turning redder and redder. After all this, she is going to die of a stroke.

'Just look into it,' Arabella snaps, surprising herself. 'Just try to help her. That's all we're asking.'

Adela looks as though she has something more to say, but at the sight of Arabella's gaze, she holds back.

'I'll look into it,' Adela says.

'Thank you,' Arabella whispers, dumbfounded. So sometimes it works when you speak up.

Her mother is clearing her throat. Next she is going to ask Adela to find a car for Sade. She knows how her mind works: You never accept victory; you keep on asking. But Arabella has had enough, and she pushes her mother off in the direction of her room.

'That woman has the morals of a snake.'

'I think we won, Mom. Let's leave it at that.' They go down the corridor to the West Wing, past an old gentleman who is still wandering around hopelessly, looking for his wife. Arabella can hear the dogs' toenails clicking in the distance and the throb of the soap opera from the dining room. She has brought some ice cream today. Her mother has had so little appetite lately that it didn't seem worthwhile to get the hamburger.

'Anyway, I don't want to talk about Adela. I want to talk about your story.'

Beneath her hands she feels her mother's flinch and knows that terrible moment of panic when someone else has read your work, when you wait, terrified, to hear what they think, so she puts her mother at ease. 'I loved it,' she says. Then they are moving past the nurses' desk and see Marvel talking to someone Arabella has never seen before. She is a young woman with a harassed look, and she is holding a telephone.

'New resident,' her mother says. 'She's bringing in her grandmother. She has Alzheimer's, but she used to be a rocket scientist.'

'Oh, God, that's depressing.'

'Tell me about it,' her mother says and cackles wickedly. The girl looks up, and Arabella smiles at her and nods.

'Welcome,' she says. The poor girl looks so sad, Arabella wishes she could comfort her, could tell her it doesn't have to be that bad, that a nursing home can be a good thing, a place for coming to terms with your life. But she's got to get her mother to her room. She has to talk to her about her story.

So they push forward, and now they are past the door with the little paper sign that reads: Mrs Vera Hicks. For the briefest of moments they both look in the mirror that hangs on the wall: mother and daughter, two people who are so obviously related that they mirror each other – their skin, their noses, their eyes. It is like looking into her future and her past; it is like seeing everything she needs to know. Then Arabella pushes her mother forward, toward the table, and pulls the story out of her bag.

'So you liked it.'

She puts her hand on her mother's. 'I loved it, Mom. I thought it was brilliant.'

It is late March, and a few brave crocuses are poking their heads out of the ground, although they are likely to be slaughtered by the next cold wind. It is hard not to admire their bravery, though, their eagerness to be alive.

'I read it to my class,' she throws in, knowing that she will see the spark of light in her mother's eyes.

'All of it?'

'I wasn't going to read it. I was just telling them about it, but they thought it sounded so good, they wanted to hear it, so I read them the whole thing.'

'I hope no one writes down on the evaluation that you wasted a whole class.'

'I think I'm safe.'

Her mother begins to click her teeth in and out, the way she does when she's excited, and peers over at the composition book. Arabella still can't figure out how she was able to write it all down or how long it took her. The woman can't pick up a hamburger, but somehow she managed to write twenty pages of a story. It is this determination that has always been terrifying to her.

'They must have noticed it didn't have an ending,' her mother says, clicking her teeth harder; the dentures are bobbing up and down with her agitation. Arabella treads warily. Just for once she'd like not to say something stupid, but she has to say something to get at the truth. Perhaps it is best to just come out with it.

'They wondered – I wondered – what happened with Dad on the night he died?'

Her mother's head snaps back, but she doesn't laugh. Her face twists, and the old bitterness reappears.

'There was no miracle, I can tell you that.'

'Were you really expecting one, Mom? Was that part true?'

Her mother points at the pictures by her bed. Arabella assumes she wants to see the one of her father, her favorite photo from their anniversary party, but her mother shakes her head when she picks it up. 'No, not that one. The small one behind that picture.'

Arabella reaches and picks up a small, ragged photo of a man wearing a suit. It is so faded, you can't see much more than his teeth and his dark skin.

'Who is this?' Arabella asks, although even as she speaks, she knows the answer. She can almost see the figure dancing in her hand; there is energy coming from the photo. 'There really was a fortune-teller?'

'I told you about the Continental Hilton,' her mother says.

'So he really existed? He really promised you a miracle on Dad's sixtieth birthday?' Arabella doesn't know why she is so surprised. She earns her living helping people navigate the line between what happened to them and how to make it into a story. She knows better than anyone the strange turns that people's lives can take, and yet she never associated her mother with this type of drama. Her parents' lives were worn down by the erosion of suffering; she had no idea there was a fireball waiting to explode. She had no idea her poor mother was waiting for a miracle.

'Then what happened?'

'Exactly what I said in the story,' her mother says. Her eyes are bright and angry, and for a moment Arabella can see her as a young woman, a newlywed, in love. 'He said there was going to be a miracle, and I believed him. I didn't see how there could not be one. I was crazy that night. Waiting.'

Those angry eyes focus on Arabella. 'We went to dinner. Then you left to go back to college, and I took your father home. He was tired that night, but then he'd been so excited. He was always excited to see you.'

Her hands are twitching, playing a guitar, singing her song, her terrible sad song, and Arabella is not sure she has the courage to hear what is going to come. She feels like putting up her hands, just as the director of the nursing home did, warding her mother off. Yet she has been doing something very like that for years, and she can't do it any longer. There is no time to do it any longer.

'It got later and later,' her mother says, her voice a scratchy whisper. 'He was tired, but I didn't think he should go to sleep because I was worried the miracle wouldn't happen if he fell asleep. So I turned on the TV and talked to him. Then I changed my clothes, and I began to clean out the closet. I made piles of new clothes, old clothes, and clothes to give away. All this time I was chattering and chattering about foolish things.'

'What was Dad doing?'

'You know your father. He didn't do anything. He just listened, smiling.'

A gentle man, a passive man, a man who was buried under his misfortune, who was left with nothing else he could do except love the two women in his life. Arabella can see him lying in his bed, those pale white hands folded across his stomach, a living death, just the way he looked at his funeral.

'What happened then?'

Her mother is quiet. She closes her eyes, but Arabella can see the lids twitching as though she is having a dream. Arabella picks up her father's afghan and drapes it across her mother's knees. Perhaps it will warm her. Perhaps it will protect her from what she is seeing now.

'He had one of his spells. He was having them so frequently then. Well, I wrote about it in the story. You probably don't remember, but he would all of sudden shut down, as though someone had turned off a switch. I never knew when he would come back on. Sometimes it would be five minutes, sometimes an hour, sometimes more. There was nothing to do but wait.'

Her eyes are closed, but a rim of water hovers underneath them, tears that have been building up inside her for a long time. Arabella's own tears have started to fall, and she feels like a child, with tears and snot and everything else dripping from her. She picks up a tissue and wipes her mother's eyes and then her own.

'Normally, I would have called the hospital. I would have taken him to the emergency room. I had already done that twice that week – not that there was anything they could do for him. They told me not to bring him again unless it was an emergency.' She begins smoothing the afghan with her hands, knitting her story together.

Then she takes a deep breath and opens her eyes. 'Was it an emergency? It was always an emergency with your father, and the fact was, I was worried that if I moved him, the miracle wouldn't come. So I didn't call.'

Her chin is up, her eyes strong, and yet her poor face is very pale and tired.

'Then what happened?' Arabella whispers, and at that her mother's face crumbles, seeming to drop into itself. 'He died,' she wails. 'He died.'

'Oh, Mom.' Arabella hurls herself at her mother, taking her into her arms. She is amazed at how frail she is; she is nothing more than bones and a little skin.

'I'm so sorry,' Arabella cries.

But her mother is convulsed with deep wracking sobs, sobs that she has been holding inside her all these years, until finally she is done. Her slight body seems to collapse against Arabella, and all is quiet save for the roommate's breathing, moans from out in the hallway, and a whimpering sound that Arabella is surprised to realize is coming from her. Her face feels as if it is melting. Water drips off her cheeks until finally they are both cried out, exhausted.

'You see why I can't end the story,' her mother says. 'I can hardly end it with me killing your father.'

'You know that's not true,' Arabella says, the words shooting out of her. 'He was going to die. Nothing you could have done would have made any difference, and you loved him for so long and so well. You know that.'

Her mother shrugs. 'There's no way to know.'

'I do know,' Arabella says. She picks up the picture of the fortune-teller and rips it in half. 'It was cruel what he did to you.'

She thinks of the way her mother was at her father's funeral – so stony-eyed, so dazed – and she remembers with horror that she yelled at her mother, that she screamed after the funeral when the two of them were sitting in her father's sterile bedroom: 'It's as though you didn't care.'

'How cruel I've been to you,' she whispers.

But her mother does not respond.

She is listing in her chair now, and her eyes are flickering closed. This is all too much for her, and yet Arabella can't bring herself to call for help. She knows her mother would not want to be seen like this. She gets a washcloth and runs it across her mother's face, wiping away the tears. Then she puts her arms around her and lifts her into the bed. She is very light.

The room is airless, empty. Her mother's eyes are closed, and she is breathing heavily, keeping the same rhythm as her roommate's labored breaths. Arabella, listening to the sound, thinks again of that terrible night her mother wrote about. She imagines her mother sitting on her father's bed, watching his white sheet go up and down with his breaths, looking all around her for the miracle that did not come. And there was the terror she must have felt when she realized her mistake.

Again the tears come, and Arabella, turning away, catches sight of her mother's copy of *Arabella*. There the book sits, on the table by the window, all pink and hopeful – the groom always masterful and loving, and Arabella always true. It is a book that brings joy.

'You don't have to end your story the way it really happened,' Arabella whispers to her mother. 'That was cruel what happened to you and Dad, but you can change it. That's the beauty of fiction. You can make up whatever you want; you can make your story end the way you want it to end; you can make it end the way it should have ended.'

Her mother's eyes flicker open, and Arabella forces herself to think, to grab at the idea that shimmers just outside her grasp. She looks again at the happy pink book, and then the answer pours into her head as it has done on rare occasions when she is writing her own story and everything is going right. It is a rare feeling and a wonderful one, the gift of inspiration. It's a miracle.

'What if,' Arabella says, 'you go back to that final scene in which the mother is feeling joy because she and her daughter have finally connected? The waiter is going to come back, right? You started the story with the waiter and you're going to end it with the waiter. It can go like this:

'It is then that Joan smells the lilies and spots her waiter walking toward them. He is also smiling, a relaxed, happy smile. His face seems different, brighter somehow. And Joan knows that he is her angel. Impossible as it is, her miracle is about to take place. So she stands up, arms out and eyes sparkling with tears, and ever so deliberately starts to walk toward him. As she does, she can hear behind her a rush of wind, the sound of Danny standing.'

Her mother's eyes creep open, and she repeats the final words: '. . . the sound of Danny standing.'

'Why shouldn't your story end in a miracle, Mom?'

'The sound of Danny standing,' her mother repeats. Her face and hair are the same color as her pillow. Her life is being leached out of her. And yet when she smiles, her face grows pink. She fingers the afghan, her thin fingers running up and down the worn wool, and Arabella, looking at the picture of her father, can almost see him in motion. She pictures him standing; she pictures him walking over to her mother and holding his hand out to her. She pictures everything being the way it is supposed to be.

'I like it,' her mother says. She looks at Arabella and smiles. 'Thank you.'

Chapter Eleven

ON THURSDAY MORNING Arabella is sitting at her computer, looking at the beginning of her novel, *Courting Disaster*, reading through the words and coming to the discouraging realization that it is all worthless. No one will ever want to buy this book; no one will ever want to read this book. Even Arabella doesn't want to read the book. She hates the characters and the plot; she even hates the words – every last one of them, so polished and cold and brittle.

She stares at them now, rows of sharp black nuggets, and thinks how unsatisfying her relationship with these words has been. It is like going out with a man who will never marry you. You date him and date him, waiting for the day when it all comes together and he gets down on bended knee. But it never happens. Eventually he leaves you for someone inappropriate and proposes to her in a week.

The only thing to do is press the delete button and move on.

'Are you sure you want to delete the full text?' the computer asks.

She presses *Ok*.

There is the briefest convulsion as the computer seems to blink, and then her novel is gone.

Arabella stares at the blank screen and feels a convulsion within herself. Then she reminds herself that she hasn't emptied the trash bin yet; she can always get it back. There's no point in being foolish. She has made her point, and she does feel better. She sets her fingers on the keys and opens up a new file. She is not exactly sure what she's going to write, but she knows something is there; it has been pricking at her for the last few weeks. Something is coalescing, something to do with the class and her mother and Chuck. It is not there yet, but it will come if she's patient and works at it.

She begins tapping on the keys. Arabella is thinking of the look on her mother's face when she came up with the ending of the story; she is trying to describe how she felt at that moment. How do you get something like that across? How do you describe a moment of happiness like that? You can say that her mother smiled, that her eyes sparkled, that her face relaxed, but how do you get across the shimmering joy on her face and the joy that flooded through Arabella at that moment? You can't really describe it. All you can hope is that everyone has felt a moment like that at least once and knows what you're talking about.

She types *Joy* on the page, and next to it she types *Mother*. Then she sits there for a half an hour typing nothing at all, yet forcing herself not to go to Spider Solitaire. She begins to think of an opening paragraph, but then the phone rings, and before she can answer it, Arabella knows what she is going to hear. Even so, she is startled by the sound that breaks from her lips when the nurse tells her that her mother has passed.

'I'm very sorry,' the nurse says.

Arabella doesn't even know who this woman is; she does know where these horrible keening sounds are coming from. She feels as though her grief is spewing from her. She looks around the room wildly, trying to find something to focus her eyes on, some picture, some image. The Hudson River flows outside her window, gray and merciless. She cannot bear to look at the questioning face of her mother that stares at her from her framed portrait, but then she catches sight of the books on her bookshelf – her friends. There is the black spine of *To Kill a Mockingbird*. She grabs it and hugs it to her.

'Where's Marvel?' she whispers.

'She's on vacation,' the nurse says, her voice as soft as a nursery rhyme. 'I'm very sorry.'

There is a brief moment of silence, and then the nurse starts to talk as if reading from a note: 'Your mother was having breakfast, and she finished eating and then closed her eyes. She was eating oatmeal. It was very peaceful.'

There's no rush, the nurse assures her. There is nothing much for Arabella to do because all the funeral arrangements were made and paid for when her mother's payments were taken over by Medicaid. The hearse will be there soon to remove the body, though she is welcome to come and view it if she likes. All that needs to be done is to set the time for the services and to clean out the closet. There's no need for Arabella to do that today, of course, though many families prefer to get it over with. There is no rush, this new nurse says as she hangs up the phone. 'I'm very sorry for your loss.'

That's it.

Thirty-eight years of struggle and love and anguish and everything else, and her mother eats oatmeal and dies. And the only thing left for Arabella to do is clean out her closet.

She calls Chuck, and he offers to come up to help her or have her stay at his place or take her to Paris. But she says no, thank you, not right now. She would rather do it herself. She doesn't mean to put him off, but she feels so fragile that the thought of having to deal with anyone, even someone she loves, is too much for her. He says that's ridiculous, and he'll meet her in the nursing home in two hours.

'That would be great,' she says.

The sky is blue, the way it was on 9/11, and as Arabella pulls into the parking lot, she remembers calling her mother on that terrible Wednesday, the day after the attack, to tell her she didn't think she could visit. Her mother said, 'Oh, that's right. Use a national disaster as an excuse to put off seeing your mother.'

She parks next to her regular Dodge Caravan and looks once more at the bumper sticker: 'Proud Parent of an Honor Student at Port Chester H.S.' She thinks how sad it is that she will never see that car again. She will never again see the pansies that gaze at her mischievously as she walks toward the front door, and never see Dotty again – Dotty who is swooping toward her like a banshee and then hugs her. Death is like having someone lop off a part of your life; not only do you lose the person you love, but you lose everything that goes with her.

Arabella is fighting off this swirling feeling of anguish, thinking that if she loses control, she will start to scream, and the sounds of her cries will slice right through the nursing home. Suddenly Chuck is alongside her, his hand under her arm, holding her up.

'I'm so sorry,' he says. His gentle gray eyes seem to kiss her. That handsome face is filled with love and concern.

'Dear Arabella,' he whispers as she sobs against his chest.

There is not much to do. In death her mother looks even smaller than she looked in life. She is all wrapped up in a sheet; there is even a sheet around her head so that she looks like a nun. Arabella kisses her good-bye, but she knows her mother is already gone. The hearse comes and takes the body away, and then they pack up her mother's clothes and put them into boxes that will be given to the Salvation Army. They throw out the cosmetics and the soaps. All that is left are the pictures, and Arabella puts those in a separate box to take home. The last thing to pack is *Arabella*, which sits pink and forlorn on the table.

'I'm going to read this,' she says to Chuck.

'Me, too.'

She looks once more at the birch tree, so white and elegant. Little daffodils are starting to sprout up at the edge of the green grass. Soon the butterfly garden will be attracting insects, the residents will be sitting outside, and the whole cycle will start all over. She thinks that, in an odd sort of way, she has been happy in this room. Had her mother never moved here, they would never have started talking about writing, and she would never have written her story. She tries to see in that a blessing, but her heart hurts too much.

The roommate sighs as she leaves, and Arabella bends over and kisses her good-bye. The last thing she does is take the little name tag from outside the door. She doesn't know what she's going to do with it, but she can't bear to think of its being thrown out. They are just heading for the parking lot when Sade comes running out. She is crying and throws her arms around Arabella. She tells her what a great woman her mother was and how brave she was in fighting to get her job back.

Then it is over, and Arabella and Chuck get in the car and drive away.

The remainder of the day passes in a blur. Chuck suggests they go to P. F. Chang's and have lunch and remember her mother. That seems as good a memorial to her mother as any, given how much she loved to eat there. She spends the next few days making phone calls to various people who once knew her mother, making arrangements for the memorial service, which goes off fine, and then the burial. At one point her boss calls to say that he heard about her mother, and he's sorry, and if she would like to miss this Wednesday's class, he will arrange for a substitute.

But she tells him she is eager to see the class – that, in fact, there is no one she would rather see than that collection of eleven people sitting in a nursery school room, sharing their space with a rabbit, and trying to learn how to write.

'You're sure?' her boss asks. She can hear the surprise in his voice.

'I'm sure.'

Tenth Class: Voice

'SO WE'VE COME all this way together, and I've saved the most important topic for last. I know, D'mon. You're thinking I'm going to talk about how to get an agent, but in the end that's not all that important – or it is, but it's not something I can really teach you about. No, the important thing I can teach you is about voice.

'Voice is the reason you write. Voice is you. It's the words you choose; It's the things you write about. It's the way you structure a sentence. It's the way you talk; It's what makes your writing different from anyone else's so that, ideally, a reader has only to look at your first paragraph and know that Arabella Hicks wrote it. Or D'mon. Or Dorothy. It's you.

'The good news is that everyone has a voice,' Arabella says, 'and the older you get, the more of a voice you have.' She can't help but think of her mother's voice – querulous, engaging, intelligent, dramatic, missed. 'The bad news is that most people are afraid to use their voice, so they hide it. They cover it up with clichés and lies. They protect themselves, but that leads to something that is bland and boring.

'You have to hurl yourself into the story, do the best you can, and pray that at the end of the day you're not slashed to death.' She catches Conrad's eye, quizzical, measuring. She did see him at the shoe store, she reminds herself.

The bunny thumps against the cage sympathetically. She has returned, and there are five little bunnies in the cage with her. Another creature defined by its desires, Arabella thinks.

'The only consolation I can give you,' she says, staring out at the hopeful faces of her students, 'is that if you are honest, no matter how embarrassing it is, you are likely to connect with someone who will be very relieved to know that there is one other person in this world who thinks the way she does.

'Many people feel alone, and they turn to writing to find a friend,' she says, thinking of the comfort she found after her mother died in simply holding books. 'And they are looking for honesty, too.

'Isn't that why you write? Because you want to tell the truth? Because you want to understand the truth, and the only way to understand it is to write it down?' Over and over she thinks of her mother's story and the courage it took for her to write it and how it transformed her life.

'And,' Arabella continues, forcing herself back from the

brink, forcing herself to look at the bright posters on the wall and the dissatisfied expression on the bunny, 'while we are on the subject of honesty, let's salute Byron because he is the most honest person here.'

That gets the class's attention. As one, they all turn and look at Byron, who is shimmering in his blacks and golds, his thick curls greasy with styling lotion, his legs spread wide apart, and his huge feet encased in cement-heavy black shoes.

'Is there anyone here who has the least doubt what Byron thinks about all the time?'

They all laugh, Byron included, and Arabella thinks that this is one of the pleasures of a fiction class. You have a man that in any other context would be considered a pervert, but in the fiction class he is prized for his honesty. She wonders what he will write on his evaluation. She has only a little bit of time left, and then she has to hand out the forms. How she hates those evaluations. Why can't she just shake everyone's hand and go home?

'Would anyone have any trouble picking out a sample of Byron's writing, even if I covered up the name?' Arabella asks.

'Would I be able to pick out your writing if I covered up the name?' She asks this of the class in general and then gives them a few minutes to think about it. Meanwhile, Arabella looks around at the walls of the nursery school, which are covered with pictures of the class science experiment. It seems to have involved popping popcorn in an open pot, the sort of thing that could end badly. The teachers are probably vigilant and make sure that all the stray kernels are swept up. Still, you can only protect the children so much. Some poor soul could wind up with a kernel in his face. Some people have no luck.

'So it's good that Byron writes about sex all the time,' Pam screams out.

'I don't know that it's good,' Arabella says, unable to stop herself from backpedaling a little, 'but it's true.' She turns to Bonita and says, 'Your voice is also very distinct, and that's because you have a way of putting together a phrase that is unique to you. You may eventually want to tone it down a little, but I can't see you ever writing anything bland.'

Bonita flushes with pleasure.

'You don't see a man, you see a stallion. You don't see a rear end, you see buttocks. The thing that makes your writing unique is that you choose the words that work for you, and no one else would choose those words.'

Bonita is radiating joy, and Arabella thinks how easy it is to make someone happy, especially if you're saying something true.

'Choose your words carefully,' Arabella says to the class. 'This is part of finding your own voice, and this means no clichés, no easy answers. If you want to say that someone's face is red, do not say, "His face was as red as a beet." '

Dorothy groans and holds her head. 'Damn.'

'When you say his face is as red as a beet, it doesn't mean anything specific unless you are a Russian farmer. You have to choose the words that get your personality across. For example, Bonita, you could say, "His face was as red as the new Lancôme lipstick." And Ginger, you could say, "His face was as red as the horse I learned to ride on." ' Arabella looks at Pam and thinks that she could say, 'His face was as red as my favorite little pills,' but she decides to hold back on that one. There is no point in being too honest. And she decides not to ask Byron, either. 'Alice, what could you say?'

'His face was as red as an explosion.'

'How about you, Justin? What book do you have with you today?'

He holds up *Haunted* by Chuck Palahniuk. 'Now he has a voice,' Arabella says. 'That's a voice you could recognize anywhere.'

Justin looks at the book, at the black-and-white photo on its cover of a person screaming. 'His face was as red as the blood dripping from her eyes.'

'Good. And how about you, Chuck?'

He has been scribbling away in his new notebook, but now he taps the paper for effect. He has good command of pacing, she thinks.

'His face was as red as his teacher's sweater.'

She blushes at that, but it's true. She is wearing a red sweater. She looks down at her arms and can't quite take it in. He insisted that it would bring out her color, and the saleswoman at Nordstrom's was so effusive that Arabella couldn't resist. She feels like a tulip, though; she half-expects people to laugh at her as she walks by, though no one has.

And now the last exercise is done. It is time to hand out the evaluations, but Arabella hesitates. She has come to like this class so much that she cannot bear to read anything hateful. What if it turns out that she has misread them? What if it turns out that they have just been biding their time, waiting to slash her to bits?

She hands the forms to Alice, who happens to be sitting closest to her, and Alice passes them around. Arabella puts a manila envelope on the desk in front of her. The idea is that the students should put the evaluations in the envelope without Arabella's seeing what they've written, and in that way they can feel free to be honest.

As a practical matter, she is supposed to read the evaluations after the class leaves because that way she will find out what she is doing wrong. 'Don't take it personally,' her boss explained. 'Just try to learn from the feedback.'

'Be kind,' Arabella throws out, smiling and trying not to look desperate. Then she sits down at her desk and tries to look as if she's thinking great thoughts while her students evaluate her.

They take it seriously. They always do. And they have so much to say. They fill in all the extra lines, they write on the back, and they sign their names. Only Chuck looks up. He winks. If he writes a bad evaluation, she is going to throw in the towel. But she thinks she can trust him enough to circle all the fives. He looks cheerful enough when he walks up to the front of the class to put his sheet in the envelope, and then Conrad shuffles up next, his shoes making so much noise that she looks down at them. They are bright white shoes with gel on the side. Flashy.

NAME OF TEACHER:

CLASS:

STUDENT EVALUATION
Please circle the appropriate number

High   Medium   Low

Overall satisfaction with course

5   4   3   2   1

Instructor's command of subject

5   4   3   2   1

Instructor's ability to teach material

5   4   3   2   1

Instructor's openness to questions

5   4   3   2   1

Overall effectiveness of instructor

5   4   3   2   1

Additional comments:

'Thanks for the class,' he mutters. She catches a strain of music from his headset, something smooth and romantic.

Ginger and Justin come up together. She is wearing jeans and a T-shirt, and looks relaxed. Justin smells of liquor. He has taken up all the vices of writers without actually doing any writing. She feels bad for him. No one said it was easy, and there's not much more she can do to help him. She has demons of her own to fight.

Dark Alice meanders up then, nods at Arabella, and folds up her evaluation into a tiny square and pops it in, which makes Arabella exceedingly nervous. What did she write that she doesn't want Arabella to read? she wonders. Dorothy comes up next and flashes the evaluation at Arabella, showing her all the fives that she circled. 'Great job,' she says in a stage whisper. Her white hair is sitting a little lower today; she must not be running her hands through it so much.

Mimi smiles at her, too. This is a little like a jury, Arabella thinks. She wants them to meet her eyes. Mimi's skin is pale and her hat is pulled down over her head, but her eyes seem sincerely merry. Byron is next. He does not so much walk as swagger. She has seen little dogs walk like that, doing all they can with their strut to prove how big they are. He has scrawled words all over the back of the page.

Pam and D'mon are last, an unlikely pairing. She is close to the edge, and he is all the way in the center, but he holds the envelope open for Pam. Then, because her hands are shaking, he takes the evaluation and pops it in.

'Good work,' he says.

Arabella expects them to walk away then. The class is over; the journey is at its end. But instead they are all sitting in their seats. Arabella is not sure what to do; she has nothing more to say. She wonders if they are expecting her to take them out for drinks; then, amazingly, they all stand up and begin to clap.

It is the most wonderful sound Arabella has ever heard. It is music, it is strength, it is love, it is a miracle. It is a sound that will reverberate in her head for many years to come. It will never end. It does, though, and then one by one they leave – except for Chuck, of course, who waits for her in the hallway. He will take her home to his apartment tonight and cook dinner for her and love her and read the evaluations with her.

But before she can go to him, Conrad is standing by the desk. His presence puzzles her. He has been in two of her classes, and he never raises his hand and rarely speaks.

'See you in April,' he says.

'Why?' she blurts out, thinking that he's threatening her.

'That's when Advanced Fiction begins. We've all signed up.'

Writing Assignment

ARABELLA HICKS – THE FICTION CLASS
(For extra credit)

Write a short story (just a few paragraphs) with this proviso: You can only use words of one syllable.

Chapter Twelve

THE CLASS IS over, and Arabella is back in her apartment, trying to sketch out a new novel. It is a feeling similar to waiting to sneeze: She knows it is going to happen, it's just frustrating to have to wait. But she is patient. She is so patient that she feels as though she has taken some of Pam's drugs. She feels muffled, dissatisfied, and ready to scream.

Chuck sits in the corner reading *Arabella*. He says he is enjoying it – or, as he put it, 'That girl's a spitfire.' Every so often she hears him chuckling over some passage, and then she looks over and watches him, relaxed and happy. A man like that could drive you crazy. She finds herself wondering how he is going to deal with old age and death. She finds herself imagining him in a nursing home, her visiting him, bringing him food, but when she got up enough courage to tell him her fears, he just laughed. 'I'm just fifty-three, Arabella. I think I have a little time.'

He has managed to become friendly with her next-door neighbors, a pair of punk rockers she has ignored for years because of their tendency to play loud music late at night. He chats with them; he chats with the security guard; he chats with the mean old lady on the fourth floor who has an 'enchantingly cute kitten'.

Arabella looks at the computer screen again and types up a new opening paragraph, but every time she starts, she sees her mother's face the way it was when she came up with the ending. Then she sees her face as it was the last time she saw her, wrapped in a sheet, and she feels a hard mass of grief growing inside her. Her mind replays her mother's death, the tawdry image of that last bite of oatmeal. She keeps thinking about what she was doing at the time of her mother's death, and she suspects she was also eating oatmeal. So much passion and life. Does it have to end like that?

She is sitting at the computer on Thursday afternoon, thinking it was just a week ago that her mother died; she has a gnawing feeling of despair. Then Arabella notices the mailman coming toward her building. He is an intriguing man who fought a lawsuit with the post office over the right to wear shorts during the winter. She doesn't understand that sort of mania, but she suspects there is a story in this man, so she always watches him carefully when he drops off the mail.

Chuck has become intrigued by him, too. He may not have a writer's dedication, but he does have a writer's appreciation for a good story. He likes to chat with the mailman and hear his stories, and he saves up interesting quotes and lays them at Arabella's feet, as a cat might give his owner a mouse.

'You have a letter from the nursing home,' he says when he returns from the mailbox.

'A bill?' Her heart automatically flops. She imagines owing thousands, finding out that the government has a cut-off on how much they will pay. She will have to declare bankruptcy.

'I don't think so.'

Chuck hands her the envelope. She looks at it, wondering what it could be. The handwriting is unfamiliar to her – a large looping scrawl that looks a little like Byron's. It is probably a thank-you note. She gave some of the staff some money to thank them for taking care of her mother.

'You should probably open it,' Chuck says.

She sits down on the couch and glances at the picture of her mother that is now resting on top of her computer. Then she opens the letter. It is from Marvel.

Dear Bella,

I am so sorry I did not get to see you after your mother passed. She was a great lady, and I will miss her.

I had to go down to visit with my mother, and so I did not have a chance until Sunday to speak to Sade. She was with your mother when she died, and I thought you would like to know what she said. I think perhaps it will be a comfort to you.

Your mother was very excited that morning. You know how she would get, yes? Her eyes sparkled like diamonds. Her color was blush. Sade asked her what she is so excited about, and she tells Sade she has a dream last night and she sees her husband. Your father. And he is strong in this dream. And he tells her he is going to see her soon. And he tells her not to be afraid.

So she says to Sade, What do you think about that?

Sade tells me she doesn't know what to say. Many residents have dreams, you understand, and I believe that is a good thing. Many of our residents live in their dreams.

Your mother's hands were weak that day, and so Sade was feeding her her oatmeal. She says your mother kept jumping and looking around, like she was expecting to see someone. Sade thinks perhaps she is expecting to see you, although she knows you do not come on Thursdays. Sade says she looks happy, like a girl.

Then, when she is done with her oatmeal, Sade is going to get her some orange juice, but your mother isn't paying attention. She is smiling at the corner of the room. Sade looks, but she doesn't see anything, but she feels something. She wants to say something, but then your mother's face changes, and she smiles and she says, Danny. Sade is watching your mother's face and, she says, for just a moment before she dies, your mother looks like a young woman.

This is all I have to tell you, Bella.

God bless you.

Marvel

Arabella reads the letter several times. She tries to picture what happened. She wonders if it is possible. Was there a miracle? She so wants it to be so. Her mother deserved it. She is enough of a realist to know that the most likely explanation is that her mother had a hallucination before she died and saw what she hoped to see. But there's a possibility, a chance, that her father did really come for her. He did love her, and she loved him, and if there was any way in heaven for him to come to her, Arabella feels sure he would have.

This is what she chooses to believe. This is what she will write.